Roo Kickkick & the Big Bad Blimp

Ryan Gattis was born in 1978 in Illinois, USA. Raised in Colorado, he lives in east London and is currently a PhD candidate in Creative and Critical Writing at the University of East Anglia. His brother Brandon lives in Colorado Springs. In addition to being a freelance artist, he works for a mutual fund investment company. *Roo Kickkick & the Big Bad Blimp* is their first collaborative effort.

Ryan Gattis

Roo Kickkick &
the Big Bad Blimp

SCEPTRE

First published in Great Britain in 2004 by Hodder and Stoughton
A division of Hodder Headline

A Sceptre Book

1 3 5 7 9 10 8 6 4 2

A CIP catalogue record for this title is
available from the British Library

ISBN 0 340 82832 3

Typeset by Palimpsest Book Production Limited,
Polmont, Stirlingshire
Printed and bound in Great Britain by
Clays Ltd, St Ives plc

Hodder and Stoughton
A division of Hodder Headline
338 Euston Road
London NW1 3BH

Acknowledgements

First and foremost, I must thank my brother Brandon for helping me create this book. Secondly, I need to thank my parents for all of their support and love. Also, many thanks go out to all my teachers who have guided me this far, particularly Mark Axelrod, Marty Nakell, Barney McGrane, Pilar Rotella, Andrew Motion, Marina MacKay, and certainly Jan Osborn, for forcing me to look out the window and write what I saw. I cannot forget all the help and encouragement of Lizzy Kremer; my gracious thanks for all of her hard work and continued patience. I am very grateful for the insight, style and constant belief of Helen Garnons-Williams, and a huge thank you to Katy Follain, Hugo Hutchison and Nicola Doherty at Sceptre. Of course, much love to W.J. Peace, C.M. Piliero, R.S. Hammill, P.B. 'Peanut Butter' Paulson and Mike E. 'Mookie' Raulston, because without you characters, Barguss would've been a lot less colorful and a hell of a lot less fun. Also, thanks to Ryan (for reading), Char (for listening and always encouraging), Lorraine (for 'thieving'), Gemma (for seeing), Gustavo (for calling me demented) and all those who were with me in spirit during my travels. Last but never least, I would like to acknowledge the wonderful generosity and sense of humor of Mr Wayne Newton, who is, and always will be, 'The King of Las Vegas'.

Contents

I

Roo Kickkick had been living in the town of Barguss, on Blank Street, less than two months before someone picked a fight with him and broke his face wide open. They curbed him. If you don't know, that's when someone opens your mouth and puts it on a curb then kicks the back of your head so hard with their boot heel that the cheek skin around your mouth tears like wet toilet paper and all your teeth come out on the cement like your pocket just ripped and you dropped all your loose change in a clump, except it's got blood all over it and you aren't so sure you want to pick it up. The person who did this to him was . . .

Raoul de los Dios, who had six fingers on his right hand and so he had to flip people off with his ring finger cuz the middle finger wasn't the middle finger on his right hand. He didn't care about 'nothing or nobody', that's what he always said. Some people say they saw him pick up each one of Roo Kickkick's teeth and put them in his pocket. One girl who had dirty sex once with Raoul swears that she saw Roo Kickkick's bicuspids and molars hanging on a cord around his enormous naked neck. But Roo Kickkick wasn't the first person Raoul de los Dios beat up. That person was . . .

Thorpe Thorpe. He had an electric/acoustic band called Autistik/Artistik, formerly named Historico Future Co., and he played harp/banjo/two-string bass and gutbucket. He wrote most of the lyrics in his basement that he sublet from his older brother. There was no heating in it and sometimes he got hypothermia so he wrote a song about it called 'The Angel of Death'. He looked like a young Salvador Dalí minus the moustache and he kinda resented that we always told him so. The other half of the duo was . . .

Thed Teldut, who had originally named the band 6T, which stood for Tee Tee Ta Tee Two Too, but no one ever seemed to get it, so they dropped it. He played the 808, a Dappa© drum machine, Neolix® Super Jam 550 portable guitar/keyboard and the maracas. Their best song, the one that everyone sang along to at their concerts, was 'Jacques Derrida, You Arsehole, I Love You' complete with British spelling cuz Thed had gotten to go to London for six days and five nights when he won a summer trip once and picked the spelling up somehow. Since then, Autistik/Artistik had achieved a certain cult status in Barguss and we knew that when . . .

Florence Mink went to one of their shows. She was born to be a star and everybody knew it. One day, she wore spoons in her hair, at the ends of her pigtails, and everyone thought it was so cool. It was then that we knew she could get away with anything. She even sang the chorus to 'J.D.Y.A.I.L.Y.' as it is known among the groupies – 'Deconstruct the difference / between you and me / and you and you and me / Monsieur bourgeois munificence' – while standing next to her boyfriend . . .

Monroe Mister Promised To. He was the kid of the guy that practically owned all of Barguss (car washes and strip malls and ice cream stands) and he always looked bored. He was captain of the ball team and a male model and he had lots of money and so people pretended not to notice when he was so mean to Florence and sometimes people even thought she liked it. Then everything changed.

That's the day the blimp came. That's when this starts.

Roo Kickkick & the Big Bad Blimp

For a year, Roo Kickkick had been healing. Not just physically, but emotionally and spiritually. At least, that's what his therapist told him. And now he had great nice big scars that made him look about like the biggest smiler in all of Barguss. Sometimes people would go and do silly things to make him smile just to see his face crinkle around his prosthetic teeth.

They were beautiful those teeth, so much better than real: white and strong, not discolored in the least. He could eat nuts or steak or even motor oil if he wanted and it didn't matter, not a single stain. 'Beautiful technology,' he would call them, and smile big and sometimes the girls with the matching jackets who hung out on Gee Street would get that kind of attracted/pitying look in their eyes and everyone knew that Roo Kickkick did all right with the ladies cuz he was a survivor.

Word from the girls was that he was 'tender'. 'Tender in the bedroom,' they would say and giggle and each one would know what the others were talking about and sometimes they would put their hands in their pockets and look down at the cracking sidewalk cement or caress each other's cheeks in imitation and close their eyes and maybe even sigh if none of us guys were around the Taco Coleslaw Hamburger Hot Dog Apple. That was the name of the restaurant at the end of Gee Street where we all used to hang out. It was a building built like a food container, all boxy and even had a painted red catsup stain on it. Not like Roo's teeth at all. But we had the sinking feeling that he was just biding his time with the other girls cuz he really had a hard pining for Miss Florence Mink.

This was certainly not good cuz she was with Monroe Mister

3

Promised To and we all tried to tell him that, but he just kinda smiled and got a look in his eye that no one could hurt him worse than he had been hurt before and we really wanted to believe him but we knew Monroe Mister would run him over with his car sixteen times and then call the police and not even get charged cuz his dad had an affair with the chief of police on the side.

So we tried to tell him that there was something broken inside Florence for her to want to be with someone like Monroe Mister. That she had always gotten everything she ever wanted and that a person like that doesn't know pain and had missed out on some growing up experiences cuz she was like a living shortcut but he wouldn't listen.

He'd just sit on that bench outside the Taco Coleslaw Hamburger Hot Dog Apple and look out into the road that went east/west through Barguss and divided the poor side from the rich side and we were all on the poor side. Then he'd look up at the tree that dumped shade all over us at the noon hour and smile and his scars touched the edges of his eyes and his cheeks got really wrinkled so that he looked super old.

Well, that was the day that Thed wandered by and reminded us about the concert going on that evening, as if we even needed to be reminded about the biggest city celebration since the state centennial sixteen years previous. It was outdoors at the Big Barguss Blimp Ceremony that the city hall had planned in the memorial park (which was kinda funny cuz no one we knew ever remembered what we were supposed to remember the memorial park was made to honor in the first place) and even though none of the older folks liked Autistik/Artistik, they were our only real band and they actually made a CD once in California and all the kids in Barguss bought it and played it out their car windows so loud it rattled their speakers like a little kid banging on kitchen pots. The blimp was meant to increase tourism funds so the city hall was paying them to play by dropping all the noise complaints logged against them from their time spent practicing at Thed's mom's house. So it was like they were playing for free but they weren't cuz they owed Barguss something around eight hundred dollars for being so loud so consistently.

Thorpe Thorpe wasn't too far behind Thed and he was dragging Staceyleene behind him and she was on roller skates on account of the fact that all waitresses that worked at the Taco Coleslaw Hamburger Hot Dog Apple had to wear them while working cuz it was their trademark. It wasn't long before someone piped up and called Staceyleene his 'Gala' and she just blushed but he got all mad at the overt Dalí reference but made us promise to be at the ceremony that night cuz they had a big surprise planned. So it was decided quickly, out in front of the stained building shaped like a food box, under a tree, with cars going by, that we'd all go.

Of course, at that point, nobody but nobody knew that Raoul de los Dios had broken out of the city lock-up by stabbing the guard with an ink pen and stealing his keys. Everybody forgot exactly what Raoul was in there for, whether it was gross bodily harm or drunken assault, but the information surprised none of us. They say he stole a car right there near the jail and drove straight across town to rob the jewelry store owned by Agghe Raine, who once flew to Africa for free cuz he gave a stewardess a ring and even though they weren't engaged she said they were and so he didn't have to pay cuz he was 'family'.

Well, Raoul stomped Agghe pretty good and left him there on the brown tiled floor of his own store and he bled to death cuz nobody came and when we found out about it later that afternoon we all said that finally, finally when they caught up with that filthy psychopath Raoul he would go away and never come back. We didn't care how it happened so long as he never came back, but it was still mighty unsettling cuz Raoul was all of a sudden on the lam and free to hurt whoever he wanted.

Meanwhile, across town, Monroe Mister pulled up in front of the beauty salon with his blue car, the really fast one, and left it running outside when he went in to pick up Florence but she was chatting and so he crossed his arms and leaned against the doorjamb. The only chair occupied in the whole place and Florence was sitting in it, talking about shopping and lung health with Doctor Nancy, who had given up a lucrative gynecological practice to pursue her first love: beauty improvement. They finished their conversation in between admiring sidelong looks at Monroe Mister lingering in a shaft of sunlight that he had purposely positioned himself in, still with his sunglasses on even though he was sorta indoors.

It only takes five minutes to walk to the big city park from Roo Kickkick's mother's apartment. So we went fast and joked and stuff and poked Roo about Florence cuz she's 'broken on the inside' and 'too pretty to be nice' and stuff like that but he just kept walking and was real good about taking our jibes. We all refused to let Raoul's recent antics scare us into not going. Seemed like the whole town thought pretty much the same way cuz just about everyone was at the ceremony/concert when we got there.

   It was really weird and none of us could remember another time when so many people were in one place around here. Since there weren't any chairs, people mostly just sat on red and white picnic blankets or old tablecloths that they had brought. Cuz of that, the crowd looked like a buncha tiny checkers games with the people as the big pieces when we came over the hill into the park. Some people even ate watermelon and spat the seeds out into other people's hair and it was gross but people were laughing and having a good time.

Monroe Mister drove up in his car and didn't bother to open Florence's door, but we all saw pretty soon that she wasn't wearing silverware in her hair and that was kind of rough cuz some of the Gee Street Girls came with forks in their hair and they had to run home to change. So the concert started without them, right smack in the middle of our two-square-acre memorial park.

The city hall people sat at the back of the roped off crowd area, except they sat on a grandstand that had been erected just for them and 'their pampered asses', that was how Thed described it. Directly across from the grandstand was the stage and it was a makeshift type that rose about five feet off the ground and the front of it was covered with black curtain and about twenty feet above the stage was a big ladder-looking thing all parallel to the ground that held a buncha lights and sound stuff. The whole thing was set between two huge oak trees and the bigger and broader tree on the left of the stage anchored the blimp.

To see it for the first time, all pumped up and hanging there in the sky, was actually quite a sight. Easily three times as big as the stage, it hung high above and it was the nastiest mucus shade of yellow we ever saw, ever. Add to that a black circle on the nose and the words 'Big, Beaultiful: Barguss!' emblazoned on the side in black block letters that made us all laugh cuz beautiful was misspelled and the blimp was basically a three-dimensional advertising billboard except bigger and a whole lot uglier. Worse cuz it seemed like such a lie. Barguss isn't big and we haven't been anywhere but Upton to compare it to, but it isn't all that beautiful either.

Well, the city hall people made a few speeches before all the lights came down, casually assuring everyone that the spelling would be fixed before the 'official launch' (which we all thought that very night was anyway cuz all the posters said so but we never pretended to understand the city council so that was that) and just then Autistik/Artistik made a huge dramatic entrance on the stage opposite them, people barely had enough time to turn around to catch sight of Thorpe Thorpe coming up through the floor and Thed Teldut flying in on wires suspended from the ladder thing above the stage. They played twenty songs and almost everyone our age sang along and they played a few new ones and you could almost see people trying to learn the words right there.

And then, at the end of their set, came the big surprise. Thed and Thorpe jumped up simultaneously and cut the ropes to the blimp with flashing silver machetes and the crowd cheered and the city council people just about committed mass suicide right there cuz we all saw their red faces even in the half darkness and we knew they spent all of that year's budget and the next year's budget on it in the hope of attracting stupid tourists to Barguss to see a blimp. And maybe they were even worried that the blimp would get away and wherever it landed the people that found it would think we were all idiots in Barguss cuz we couldn't even spell the word beautiful right but they didn't do any of that. They just got angry and then got even.

They called the riot police, which in Barguss consisted of only the MarMartuchy family, the father and eight sons that probably tipped the scales at a ton and a quarter all together and went hairy shirtless out into the crowd but wore gas masks and carried shields and clubs and just started beating people 'til we gave up.

So everyone sat down and put their hands up, nice like. Except it was then that we saw Raoul de los Dios was on the blimp, just behind the nose and he must have been hiding cuz no one knew what madness he was up to. He was kinda far away up in the air and waving his arms around as the blimp drifted but there was the cut bit of rope hanging down

8

from it and we all held our breaths when Roo Kickkick looked Florence Mink square in her pigtails from across the checkerboard crowd and jumped on that old rope.

People turned more lights on the sky and we all saw Roo climb up to try to help Raoul down, to try to get him to safety, though none of us knew why cuz we all would have thrown our shoes at him 'til he fell off and died but Roo was so nice and trying to be good in front of all those people and then we figured it was cuz he wanted Florence to like him.

And then everybody was quiet and just staring up at the night sky, all the stage lights were on the blimp that floated weird cuz it was kind of strung up in the other tree across the stage and looked like it was trying to break free and even the MarMartuchys stopped and then Thorpe Thorpe and Thed Teldut emerged from their hiding hole in the stage and started playing music. Nice and slow and scoring the action, all impromptu.

Roo had a rope around his waist and he was trying to reach Raoul de los Dios who was hanging off the edge cuz he had slipped and when that happened, Thed Teldut did this echoey breakbeat on his Dappa© and the crowd clapped and stuff and none of us could tell if it was cuz Raoul might fall on his immense head or cuz Thed was a musical genius.

But the blimp swung around, right over the crowd, pushed from a breeze like, and the crowd 'ooooooooooohed' and we thought we heard Roo screaming something heroic like, 'grab my hand,' cuz he was leaning over the side and trying to grab Raoul. But then de los Dios's grip slipped and he fell head first right into the crowd and by some lucky twist, his skull crushed Monroe Mister Promised To's skull and none of us believed in fate or 'kharma kharma kharma / now bring me the women of your sangha', as Thorpe Thorpe was screeching into the mic just after it happened cuz the music hadn't stopped.

9

After That

We believed in just desserts though and later that summer we all had to endure a march in a parade honoring Monroe Mister Promised To. It was organized by his dad and we went but we all made bad remarks cuz, after he died, it all came out that Monroe Mister used to beat Florence and he was the one who had at least suggested that Raoul de los Dios curb Roo Kickkick cuz he was a rival and so there was even a nice song played at the funeral called 'Sugar Dog Monroe' and Thed sang the vocals and Old Man Promised To just stood there all dignified with a tear in his eye but he didn't know that it was ironical and we were making fun of his worthless son and we were glad he was gone.

They made a big movie about it, the blimp and everything, two years later, all Hollywood and stuff and some new kid played Roo Kickkick but his scar make-up was really bad and the only thing that saved it for us was that Roo Kickkick was given a credit as an advisor on the film, Florence Mink played herself, and Autistik/Artistik got to do the score. It didn't make much money at the box office (not in America anyway) but it did make a lot in Barguss. It ran for three years in our local theater and a coupla times people actually dressed up like people we knew in the movie and we always thought that was kinda strange.

Roo Kickkick and Florence Mink, well, they kinda got . . . actually, it's really complicated and sorta hard to sum up right here so maybe it isn't so good to tell you about any of that just yet.

As for Raoul, he died, that you already know. We still make jokes though that his extra finger didn't make his grip any better and sure as heck didn't save him from falling.

Thorpe Thorpe moved to Hollywood and lived the high life for a while before embarking on a new Autistik/Artistik album and the subsequent North American and World tour.

Thed Teldut did much the same as Thorpe. They were inseparable for the longest time.

Under pressure from Old Man Promised To, the town council erected a monument to Monroe Mister in the park where he died but we all used to spit on it when we passed by, and every so often someone would throw a bag of flaming poo at it, cuz we never liked him and he didn't deserve a statue. It sure was a good thing when it disappeared.

Plenty of tourists came to Barguss anyway though, on account of that movie. It was called *Roo Kickkick & the Big Bad Blimp* and we'd still be watching it right now if the print didn't get too hot one night in the projector and get blamed for burning the theater down, but that's a whole different kinda story.

2

We've known pretty much everybody mentioned so far since our mama was still picking out identical speckled green pants and sweaters (cuz that's how most moms dressed their twins back then) for us to wear and getting kinda mad and putting ice in our hair when we came home from grade school with gum wrapped up in the strands that we had previously tried to cut out with left-handed scissors but we were both right-handed and so only hair came out in clumps on the floor by our Velcro shoes but no gum. So the next day we'd have to get haircuts and the barber's place always smelled like smoke and burned hair where the ash got dropped on it. So we figure that's a real long time.

Early on in junior high school we found out just how talented Thorpe Thorpe really was cuz he played all the instruments in our 'developmental' music education classes on late Tuesday and Thursday afternoons, that had been created by a new policy in our school: no detention, just mandatory music class on account of the school board thought it would have a more positive effect on us as people if we could learn to appreciate music rather than sit around in a hot room after a regular school day and do nothing when we shoulda been doing homework.

During those classes we were encouraged to try as many

instruments as we liked and eventually pick one to learn, that was the point of the program anyway. So Thorpe Thorpe would play our old favorite, 'Talk Dirty to Me', on the xylophone and it was a real good thing the teacher didn't know that song cuz she would have been mad due to it not being 'classical'. But it was classical to us and we always laughed in awe when he played it and closed his eyes but still hit the pegs or whatever they're called.

After music class on Tuesdays and Thursdays, we would hang out in the empty red dirt playground of our old primary school that happened to be just across the street. The only trees around were outside the tall metal fence. The sunny days were the best days outside. Especially when we didn't have to wear coats cuz sometimes we fell while playing football and ripped them right up, though mostly that happened when we played our favorite game: Hooty Mack versus The Rogue Pimps (everyone always wanted to be Hooty Mack, the legendarily righteous vigilante from Upton, but only one person could be him and it was usually Thorpe, then Thorpe/Hooty got to beat everyone else up good and even if it was play, sometimes you got hit and hurt for real). Our mama hated that always. It didn't matter, though . . . we did it anyway. We were all caught up in the spell of Hooty Mack.

Probably when we were about eleven or twelve, a play was put on in Barguss in a converted movie screening room. Beau Thorpe (Thorpe's older brother) took us and Thorpe to see it twice. It was a traveling show written by some college kid playwright from Upton called nothing less than HOOTY MACK. It was like a blaxploitation/Greek tragedy with a killer soul soundtrack and it included all the stories we had heard as little kids, like the time Hooty beat up eighteen men with nunchucks just like Bruce Lee did in The Chinese Connection, *or the time when Hooty had a stand-off with Pimp Tall (a very infamous bad guy) and a live grenade in his own kitchen and he threw it in the oven and jumped out the window just in time but Pimp Tall didn't quite make it . . . oh, they were all there, and we ate it up!*

From then on we played Hooty Mack pretty much every day and we acted out all the stories we had heard: sometimes we were Hooty's company in Viet Nam, fighting to save his life and get him back to base after he suffered a nasty injury that he got a purple heart for, or maybe sometimes we'd play Hooty Mack and The Pimps of the Round Table and everybody'd have to be a different pimp for Hooty to defeat and nobody wanted to be Pimp Tall cuz we always had to simulate the grenade with rocks as shrapnel, or sometimes we even played at the most crazy showdown in the history of Upton: Hooty Mack against The Scarlet Pimp, Arnell, the overlord of all the pimps on the round table, the King Arthur guy (except evil), the man who ordered his serfhookers about in his fiefghettos under the collective eyes of his ducalpimps, and we'd all re-enact Hooty's infamous storming of Arnell's downtown warehouse on the portable trailer-looking building that doubled as our elementary school music classroom, but we couldn't actually start a fire so we just made fire noises with our mouths and had to jump out of the way when imaginary walls of flames came toward us. Sure, all this probably sounds super silly but really, we never had sports stars to want to be like, never really had anyone to want to be like outside of Hooty Mack and take our word for it that every single one of us wanted to be him more than anything, ever.

If we weren't playing Hooty Mack in the playground of our old primary school those days after music class, we would sometimes tell stories about the time we all used to have fantasies about saving Florence Mink (she was always the prettiest one in our class) from a wayward kickball flying in through our old classroom window so hard that it broke the glass into a brillion pieces and endangered her life and then

14

she would love us cuz we were her hero and had dived in and saved her from death. It would be just like that, instant bang boom love, at least that was what we thought.

She was so blonde in grade school (our mama says it's cuz she played outside all the time and the sun lightened her hair) and the back window of our classroom was so big and she would stand by it when she got up to go look stuff up in the dictionary in the back. While we had to copy off the blackboard she would stand there, leaning over the book on the brownish counter in front of the big window that was always covered with horizontal blinds, so if a ball were ever to come through there, she wouldn't even see it.

Back then we had thought about staging it, but no one could kick it hard enough to break the window. We know cuz we tried a few times during recess and the only thing that happened was a rubbery 'bwong' sound as the window vibrated and the teacher came out and looked at the window then told us to be more careful. Besides, no one wanted to be left out from saving Florence. We wouldn't even draw straws back then.

Funny how far away that kid stuff seemed to us, or at least we wanted it to be, when we played our Tuesday and Thursday football games (and even on those occasions when we couldn't keep ourselves from wanting to be like the toughest, most baddest dude in the whole history of the world, the man who in our minds was exactly a cross between Bruce Lee and Shaft and could whoop anyone with a pair of nunchucks . . . as Thorpe was known to scream and pretty loudly too: 'Hooty Motherfuckin' Mack!') on the clay dirt of our old primary school, still humming the tunes that Thorpe Thorpe stuck in our heads with that xylophone.

Things didn't stay like that for long though cuz that was definitely about the time when . . .

Thorpe Thorpe Has Himself an Accident

Must've been the Fall quarter of our second year in junior high school when it happened. That was when we got a new student in developmental music class. MacJohnson Fern-Micklewhite was his name and he got transferred to our school halfway through the year and we were told to be nice to him cuz he was new and would have 'new kid problems'. That's what the teacher said but we didn't quite know what it meant although pretty much everybody knew he was a bit slow in the head. He was actually a year and a half older than us but was still in our same grade. We did know that we had wound up in developmental music education class cuz we told our English teacher she 'sucked' when she was being mean about adverbs and embarrassing us in front of the whole class cuz we mixed them up with adjectives.

And Thorpe Thorpe had been added to the list cuz he showed up to laboratory science class in a big cape and a mask and made everyone laugh cuz it wasn't Halloween and he ran around the classroom bounding off of the desks and lab tables with gas outlets for Bunsen burners while the teacher tried to catch him but he made a dash out into the hall and started screaming, 'free as a bee/oh to be free', until the Principal Who Is Your Pal caught him hiding in the janitor's closet and hit him with a ruler on his thin fingers 'til he promised not to do it anymore. We knew cuz we saw the marks on Thorpe's knuckles and secretly decided never to get caught cuz the Principal Who Is Your Pal hit with the warped metal part used to guide the pencil and not the flat wood with the centimeter and inch numbers and lines. And we reckoned that was the most unfair thing to do when someone wasn't allowed to move out of the way or even given a sporting chance. So that sums it up, developmental music education class wasn't for the gifted in Barguss, it was for the troublemakers and as we figured out, MacJohnson and his 'new kid problems' fit right in that box.

Someone said he had a Mary Poppins-type nanny/caretaker except she was from El Salvador and none of us knew where it was but we guessed it was somewhere big and he must have learned Spanish from her. Maria was her name and apparently she did everything for him, cooked his meals and did the shopping for his clothes and told him stories, all while his real parents were off in New York or somewhere fancy in the Caribbean.

One rumor went that the Fern-Micklewhite house in Barguss wasn't even the family's permanent residence; instead, his dad lived in New York City with his mom and they would visit sometimes cuz they felt they needed a dose of 'small-time America to help keep their priorities straight', or something. Even though it might not have been true, it stung us to hear it and we felt a little bit sorry for MacJohnson and we kinda understood when he changed his name officially a coupla years later when we got to high school.

But back then in developmental music class it was still MacJohnson, and the music teacher assigned him to a seat in Thorpe Thorpe's row and it was obvious from the start that he wasn't the smartest person ever and we think Thorpe Thorpe was the first person to see that cuz he was really smart, too smart even.

That said, what happened was kinda Thorpe Thorpe's fault really. He had been teasing MacJohnson that he was slow and stupid for being older than us and stuff and Thorpe said that his parents didn't even love him cuz he had a caretaker (and he would call her Maria Poppinez or something similar) that wasn't his mom or dad and she couldn't even speak English so she wasn't American and stuff like that. Not nice things and we even felt our stomachs curl over on themselves sometimes when he opened his mouth and said something mean and ignorant to MacJohnson. None of us had much of a grudge against him cuz he was a pretty quiet kid, just with a wild look in his eyes that kept us from trusting him or even talking to him too much.

We said something to Thorpe Thorpe about his remarks once but he just laughed and said it was just joking and if MacJohnson couldn't take a joke then he was dumber than everyone thought he was and if we couldn't take a joke then we were dumb too. Looking back on it, we're sure that Thorpe's teasing about MacJohnson's parents was no big deal cuz he hated them anyway but it was the awful remarks about Maria that turned his insides to stone cuz he loved her like she had given birth to him. Well, the teasing continued for two straight weeks and nothing happened at school cuz Thorpe Thorpe was too popular, especially after developmental music class and what with us playing football and Hooty Mack and everything. But then it did happen, on a Monday, quick and nasty-like.

As far as we could trace it back, it happened in the cul-de-sac by Thorpe Thorpe's bus stop. MacJohnson Fern-Micklewhite followed him home and before he got there MacJohnson threw him up against a 1976 Volvo 244 DL (navy blue with sunroof) parked the wrong way on the road and it bent one of the side mirrors inward 'til it touched the window. Probably that was when MacJohnson/Raoul decided he had a taste for violence.

Or maybe it was when Thorpe Thorpe was on the ground coughing from a kidney punch and Raoul found a rake that someone had left out in the yard and he used the back end to hit Thorpe Thorpe in his legs and shoulders with big overhead swooshing strokes that made cutting sounds in the air before landing on Thorpe Thorpe with slapping echoes rebounding off of the houses in the neighborhood. Well, at least he did before the owner of the house, rake, and car came out. He was

18

a big kind of drunk named Hasselzwell Smol and he promptly took the rake from Raoul – sorry, he was MacJohnson still back then. We get confused on account of that's the same behavior we always knew of Raoul.

So anyway big Hasselzwell had a generic white-canned beer in one hand that just said 'BEER' on it, at least that's how we picture it, and he took the rake with the other and smote MacJohnson down with one blow and then picked Thorpe Thorpe up and handed him the very same rake before turning around and heading back inside without batting a sticky eyelid. Apparently, Thorpe Thorpe kinda stood over the stunned MacJohnson before dropping the rake and running home crying without ever getting a solid good lick in on the bully.

Later, he must have regretted not hitting him with the butt-end of that rake when he had his golden chance cuz he was always a nice guy and wouldn't hurt a fly but he wanted to hurt Raoul physically like Raoul hurt him and besides Thorpe Thorpe always talked big and had a big ego, so sometimes that got him in the wrong kind of trouble but we've all got to learn those lessons young we guess or it gets to be a bigger problem later on.

Anyway, Thorpe Thorpe missed two days then came to developmental music class the next Thursday and wouldn't play anything, not even 'Look What the Cat Dragged In' or 'Unskinny Bop' on the recorder, the one we all sang the chorus to under our breaths in class cuz we knew every single word. And he never said who did it but when we grew up, we all knew it had to be Raoul de los Dios even though Thorpe always just said he 'had himself an accident'.

After that incident Thorpe Thorpe kinda withdrew and spent more time at home, all alone in his room. He learned bass from his brother and we're pretty sure that was about the time he changed, cuz to ask Thorpe nowadays about that time in his life, he just says that it was when he ceased being 'a performer, only concerned with getting a reaction' and became 'an artist', getting in touch with his anger and 'dissecting his inner life for everyone to see'.

It was then that he actually wrote his first song and it was called 'When I Get Big Enough I'm Gonna Punch You in Your Fucking Face Not Hit You With a Rake 'Cause I'm No [and he would drawl this next bit] Sissified Coward' and it was a punk song cuz he just had stolen a scuffed Buzzcocks 45 from his older brother's record stash and been so inspired that he listened to it 'til the needle on his portable record player broke. We guess the only good thing to come of it was that Thorpe Thorpe learned that words can hurt and that idea obviously translated into his songs.

'Kismet' was the word that Thorpe Thorpe blurted into the mic before launching into his song and we'll always remember it cuz it even made the adults get funny looks on their faces, all cuz they didn't understand either but it turned out to be really appropriate in hindsight. Well, he played about nine seconds of his first song ever for the Zebulon P. Barguss Junior High School talent contest two weeks after Raoul thumped him good, nine seconds of screaming was all he could get in, which was good considering he screamed the chorus – which was basically the title and nothing else – five and a half times in that duration, before being dragged off stage in the middle of screaming the word 'face' so it sounded like 'fa—' as the janitor and gym teacher yanked his legs out from under him and he knocked the mic stand over on his way down. Right after that, he was sent directly to the Principal Who Is Your Pal and didn't come back for two weeks and it's kinda funny cuz that's how he met Thed Teldut.

As it turned out, Thed liked the performance so much that he sought out Thorpe Thorpe about forming a band. Thed was new in school back then, having just moved from Orange

County, California, so they formed a band right after that but no one remembers the name of it, not even Thorpe Thorpe or Thed. We always tell that story cuz in a really indirect way that's kinda how Autistik/Artistik was born.

3

Barguss got an 'Infestation of Drugs', that's what our local newspaper the Telegraph called it, in the late eighties/early nineties. It was sorta true. Seemed like overnight, drugs were available and people were doing them. Everyone was. Our mayor got convicted of cocaine use and then got re-elected after serving a short jail term in a cushy white-collar-type prison. Typical stuff, really. It's hard to explain to people that there wasn't anything ever to do in Barguss and so people either watched lots of TV or did lots of drugs until that big national campaign to end drug use finally caught up to us.

Which was actually kinda a blow to our economy cuz we had some really good drug dealers like The Peteness who made a big deal of putting money back into the community; like buying gold rims for his car at a local shop and also buying a house with cash and paying local guys to guard it. So it was kinda funny and sad that the war on drugs actually hit the small Barguss economy pretty hard cuz we all sorta profited from guys like The Peteness throwing money around. He was a kinda shadowy character but people who'd seen him said he looked just like Gary Oldman in True Romance, fake dreads and awful shirts and everything. But he wasn't as prolific with his money throwing or community improvement as . . .

Sassa Medusa Belle. She was the only female drug dealer we

had ever heard of cuz we thought you had to be a guy and be all tough to sell drugs and keep your turf but she changed us from thinking that. She was a local girl and used to play basketball for our high school and they got second in the whole state behind her quadruple-double: assists, rebounds, steals, and blocked shots, but it wasn't quite enough to win. They lost by four points and she only scored nine, one point away from the first-ever quintuple-double in state tournament history. Though it's still the only big plaque we have in the high school trophy cabinet and it's a second place one but we're pretty sure it still haunts her.

Anyway, she was really tall and jackknife smart and she used to take her extra money and put it into kids' clubs and stuff, which was kinda weird cuz she made a lot of money from school kids doing her 'merchandise' but that's what she did and she also built a little park and named it after her mother: The Mrs Irma Lorna Belle Park for the Recreation of All Barguss. And she even forced some of her clients who had debts to clean up that park on account of their inability to pay and some still credit her for having the idea about citywide community service for debtors. We think the city hall old folks stole that idea from her.

'Course even Barguss isn't big enough for two big-time drug dealers, much less all the other little ones that tried to horn in on the bizness in our 'suburbs' like Krakatowa Proper, the yuppie housing community which had a penchant for speed. The California boys brought speed in by the truck-load for them and for a little while it was fine until The Peteness and Sassa Medusa Belle banded together to push out the 'California influence' as it had been dubbed, but by then both of them had big heads and didn't want to share. We think it was The Peteness that didn't want to share but either way they had a 'war' which lasted two days and left two maimed (but they got better) and one *dead (he didn't). Not much of a war really, kinda civil in retrospect.*

So Barguss's only gang war ended in the late eighties when The Peteness had his throat slit at his own house. Rumor was Sassa or one of her goons (probably even Thorpe's brother, Beau) did it, of course we could never prove that but everyone knows. For a while she was just a local benefactor cuz she made wise investments and got out of the housing and urban development thing before it went belly up to the sun. She even sat on the town council every so often cuz she got out of dealing and occasionally lectured at the community college just up the highway about social responsibility, entrepreneurial stuff and economics. We thought that was funny.

So there, really we couldn't tell this next one without you kinda knowing the background around when this story was told to us.

Thed Teldut Blasts Off into Outer Space!

Back when Thed Teldut was sixteen, which must have been 1991 cuz we all pretty much turned that age then, he worked his first summer job in the Barguss shampoo factory as a stirrer and it wasn't long before he started having bizarre theoretical thoughts about the Fibonacci sequence and how circular patterns appeared in everything natural, like plants and rocks and fingerprints, even the stirring of a giant vat of blue shampoo. It wasn't a real shampoo factory but more like one that got subcontracted from the bigger companies so it wasn't 'official' is a better way of saying it, which basically means that the giant vat of blue shampoo that Thed stirred for eight hours a day could end up in any one of thirteen different brand name bottles cuz the same parent company owned 'em all.

It's pretty safe to say that Thed hated that job. Many people just take this as a given as all of us kids just out of school for the summer ended up working long awful jobs like at the shampoo factory or the grocery store or the local telemarketing company just up the road in Pinecone County. There wasn't much industry in Barguss and it generally tended to be of the variety that other towns didn't want, like the toxic-smoke-producing all-weather radial and snow tire plant on the outskirts. We didn't really want it either but we just never happened to be in a position to turn it down.

So the way we hear it, tired ol' Thed went home one night after work and ignored his mother's orders to clean his room or take out the garbage and went up to the attic that he had moved his bed and stuff up to from his old room downstairs and sat down with a broken strobe light he had for years and decided to finally fix it but then he went one step further and he made a drum machine with the circuit cuz he read about Thomas Dolby doing it once in a magazine.

Well, by then it was late and it was dark outside and Thed wanted to go out and tell Thorpe Thorpe what he had done, so he walked down Gee Street humming 'One of Our Submarines' 'til he cut through the half-full parking lot of Taco Coleslaw Hamburger Hot Dog Apple to get to Thorpe's brother's house. He knocked and knocked on the basement window where Thorpe lived but got nowhere. There weren't even any lights on inside.

Soon enough though the front door of the house opened and out into the light stepped Thorpe Thorpe's brother, Beau Thorpe. He was bigger than Thorpe and handsomer and always had lots of girls over but we all knew he only ever cared about himself and, cuz of that, never treated them so good. He also happened to have a shotgun in his hands and called out something like, 'step out from there, you rat,' to Thed and Thed just kinda stood straight up and put his hands in the air.

When Beau Thorpe's eyes adjusted to the darkness he could see the light reflecting off of glasses and it was just little Thed and he laughed and put the gun up on his shoulder and told him to come in if he was cold. 'Who do you think you are sneaking around in the dark out there . . . Hooty Mack?' and Beau laughed at his own joke, turned around and motioned for Thed to follow him into the house. So Thed did and as he walked in he just said that he was looking for 'Thorpey Thorpe de Ville', as he sometimes called him, and he had just made a drum machine from scratch with an old strobe circuit.

Thed tried to say those words while looking at the crooked stained floor mat but looked up and swallowed half of 'em cuz he saw a girl with her shirt off and no bra either just sitting out in the middle of the living room, wearing a long faded red skirt over dirty white socks that came up to her knees, just kinda giggling. She was leaning over a big glass container that had a few rocks in it and a big tarantula spider all up on its hind six legs and she was feeding it live grasshoppers and crickets from her hand. Apparently she'd been giggling cuz the crickets tickled her palm just before she stuffed 'em through a small hole in the top of the spider container.

Thed had never seen breasts in person before, so that occupied him more than what she was doing. In fact, the only previous time he had even seen boobs was in a magazine that Thorpe had loaned him, and so of course he stared and didn't notice the rest of the living room until a metal-on-metal banging sound from the kitchen kinda startled him into awareness. The curtains were drawn and their color was not immediately recognizable as the TV piled blues and greens on them, not to mention the couch and the bookshelf behind it too.

'Twerp Thorpe's gone out with Staceyleene,' Beau Thorpe said nice and loud from the kitchen, still banging some unseen surface and laughing, 'but we're having a party and you are more than welcome to stay pa'dner.' Still with the shotgun in his left hand, Beau Thorpe took some beers out of the fridge that just said 'BEER' on them.

Thed could not take his eyes from the breasts of that giggling girl and he knew it was bad and his cheeks were turning red when she squealed and threw her head back and his breath caught when her chest heaved with the accented words: 'He ate two legs off and they flap their wings in the corner!' She smiled at Thed and he was able to lower his eyes and nod his mild assent though he said later to us that he was glad she hadn't progressed to feeding Beau's boa constrictor – Beau Junior, of course – live mice, squirrels and 'found' stray kittens, as Beau used to brag about, 'if they were small enough,' he would say.

It turned out the semi-naked girl was named Linnelisse and she was only like sixteen too but she was plumpish with pretty eyes and eyebrows. Apparently she was some kind of exchange student from Scandinavia somewheres in Europe and she had been pouting for weeks cuz Barguss was so damn boring but then she met Beau Thorpe and hadn't complained since.

It was then that Thed noticed that there was someone else in the room. Sassa Medusa Belle sat stock still in the corner and looked really tough. Apparently she was just back from Upton Junior College at the time, still playing basketball; that's what Thed said cuz she was wearing her b-ball shorts over her long muscled legs and lounging silently in the dirty barcalounger that looked like 'cushiony frooty loops vomit', as described by Thed Teldut himself.

Sassa didn't say anything, she just sorta sat there and took long drags off of something smoking in her hand and Thed guessed it was a roach or skunk or other like animal that described the drug and he knew that this was just the sorta situation Moms Teldut had warned him about but he didn't care. He just sat down across from Linnelisse and waited for something to happen.

'Somebody pitch that kid a slow ball,' Beau Thorpe said, sitting down on the couch behind Linnelisse and looking at Sassa, 'come on!' he said, 'it's his first time . . . let him never forget it.' Thed reckons Sassa just watched the TV for the sports report, then without saying anything, she put two pills and a big vial on the table and Beau got all excited and said, 'you ready, kiddy?' all fast to Thed while laughing manically, and Thed got shit scared but he nodded.

Beau Thorpe got a spoon from the kitchen and came back and somehow in that short time he wasn't wearing a shirt either and what's more, Linnelisse put some white stuff on Thed's gums after she made him open his mouth and her boobs swayed inches from his face as it went completely numb from chin to hair and he laughed cuz it felt like the time he woke up from having surgery on his ears and couldn't feel anything above his neck.

Well, the two pills went in the spoon and the liquid in the vial was poured over them 'til they dissolved to a chalky kinda substance and Beau said, 'now take your medicine like a good little boy,' and Thed took the spoon and without spilling a drop, swallowed it all and everyone in the room clapped (Linnelisse even crushed a cricket between her fingers by accident while doing so), everyone, except for Sassa. She was putting music on the record player just then and Thed said he didn't like it when it came on cuz it was The Specials and he didn't really like them cuz he thought ska was 'deader than dead', but he drank up the beer Beau handed him cuz anything would have been better than the taste of the spoon concoction, even crappy beer.

The last thing he remembered was Beau Thorpe laughing words out of his mouth, 'Enough LSD, benzo and morphine to kill the whole damn Brady Bunch including Alice!' and then it was the song 'Nite Klub' on the stereo but just the first few lines. 'Is this the in place to be? / What am I doing here? /

Watching the girls go by', and he said he remembered thinking that it was one of those perfect moments in life when the music fits your life like on purpose but then the needle slid acrosst it and Sassa pulled down another record, a twelve-inch, and it was 'Ghost Town' and by the time the beat and organ came in, you know, after the windy bit, he felt like he was sinking.

Supposedly it was the first time he ever tried drugs. We wouldn't know, we never tried them exactly but we liked to talk about them and try to be cool. As Thed tells it, his trip was a blast-off in a rocket where he went up to the moon and flew around it a thousand times in a stacked six-wing WWI-era prop plane with the visual incarnation of a story character his brother and him had made up in the back of the family car when they went on long journeys.

'Pouse and his Flying Pigpen', that's what Thed called it. That was the name of the aeroplane, the Flying Pigpen, and Pouse was the pilot up there flying around the moon with him and they threw tomatoes into the big craters and they laughed at everybody cuz the moon wasn't made of cheese at all, it was just a big rock and Pouse was animated like a 1960s cartoon and Thed said his eyes felt like rolling dice that always came up sixes. Then, he said, he can't remember, he just woke up and no Sassa, no Linnelisse and no Beau Thorpe, only the sound of a loose shutter banging against the kitchen window.

It was light outside though and so he walked out into the yard after getting a drink of water from putting his head upside down and his lips on the faucet and grabbed some bread from the breadbox cuz he was uncommonly hungry and thirsty. With heavy legs, he crunched on some fallen front yard leaves 'til he got to Thorpe Thorpe's window and knocked but no one was there, so he went home after using the last of his pocket change to get an order of fried beefsteak tomatoes from Taco Coleslaw Hamburger Hot Dog Apple cuz he said his trip had made him super hungry for tomatoes.

But he felt okay, aside from groggy, and he crossed Gee Street and went home, just figuring it was the next day, but it wasn't, it was two days later and everyone was wondering where he was cuz the cops were searching for him and everything. Well, Moms Teldut gave him a Cerberus-type treble-tongue-lashing but was actually really glad to see him and the lie he told must have been extraordinary cuz she never even grounded him but maybe that was cuz she had to go to so much trouble to get the police to call off their search that had expanded to three counties, we aren't so sure.

Later, we all found out the whole sordid story (well, at the time, we thought it was the whole story but later we found out much, much different) from Thorpe Thorpe that Beau and everyone had thought that Thed Teldut was dead, so they took off on account of his not moving at all for hours and hours. We can only guess that they figured Thorpe Thorpe would eventually find him and make the necessary arrangements, so we guess it was a good thing that he wasn't dead. There is a kinda funny sidenote to the tale though cuz Thed said the event actually inspired his first electronic instrumental song, 'Frank Sinatra Could Never Fly Me to the Moon'.

4

Donny Barn came to Barguss in 1972 as a Canadian immigrant with a good sum of money. Growing up in western Alberta, Donny had played hockey and box lacrosse, but those were hobbies compared to his passion for Western films. He had two dreams back then. One, to construct a movie theater in which he could show all of his favorite films and two, to build a large number of Western-themed clothing chain stores throughout Barguss and the surrounding area, with an eye to taking it national one day.

Donny had one more dream though. His third dream, which remained unvoiced in public places while sober, included going down 'in a blaze of glory', but none of us were too sure what it meant and he only screamed about it when he had had one too many at Paulson's Cocktails on Cole Street, the local dive bar. Well, he accomplished the first two, unveiling the Exclusive Donny Barn Theater and its 'fabulous eight screens of wonderment' in February of 1974, with the first ever showing at the theater being a Peckinpah double bill of Bring Me the Head of Alfredo Garcia and The Ballad of Cable Hogue. Shortly thereafter he opened the first of his Western-themed warehouses: Barn's Barn (For Western Wear).

Though it wasn't so much a problem, there was a catch: Donny was crazy, certifiably. The United States had almost denied him a green card cuz of his having spent time in a mental institution in Calgary between 1969 and 1970. Our mama says it wasn't an unusual sight to see Donny flying down Gee Street going 110 miles per hour on one of his recently purchased motorcycles wearing only a diaper and screaming unintelligible gibberish that most folks just wrote off as some 'damn Canadian dialect'. Three motorcycle accidents, one stint in traction, and three broken collarbones (he broke the left one and the right one after a nasty accident with a runaway Cooper Market dumpster, and the second time he broke his right one is a real nasty story too, but we'll just have to tell that later), but all that never deterred him from riding his 'two-wheeled demons', as he referred to them. There was an upside to his insanity though, as it provided some of the most entertaining and infamous commercials ever to come on local television.

Yup, it was a common occurrence to see Donny announcing one of his typical 'price drop' sales by yelling and spitting, '$8.99! $7.99! $6.99! Awwwww heck, $5.99!!!' at the camera while actually sinking his teeth into the latest collection of functional boot-tapered jeans to somehow prove their quality, before lobbing the garments over his head and into the hat rack crammed with ten-gallon cowboy hats at one of his Western-themed warehouses.

Donny was a well-appreciated local celebrity, perhaps due mostly to his eccentricities, long before Florence Mink got famous but he sure knew the people of Barguss, crazy as he was. So when he decided to hold The First Annual Florence Mink Film Festival at the Exclusive Donny Barn Theater in the summer of 1998, the tickets sold out within two days and in Barguss, that's really, really fast. Florence Mink got famous real quick after Roo Kickkick & the Big Bad Blimp cuz a famous producer scouted her out of the movie. He was even quoted as saying she was the only good thing about it. Then again, she was playing herself but she didn't wear spoons in her hair in the movie. Well, after it, she made a buncha films in the next four years though she was always making noises about 'retirement'. Which was quite odd cuz we all knew how she adored the attention and how she never came back to Barguss once she got famous. She just moved all her relatives except her dad (everybody thought that was kinda weird at the time) out to California, wholesale like.

Generally, people in Barguss go see all of Florence's movies when they first come out cuz she's our only real kinda celebrity after Thorpe Thorpe and Thed Teldut, even though she completely disavows us and even says she is from Texas sometimes in her interviews but she was born and raised here, and Barguss isn't in Texas so we don't understand it. We guess it was predictable then that Florence turned down an invitation from Donny Barn to show up at the first annual film festival held in her honor. We were some of the first to buy tickets and definitely the first coupla people in line even though we've seen all of her movies, some three and four times even but everybody else had too.

The festival was held over a weekend and it started late on a Friday night with a showing of the first film Florence did after her debut. It's a big budget thriller called The Gone Town Boys and it's about a group of teenagers that run away from home after they do something stupid like kill somebody by accident while they've been drinking. So they run away and go live in a deserted mining town in the mountains cuz they need shelter and they figure no one will ever find them there. Only problem is it's haunted (cuz they always are) and Florence was the head miner's wife that got killed a hundred years ago with a pickaxe and is looking for revenge. It's really, really scary though and in the viewing we saw, two girls left crying with their boyfriends running behind and trying to comfort them. We thought it was funny cuz just about everybody in Barguss has seen it and yet people still get scared like that at the scary

33

parts. Some Spanish director directed it perfectly and we won't ruin the ending but it's poetic.

On Saturday, they showed a noontime movie; it was a dark romantic comedy drama about two lovers and one is dying and it's called The Last of Me, and we're ashamed to admit it but even we cried when Florence croaked in that one. We couldn't help it, everyone else was crying too and during the crucial death scene we could barely hear it cuz of the sniffles in the theater. It's really weird when you know the person dying on the big screen cuz it's real but it's not real at the same time.

After that, we bought more popcorn at the concession stand and waited for the 3:00 p.m. movie, The Lloyd Krekenburg Letters, it's kinda like a mystery comedy. Florence is really funny in it (we thought so anyway but it might just be the writing cuz we laughed a lot and couldn't remember Florence ever being so funny in real life) even though she isn't in it for very long, which pretty much meant that everybody hooted and hollered at the screen as she popped up and then they laughed extra hard when she delivered her punch lines even when they'd heard them before and it kinda made us feel nervous but we didn't know why.

At 5:30 p.m. the D-BET, as we've always called it, showed Florence's brand new movie (at the time) and we think it's her best, that would have to be The Burning Bend, behind the movie about Barguss of course. The Burning Bend though was so good in a different way and it's about a Southern family in the Civil War and they live in rural Georgia and they get caught in the middle of Sherman's march through the state and it was heart-wrenching and sad but the good kind of sad and it said a lot about the United States even though it wasn't historically accurate and kinda made up and changed facts. Florence was the daughter who loved a slave and later she even got an Oscar® nomination for it, which we thought was great cuz Florence pulled off a terrific

34

Southern accent that surprised us too, cuz Barguss isn't in the South either.

Funny how just after the emotional roller coaster of The Burning Bend, Donny Barn decided to show Florence's worst movie ever at 8:00 p.m., but still the theater was pretty full. Nickel, Nickel, Dime is about small-time hustlers banding together and forming a syndicate or something like that and she plays some pimp's girlfriend/hooker. It suffered from a 'lack of direction', that's what Florence Mink said later in an interview cuz Oliver Stone was gonna direct, but then he didn't, and then they talked about all sorts of names and nobody would direct, then someone nobody ever heard of (Alan Smithee, we think his name was) just kinda filled in. Supposedly he had done lots of TV and horror movies, but that didn't help cuz the plot has big holes in it and it isn't funny when it's supposed to be. The showing wasn't so bad though cuz we sat next to Donny Barn himself and he cracked jokes about the movie into a microphone the whole time and he must have written 'em down or something cuz he had everybody rolling in the aisles by making fun of some of the one-liners and crappy acting.

We're pretty sure everyone had been waiting for the 10:30 p.m. screening more than any of the others on Saturday cuz when people say Florence Mink's name (anywhere but Barguss) they always think about Caddywoddle. It's a lot of people's favorite cuz it's kinda like a Frank Capra movie but it isn't, on account of he was dead when it was made but Florence plays Dorothy James, a high-powered executive who is ruthless in her bizness and she is really rich and good at her job but she's also mean. Well, one day, when she is really mean to someone she shouldn't be mean to, her childhood invisible friend Caddywoddle comes back to teach her a lesson in how to be a better person. Caddywoddle isn't invisible to her but to everybody else he is and they are friends and she changes to

35

be nice, by the end of the movie anyway. Everyone said she was robbed when she didn't get any awards for her performance even though it sounds cheesy but apparently it sells and rents really well on video . . . our mama says it's one of those 'late bloomers'. Maybe due to the fact that it makes you feel really good inside when you watch it. But it is so much better to watch at a movie theater especially in Barguss cuz at the end the audience people were actually mimicking Florence's dance in Times Square just before the credits and dancing in the aisles and almost everybody sang the songs perfectly in time with Florence on the screen but they're good enough just to mouth the dialogue to themselves the rest of the time.

The festival closed with a viewing of Roo Kickkick & the Big Bad Blimp *and in the showing we went to, everyone just had the best time and it was bizarre but people talked throughout the whole movie, shouting comments from the gallery at the screen like, 'that's my house!' and 'I remember that different!' but everybody was laughing and smiling irregardless of what came out of their mouths. We found out later that Donny had to run the movie fourteen separate times on two different screens on the last day of the festival, which was a Sunday, just so everyone in town could see it again. That is what a big success The First Annual Florence Mink Film Festival was.*

But this story happened way before Florence got all famous and was kinda like a mirror into her future.

Florence Mink Is a Pretty, Pretty Princess

She was, really. So pretty her father couldn't keep his hands off her in the bad way and none of us knew it at the time, which made sense cuz we would have stopped it if we'd known absolutely anything about it. Called the police or something, that's what we would have done. Her dad's brother was in the police though so maybe that wouldn't have worked. Well, we all found out when Florence went public with the news and caused an awful big fuss and she got lots of sympathy. Come to think of it, that was after *Nickel, Nickel, Dime.*

'It always happened when he put Leonard Cohen on,' we are just quoting from the national tabloid newspaper interview with Florence, 'when he was in the moods.' In the moods, she called it, and we weren't sure if it was a typographical error or not but it's somehow more chilling to us than if it were just 'the mood'. Hopefully, Mr. Cohen didn't get mad or anything cuz it doesn't say much about him but just what a sick twist her dad was. He's dead now, killed himself after the secret became public.

Eventually, we had forgotten about how we all used to think that she was broke inside cuz the only time we ever saw her was when she was on the big screen but that article changed how we thought about her a little bit. The article also said that the only person she ever, ever told was Mumartin Rigglesby, even though he isn't a person at all, he's just her teddy bear. And he couldn't do anything to stop it cuz he was stuffed and it would have been great if he were like Caddywoddle cuz he would've saved Florence. We're pretty sure of that.

Maybe there were signs but we never saw any apart from Mr. Mink always fawning over her and her outfits and making sure her bows were tied and dress was just right but it gives us a shiver to think on it now. We do remember how Florence was always the star of the talent shows, at least the favorite of the judges anyway, cuz Thorpe Thorpe was a damn legend after his performance and we always wanted him to top it but he was never allowed to compete again after what he did, so we didn't see him perform again until he got old enough to not be in talent shows anymore and he did some crazy things on stage with Tee Tee Ta Tee Two Too and Autistik/Artistik but he writes it off now as reckless youth.

In fact, the same talent show that Thorpe Thorpe got thrown out of was the first one where we truly saw Florence's talent. Her father sat in the front row (as he always did) with a really straight back and he was tall so there was a gap in the chairs behind him cuz no one could see over his head or shoulders. He didn't ever seem to care what people thought.

Well, the 'auditorium' that the talent show took place in was actually our gymnasium with a giant big sheet over the basketball court so they could put chairs on it without scuffing the wood and also the basketball hoops got put up and presto! It was an auditorium and the parents came and filled in behind Mr. Mink and looked generally approving. The only disconcerting moment was Thorpe's appearance and we had to get hushed for cheering and the parents all looked like they had eaten something spiky that got caught in their throats and they tried to act like it never happened, especially Mrs. Thorpe, who snuck out the side door afterward. With a really red face, she blabbed something about 'going out for a smoke' but she never came back that day and she never went to PTA (that stands for Parents and Teachers Association) or anywhere else in Barguss after that.

The chairs faced the stage that was a portable one of course, and not very tall and had red carpeting on it and 'it hurt', that's what Thorpe Thorpe said cuz he had gotten rug burns on his elbows and knees from being dragged off it so fast. Anyway, the show had re-started after a brief delay following his performance. Two girls had already gone and sung dressed up like Whitney Houston and Madonna respectively.

The first one sang a really bad version of 'I Wanna Dance With Somebody (Who Loves Me)' and the second one sang 'Cherish' to a tape with Madonna's voice on it too and we reckoned it was cheating but she also twirled a baton at the same time and it was okay cuz that was hard to do. We didn't know her name, as she was older than us.

Then another girl, Lucy Trucey, we remember her cuz we used to have a crush on her for awhile, lip-synched 'Like A Prayer' and just bounced up and down for the whole song but she got disqualified for having a skirt that was too short even though she wore weird green leggings underneath but they had tears in them so that must have been why the judges didn't like her look.

And Oliver Martin Rivelo, he was the kid in the other class but still in our year, got up and juggled three soccer balls to a tape on his boom box that he set at the front of the stage right in front of Mr. Mink who just looked really mad when the lyrics came out and we think it was 'You Talk Too Much' by Run DMC but we figure he didn't win cuz the judges always said they hated that 'rap crap'.

Florence Mink was next and she didn't bring on a tape player, instead she just kinda nodded to someone behind the curtain and the music came on, just instrumental and it was 'Express Yourself' and Madonna wasn't singing in the background cuz it was all Florence's voice and we thought it was great but it really got good when it became a medley and 'Oh Father' came on and she sang it directly to her dad and it was then that we knew she was a real Madonna fan and not a fake one cuz she knew the songs not everybody knew but it was kinda strange to notice that Mr. Mink kept smoothing his hair down over his balding head, over and over again which was annoying with all that motion since he was in the front row but he stopped and sat real still for her third song, which was a really great rendition of 'Like A Virgin'.

Seeing *Caddywoddle* at the film festival reminded us of her performance in that talent show cuz she sings and dances with Caddywoddle in the film and it's so well done and it feels good to know that we knew she had talent before everybody else did. That scene in the movie was her first time ever singing and dancing in the movies but we could have told them she could do it even before then.

The day of the talent show though she wore this fluffy white Madonna dress but without the 'boy toy' belt cuz she took it off backstage so she wouldn't get disqualified like Lucy Trucey, we think. But she danced really good too and she even did some real Madonna moves and when she was done we clapped hard and her father even stood up and clapped louder than everybody else but nobody thought anything of it at the time, though now it makes our stomachs hurt.

So Florence won the talent show despite her songs being 'racy' as one judge said; actually he leaned too close to the mic to say it and the *cee* sound in the middle bounced all over the tinny gym speakers. But she really was the best though and she didn't lip-sync at all. And then when her dad lifted her down from the stage with her blue first place ribbon, we all heard him say that she was his 'pretty, pretty princess'.

5

Even way before he had the blue fast car, he always got all he ever wanted. Money, clothes, girls, it didn't matter cuz he got it. Maybe it's just our sour grapes but we think that when circumstances conspire like that, people get used to being the center of their world and little bits of 'em get all shrunken on the inside, kinda like Florence too, we guess. It's almost as if the real important parts get shelved in favor of just getting one's way all the time. Character, we guess that's what's missing; character.

Monroe Mister Promised To Gets It All

We guess it must have happened as soon as he was born, getting it all, we mean. He was lucky enough to be born into a rich family, so that's nothing real, real new. Monroe Mister's mother was Miss Alabama in 1974 or something and she even got first runner-up for Miss America that year so that's one of the reasons why he's such a good-looking guy, good genes. But anyway, his father was like sixty-two when Monroe Mister was born and it was his first child so he completely spoiled the boy even after his wife left him to found a nationwide frozen food empire specializing in high-quality seafood and chicken in herby sauces.

So growing up, little Monroe Mister got all the He-man action figures including castle greyskull and those laser guns every kid wanted but no parent could afford and he got those little drivey-type cars that fit kids perfectly and you could go up hill in the street and not have to walk cuz it had its own little motor and sometimes Monroe Mister would throw stuff at us from inside the little green one shaped like a jeep and laugh. We'll always remember that.

His dad really loved him though, he must have, cuz he always gave him big presents like on his sixteenth birthday he got the new real jeep that everyone fell all over themselves for but no one could ever afford except for the Promised Tos cuz 'once money gets up that high it doesn't just go away unless you are really stupid with it', at least our mama says so anyway.

Apparently someone said the Promised To family was 'old money', but none of us ever understood that cuz this isn't new or old England and most people around here have to earn the money the hard way like working on the Promised To Car Wash or something, instead of sitting around and stacking up interest while they sit on their butts. Workers had been trying to form some kinda coalition or union against Old Man Promised To for some time cuz he always paid bad wages and there wasn't much in Barguss he didn't own. So he could do pretty much whatever he wanted.

We kinda like to think of him as the town bad guy but we think he's not so happy in his castle on Hill Street. That enormous thing he got built after Monroe Mister's mom left and everyone's called him 'Citizen Kane' ever since and he's never liked being called that, so he's just never left his 'Xanadu'. It was named Emmoly House or something silly like that and there were no other homes flush up against it like in our neighborhood·but there were some nearby (all the other ones on 'rich people hill', as we knew it, but Emmoly House is the one on the very, very top) and one rare person who had been outside of Barguss (besides to California) said how it looks like One Tree Hill in Auckland used to look except it's the tree and the hill, which to us is a kinda funny description cuz it makes us think of Doctor Seuss for some reason but since we don't exactly know where Auckland is we mostly just smile and nod when people make worldly observations like that.

He really isn't the town bad guy cuz he's our only really super-rich resident and he does give a lot to the community but in such a different way to Sassa Medusa Belle. He gave money to anything his son was doing, like donations to football and basketball and tennis and golf and they even founded a golf club in Barguss and built a new course just on account of Monroe Mister's dad wanting to play eighteen holes and then drink martinis with a triangle slice of melon that just sinks awkwardly to the curved bottom of the funnel-shaped glass in a state-of-the-art clubhouse bar.

And one time, Old Man Promised To even launched a disastrous bid for a semi-pro ice hockey team cuz Monroe Mister wanted to play but then the whole thing fell through when Monroe Mister lost interest in it after failing to learn how to ice skate backwards and so there were never any 'Barguss Blades' as the poster with the really cool logo promised us if we voted for a tax break on an arena. That made a lot of people angry cuz lots of people voted for it and nothing ever happened.

But it was just after that, maybe a month or so, on a real dark night that most of us remember the event that kinda solidified Monroe Mister and the way he always gets treated in all of our minds.

Zeeda MarMartuchy and Monroe Mister had been out drinking down at Paulson's Cocktails in the old strip mall on Cole

Street cuz that was a real dirty place that Monroe Mister could get served in on account of him not being of age to drink yet and it was the kinda place where guys who had changed their names to 'Rebel' or 'Snakeskin' challenged the odd person to arm-wrestling competitions on the bar for a double whiskey.

Our mama says Paulson's hasn't changed since it opened in the early 1980s. It's poorly lit and has several low beams that drunks always forget about after a few of the 'Three Wise Men' (named for Jack, Jim and Johnnie, and that would be Jack Daniels, Jim Beam and Johnnie Walker), not to mention a buncha faux wood interior and a wrap-around bar that barely fits in the place cuz it hadn't been built in the location but had been purchased separately from the Grizzly Bear Bar in Upton's going-out-of-business sale. When they finally got the thing down from Upton in a big semi-truck, they found out they actually had to buy the adjacent empty space and knock down a wall just to fit the gigantic bar in the bar.

So they chucked a pool table in the room cuz the bar only took up like one-eighth of the purchased adjacent room area but it still didn't matter cuz no one, no matter how small, or how short the stick, could get a decent shot in that room due to the stick hitting the wall or the giant neon signs crammed all over and sometimes those signs got really, really hot and burned you when you were leaning back and trying to sink a bumper shot. Paulson's expanded twice from there, buying two more spaces to expand into, one to the other side and one behind, so walking in feels like walking into a poorly designed house where the big trough bathroom is right next to the tiny kitchen.

Well, even those guys who hung out there and thought they were so tough they could go through life with names as silly as 'Cleaver' and the like, never were dumb enough to challenge someone like Zeeda who was all of six and a half feet tall and easily as heavy as a quarter of a rhino, and the back quarter

44

at that. It wasn't the first time Zeeda had gone in there with Monroe Mister cuz they'd been known to roam around that part of downtown Barguss in the early morning and throw heavy things through windows and no one batted an eye too much cuz if there were ever any fuss the people got twice the value of their windows in a personal check from Monroe Mister's dad the next day.

Anyway, Zeeda and Monroe Mister sat down at this rounded-off bar and it just so happened that 'Rebel' was drunker than usual and he was screaming things out like, 'you ain't nothin' but a pretty boy,' and 'why don't you come arm-wrestle me, you bastard rich kid's son?' and 'your mommy sure is pretty in those commercials, s'good that she's for sale but not so good she's frigid,' and that brought some big laughs from all over the bar and even a smirk from the bartender who had to turn away from Zeeda and Monroe Mister just to disguise it. Yep, 'Rebel', in a bright white t-shirt that said 'BLASTER' on it, said all kinds of stuff like that just to get a rise out of Monroe Mister Promised To and you know what? It worked.

We weren't there but the way we hear it, Monroe Mister slammed his shot down his throat and then back on the ex-Grizzly Bear bar in one motion and looked all tough like in the movies cuz he was sitting in a half-lit corner of the bar and he was James Dean but the weirdo James Dean that flies off the handle in *East of Eden*, except just before the transformation and he walks over to 'Rebel' and sits down like he's Stallone in *Over the Top*, except the kid isn't around and it's just Sly Monroe Mister and the guy who changed his own name to 'Rebel' to scare people.

And Paulson's always gets real excited for stuff like that, so the two guys playing pool in the back on the crooked table that slants right and always pots the eight ball or the cue ball by accident during the last shot of the game and the sauced couple dirty dancing to the jukebox that wasn't even on came over and formed one of those interested kind of half-circles around 'Rebel' and Sly Monroe Mister who sat underneath one of those lamps hanging down from the ceiling with a dirty finger-printed green lampshade on it cuz the owner thought it made it look 'classy, kinda like a real pool hall', and they squared up on this super-cheap table that had to be steadied by elbows with a tin ashtray in the middle that had three smoking cigarettes in it.

And then one of 'Rebel's buddies, some guy unmenacingly named Mikey, handed him another ashtray. So 'Rebel' put both ashtrays on either side of the table after he measured out the length of his and Monroe Mister's forearm, then put some little weirdo sticks of incense or something in there and started 'em both to burning and they had little fires in the ashtrays and it looked like some ritual and everyone knew this was way too melodramatic for arm-wrestling but nobody cared even though the bartender snuck back to the jukebox and put on the 'Bad Nite' song from *Over the Top*.

When they locked hands and Mikey held them still for a sec, everyone thought it was going to be the ultimate grudge match and it was . . . for about the four seconds that Monroe Mister played with 'Rebel' before slamming his hand down onto the flaming ashtray that meant 'Rebel' lost but kept it there for long enough to wink at him and then 'Rebel' went to the bathroom to wash his toasted hand and Mikey helped him and the guys went back to playing pool and the couple danced to Frank Stallone crooning through the juke.

'Course that wasn't the end of the evening cuz Monroe Mister won the double whiskey and then a few people bought Monroe Mister a few more shots and one even made him down a 'rusty nail' and if you've never had one of those, count yourself lucky. Well, Zeeda hauled him out of there real late like but Monroe Mister wanted some fun for himself and even though he was dating Florence during that time he called up one of his girls on the side, Jo Mary Jo, then picked her up in the covered jeep that he got for his sixteenth birthday.

Zeeda was smart enough to get out before she got in but he followed them down the block to the man-made lake in the memorial park cuz Monroe Mister was driving real slow and never even braked before the jeep went right into the lake in the middle of the night and it was amazing how Monroe Mister made it to shore but Jo Mary Jo didn't, even though Zeeda jumped in to look. She died that night but the police didn't find out 'til late in the next day when Monroe Mister's dad told 'em and there wasn't much of an investigation and Monroe Mister didn't even get charged so we suppose we don't even need to mention that Jo Mary Jo lived on the poor side by us, south of Gee Street. We're sure all of this is true cuz Thorpe Thorpe swears that's what Zeeda said one night at his brother's place when he went out of his head on some leaf drug from Yemen called gata or something like that.

Well, we don't have any reason to disbelieve Thorpe Thorpe or Zeeda MarMartuchy even, cuz considering what happened bore a pretty awful resemblance to the Chappaquiddick incident with the Kennedys all those years ago in Massachusetts, so much so that the *Telegraph* even referred to the accident and 'subsequent investigation' as 'Barguquiddick' just to be witty or something (Old Man Promised To condemned the term cuz it had 'absolutely nothing to do with politics or any past event,' he said, 'because what happened was a very terrible accident in which a bright young woman lost her life and my son barely survived, nothing more,' which didn't make a whole lotta sense to us but the *Telegraph* up and printed a retraction anyway) and even though Monroe Mister was never charged, there were always rumblings that something would happen sooner or later to help make up for Jo Mary Jo's death.

None of that seemed to faze the Promised Tos though cuz after that Monroe Mister got that brand new fast kind of sports car on his next birthday cuz his dad loved him and appreciated him, too much, if you ask us. We never forgot it and many of us were real bitter about it and we didn't really ever forget that bitterness and especially not when Raoul de los Dios flew down through the air and landed right on top of Monroe Mister Promised To and squashed his head.

6

Maybe Roo's dad was weird cuz he was in the military and moved around a lot, we aren't exactly sure, but we still remember the appropriated army jeep that his dad had painted light blue and you could still see the camouflage underneath it when he drove the thing up Feat Street, knocking a few garbage cans off curbs along the way and screaming that there was 'a new dog in town', or something like that. Our mama always told us that he was as obnoxious as he was likeable and that she had no idea why Roo's mom ever put up with that kinda behavior. Well, we guess the good news was that she didn't have to for too long.

Roo's dad had a habit of leaving things half done, or getting himself in 'strategically indefensible positions wherein retreat was the only viable option,' were his exact words for it. The first time he was with Roo's mom was on a rebound cuz he got some other girl pregnant but of course, he only stayed around for a year, just long enough to get Roo's mom pregnant with a little Roo baby and leave just after he was born. In fact, that was when he first joined the army. After basic training, he was transferred to Japan for three years before he secured a transfer back to the U.S. shores where he hooked up with Mrs. Kickkick again, except she wasn't Mrs. Kickkick yet, she was Darlene Hoyt but Roo's last name was always Kickkick

49

cuz that was his dad's name. Well, Lt. Kickkick was able to hang around for five years (and get a promotion to Major) 'til Roo was about eight, before lighting out again.

It was to the Philippines that time, and he stayed there for two years before eventually wrangling another transfer back to be near Roo and the-still-Ms. Darlene Hoyt. Now don't get us wrong, Roo loved his dad and he missed him dearly but even shy of his eleventh birthday he wondered why his mother kept taking him back. 1986 was a real hot year in Barguss, and that was when the family first arrived to be close to nearby Bolton Army Base. Roo's dad had promised to marry Roo's mom just as soon as they got settled. Two years later, they went to Las Vegas and tied the knot, but by then, Roo's dad had already been spending way too much of his downtime and money at Dixie's Gypsy Den in downtown Barguss.

Which was a real shame cuz apparently, when he was around, Roo's dad was a good father and great husband on a daily basis and he treated them real nice and always had charisma, he just had a real bad attention span. In fact, when the three of them made the trip to Vegas, Roo says that his dad booked them a great room at the Mirage with two separate bedrooms and their first night in the famous hotel casino they went to see Siegfried and Roy and his dad even got picked to participate in a stunt. That was a big mistake, it ended up being the only failed stunt in the history of S & R's illustrious illusionary career cuz Roo's dad laughed so hard and so loud that everyone in the audience could tell that he was right under the stage and hadn't disappeared at all. Roo's dad always did stuff like that. He had a real infectious laugh. Roo laughs just the same way too.

'Don't blame and don't complain . . . you hear me, boy? Do not blame others and never complain, no matter how hard it gets cuz no one ever – you hear me? – ever likes a complainer, you lose the respect of others if you do that.'

Those were the last words that his father left him with. Fourteen-year-old Roo, shocked as hell, just standing there on the fall crabgrass, with no sandals on, in front of what was their family home. Nervously plugging the half-buried sprinkler head with a big toe, Roo started to cry as his father's jeep pulled away with a jerk cuz of its bad transmission and his mother told us that his father stopped the jeep and barked at Roo through the open passenger-side window that 'crying was the same as complaining', before stepping on the gas and leaving a cloud behind. Roo never talks about it anymore, so we have to ask his mom questions about it sometimes just to get it clear in our heads.

Yep, that sure was the day that U.S. Army Major Lem Kickkick finally left them for Juanita Po-Hutchins, the 5 p.m-to-2 a.m. shift cocktail waitress and occasional bartender at Dixie's Gypsy Den which was located on Gee Street diagonally across from the Taco Coleslaw Hamburger Hot Dog Apple in a building shaped like a giant pillow with a hookah chimney that was nearly falling over onto its neighbor, Lupe & Family's Mexican Restaurant, which was just shaped like a normal redbrick building with windows and not like a burrito or anything.

Well, the good news was that he didn't completely run out on them, Major Lem was kind enough to pay for six months' rent on the house and six months' worth of groceries but that was it; when his next assignment rolled around, he left for Germany and took Juanita with him. Later, we did all kinda wonder how it was so easy for him to walk out like that cuz we heard he had married Juanita. It turned out that he actually got the marriage to Roo's mom annulled.

Don't worry too much though, there is justice cuz Juanita moved with him to Germany and the climate and country really agreed with her, so much so that she left Major Lem twiddling his thumbs on the base while she shacked up with a famous music producer named Wolfgang or something and supposedly he had worked with Kraftwerk and/or Can and all those other really big, interesting and totally incomprehensible German bands cuz Wolfgang was an intellectual with a capital I and an artist with a capital A. That kinda makes us wonder how he and Juanita Po-Hutchins-Kickkick got along so well in the first place but some things are better left alone.

Back in Barguss, Mrs. Kickkick (who refused the expense of changing her name back to Hoyt) and her growing son lived a comfortable and quiet life in Barguss. The usual family pattern consisted of Mrs. Kickkick working two, sometimes three, jobs and Roo pretty much fending for himself at home after school. Mrs. Kickkick never dated anyone else cuz she didn't have time to on account of working all those jobs to keep the house and Roo spent lots of time drawing and making things up for all of us to do. It wasn't really the best time for him. He spent a lot of time at our house back then actually, which was a good thing. Especially when a few letters came in the mail from Okinawa and Manila and they had pictures in them and the noses and chins of the children 'looked really familiar', Mrs. Kickkick said with a weird look on her face and we're pretty sure she was thinking that those kids maybe looked too familiar but she never said anything else about it and neither did Roo so we kinda forgot about it for awhile.

So now that you know most of the story maybe this isn't the best title . . .

The Kickkick Family Moves to Barguss

So how about this one?

The Kickkick Family (Minus Father) Makes a Life in Barguss & Roo Becomes Roo

Everyone always asks us how Roo got his name. It was just after his dad left for good so it must have been 1989, had to be. That was just before high school started and we were all still wearing really silly shorts. Back then Roo's real name wasn't even Roo, it was Ronny and even though his mom calls him Roo now on account of it sounding so cool, it really used to be silly old Ronny before we changed it by committee.

You should know that Roo isn't short for anything. We didn't change his name on account of any physical similarity to the abbreviated nickname of the hopping marsupial known as the kangaroo and we didn't change it cuz he always wanted to go to Australia or something. No, it was much, much simpler than that. We were all in junior high school at the time and we were old enough to have organized gym times now instead of just recess, which was a shame but some of us really excelled in stuff like that, with Ronny being one of them.

That was really good too cuz Ronny's mom had to work two jobs then, one at the all-purpose apple factory where they made pies and tarts and even put caramel on whole ones, just about every way apples can be prepared for mass consumption all in one factory. She was a supervisor there having had 'green apple experience' growing up in Washington state and she also worked nights at Grover's Midnight Liquors where she monitored security and got to carry a gun and hide behind the pane in the back near the bathroom that everyone thought was a mirror but it was the two-way kind. Anyway, the fact that Ronny liked and played sports made it easier for her to work and not worry too much about him.

Well, we were playing baseball at school and it was actually a really nice day, one of those ones where nobody plays basketball or foursquare cuz the blacktop is too hot. We all gathered at the chain-link backstop that was opposite the school and the walls that the girls played wallball on. In between were the tetherball poles and the soccer field but nobody was on them either. The blacktop stopped just after the tetherball poles and then it was just a red gravel/dirt mixture for the baseball and soccer fields.

Anyway, that day was our first day using a real baseball and not a softball cuz our teacher was sure that we could handle it on account of we had done so well with a softball and we were pretty sure he just wanted to see Ronny hit the baseball cuz he coached the all-city baseball team during the summer and it was kinda like a tryout of sorts.

Everyone called him Coach J cuz apparently he had what he called an 'Eastern European last name' that was difficult to pronounce for kids like us so we never tried, he was just Coach J and he was great. He had thinning blond hair and a moustache and when we played baseball he always wore his team cap that said 'Coach' right above the Upton Uraniums logo. They were a double-A minor league professional baseball team until they pulled up stakes and moved to Vancouver, Canada, but Coach J used to play catcher for them until he blew out his knee. We always knew he coulda gone to the big leagues if his body woulda let him.

He always watched behind the backstop when we played and it seems weird now but none of us ever thought anything of it at the time. It happened on the first pitch really, it was that fast. Raoul (it was MacJohnson still but he's Raoul in our memory) was on the mound and he was primping and strutting by kicking the dirt and making wobbly motions with his legs and we all just wanted him to pitch the ball to Ronny cuz we were sure he would hit it where no one could catch it. He could hit that soggy old softball over the fence so we were sure he could clock the tightly wound baseball even farther.

Even Coach J had to yell at Raoul, something like 'just pitch it down the middle, son,' and none of us knew at the time that Raoul's big dream was to play baseball for the all-city team and then play baseball for the New York Metropolitans so he was kinda looking at it as a tryout and he knew if he could strike out Ronny he would be a shoe-in for Coach J's team. He was scared though cuz he knew Ronny could hit to all fields and beat out grounders with his speed so he decided to throw his best fastball three times, an all-or-nothing type thing.

We all remember pretty clearly when he reared back with his leg in the air all exaggerated like Nolan Ryan and Raoul was pretty tall so he looked imposing throwing down at you but Ronny never flinched, even though the pitch was a bit high; he smashed a line drive right up the middle, straight at the pitcher's mound and straight at Raoul's mouth. It hit him bang on the button too, even the outfielders could hear it, even Thommy Mazzaleenck, who was duck-walking his last name into the red dirt of right field by dragging his left heel behind him, heard it halfway through the first 'z'.

We're pretty sure that rebounded fastball broke Raoul's jaw instantly and he lost a few front teeth too, we know cuz they dropped right into the dirt with a mouthful of blood that really didn't stain the dirt all that much on account of it being so reddish to start with, so the blood just looked kinda brown in comparison. He reared back, then forward, and picked up his teeth and put them in his glove, then he went after Ronny. 'You! You!' He must have been trying to scream those words as he pointed at Ronny but it just came out 'Roo! Roo!'

Ronny tried to say he was really sorry and that it was an accident but we all laughed at Raoul and couldn't stop calling him 'Scooby Doo' and that sure didn't help cuz Coach J needed to restrain him from going after Ronny. The name stuck though and Roo made the team that summer, while

Raoul never played baseball again and he not-so-secretly vowed revenge.

About two years later, Roo's mom sold the old house on Feat for a nice little apartment on Blank Street cuz she was struggling too much with the payments.

7

Even just after he beat up Thorpe Thorpe we were sure he had no soul cuz his eyes were like glass eyes the way they were always blank, except he could move them and they never seemed to stay still. He was a genuine fidgeter, that Raoul, if it wasn't a tick in his leg or his hand, it was his eyes that were moving continuously. We tried for years to figure out why exactly Raoul was the way he was, we tried to cut him some slack like maybe he had a really nasty childhood like Florence or something, but he didn't as far as anyone we ever asked knew and so we finally came to the conclusion that he was just the crazy kind of psychotic and always dangerous and careless no matter what the circumstance or time of day.

But that was before Maria died, cuz it was after that when he really lost it. She was basically the kid's de facto mother for as long as he had ever known and he lost her in the worst traffic accident modern day Barguss ever saw. It happened on South Gee Street on the hottest of mid-spring afternoons. Maria was returning to the Fern-Micklewhite household from the Cooper Market, as she had just finished her shopping for specialty items like capers and kalamata olives.

Shopping on Tuesday afternoons was her usual pattern, that's what the Gee Street Girls swore, and they woulda known cuz they always said a casual 'hello' to her when she passed by. They had done that ever since Maria (on a whim) bought ice creams for all five of them and even learned their names: Candy, Mandy and Brandy Mulryne, not to mention Luanne and Lily Lukash. They still recount with a tear or two in their eyes how Maria would add the affectionate Spanish language suffix of '-ita' to each one of their names when she said 'buenos dias': Candita, Mandita, Brandita, Lunita (which she changed only slightly from Luannita so that it would mean 'little moon') and Lilita. Yep, those young ladies always had the nicest things to say about Maria even though they didn't like Raoul at all.

Well, Maria never had access to a car so her walk back to the house took her across Gee at the perpendicular Hotblack Road stoplight. Patiently, Maria waited for the crosswalk signal as she always had and then proceeded across as it turned to a 'walk' signal. From there, the police report gets hazy. For some reason, it could never be determined whether Oliver Martin Rivelo was blinded by the flash of the sun off of a pane of glass being replaced across the street by two workers or if he, indeed, was under the influence of some substance. One thing was certain, the music in the car was too loud and the officer on the scene suggested it had a 'distracting influence on the driver'. Monroe Mister Promised To was also in the car. Now we weren't there, but we'd bet a dime to a dollar that he was driving and not Oliver, but that's not how it goes.

The official story goes that the brand new black Ford Mustang convertible went through a 'yellow' light (which already doesn't add up cuz the Gee Street girls say they'd seen Maria cross there every Tuesday for nearly a year and she always waited for the signal) and then the car struck Maria in the hip at approximately 43 miles per hour, sending her back nearly twenty feet and spraying luxury groceries all over the searing asphalt (this little detail apparently gave the police the opportunity to discredit the Gee Street Gals as eye witnesses cuz they were more than sixty yards away and at that distance, the heat rising from the street would have 'bent the light', as the report said, and made it very difficult to 'tell with a hundred per cent accuracy, the hue of the traffic light').

That wasn't the end of it though. The driver of the Mustang stomped on the brakes and the car fish-tailed into the other side of the road just as Donny Barn (still in shock, as he stared at Maria's flying body) was guiding his motorcycle through a right-hand turn. The rear end of the car clipped the front wheel of Donny's motorcycle and he went airborne over the handlebars and everything else, landing hard on his shoulder and breaking his right collarbone for the second time.

'Then everything stopped,' said Candy and Mandy who ran to call 911 emergency from the Cooper Market payphone while Brandy and Luanne and Lily ran toward the crash to see if they could help. The Mustang had skidded to a stop in the middle of the intersection and both doors were open with Oliver and Monroe Mister both on the far side of the car and completely silent as they saw that Maria was not moving and Donny Barn was cussing up a storm and picking bits of black rock from the wound in his chin. Out of the open Mustang doors poured the music from the tape deck: the end of MC Hammer's 'U Can't Touch This' and then the briefest silence as the song ended and 'Have You Seen Her' started, Brandy, Luanne and Lily all swore to it.

The blow to the head that Maria received when her skull rebounded off the asphalt sent her straight into a coma and she died at the Barguss General Hospital two days later from brain injury complications, with her tiny hand tucked completely inside Raoul's baseball-mitt-sized paws and if he ever was a human being before that accident, he wasn't afterward. Not even close.

We almost don't even want to, but it's about time we finally came clean about the awfulness that Raoul perpetrated on Roo

Kickkick cuz it's no fair holding it back much longer. You might want to skip this if you have a kinda weak stomach.

Raoul de los Dios Makes the Worst Bloody Party

It was the summer after our freshman year in high school and we were officially sophomores when there was a little party at Florence Mink's house cuz her dad was out of the country on bizness and even though we weren't exactly invited by the hostess, we seized the rare opportunity to visit the rich side of town and went with Roo cuz we knew she wouldn't throw him out. This was before Florence had decided on a boyfriend just yet and we suspected she was playing Monroe Mister Promised To off against Roo but we all knew it was a sucker's bet to back Roo even though he was our friend.

Despite all the eyes she made at him, we knew that Florence never turned down Monroe Mister's advances cuz he was so rich and powerful and handsome and all that. They weren't a public couple yet and she was just trying to make him jealous enough to settle on her and stop messing around with all the other girls he had. Anyway, when we got there, Florence opened the door and even though the look on her face basically appeared as if she smelled something bad, she let us in.

The living room was huge and had a bar and everything directly underneath a too-big reproduction of a Salvador Dalí painting, which briefly made us chuckle about the painter and Thorpe Thorpe before Florence told the curious-looking Roo that it was the 'Young Virgin Autosodomized by Her Own Chastity' and we overheard him say that it was nice even though we had no idea what the words actually meant but it kinda made us feel sick even then and especially when we found out about the definitions later. Really really sick, like stay-in-bed-and-close-the-blinds-for-a-whole-week sick.

We knew Florence was in charge of the music cuz Madonna was on the stereo and it was 'Vogue' and it sounded kinda weird when looking around the room at the couches and chairs where just about all the rich kids in the town were eyeing us over their bottles of imported English beer or big pink and blue plastic cups full of coconut rum and brown sodapop or vodka and orange juice. They were in the midst of their binge drinking and everyone did it, we all did, cuz the only way to get alcohol when we were that age was in big quantities and it had to be drunken fast so we could feel it and it was fun to be out of control but we didn't find out it was called 'binge drinking' and it was bad until later.

We asked Florence how she got the beer and she just pointed to the screen door that led to the backyard and we could see good ol' Thed Teldut stumbling around in the grass and even from inside it looked like he was acting like a cat and walking around on all fours. Pushing the screen door back, we filed outside without Roo cuz Florence had pulled him aside and everyone was laughing out there at Thed as he rolled on his back, meowing and purring, we'd never seen him so drunk, before or since. It turned out he had gotten Sassa Medusa Belle to buy the beer as a guilty-type payback for almost killing him that night at Beau's house.

To everyone's upset, we pulled Thed to his feet and he told us in a moment of clarity that the word 'sophomores' meant 'wise fools' before passing out while still standing up, only to fall butt first onto the ground right there in the backyard grass of Florence's dad's house. We went and put a table cover over him when we discovered we couldn't move him inside without him threatening to puke his guts out all over us so we just left him.

When we got back into the house something was wrong

cuz nobody was inside anymore and the front door was wide open. Screams and shouts came right through the space where the door shoulda been and for a moment it seemed like a gigantic rectangular opening and nothing else, not even a doorway anymore. It was with dread that we bolted out into the front yard only to see Raoul leaning over Roo's bleeding body and it was like slow motion the way we flew across the lawn at him punching and kicking 'til he backed off but he had such an unchanging look in his eye and he kept laughing and saying stuff like 'now who's Scooby fucking Doo?' We ripped out fistfuls of his curly red hair and he still said, 'Ruh Roh Rhaggy!' and 'Roo Rot Ro Reeth!' and laughing all like Scooby Doo woulda done and it was really blood curdling. Sometimes, in nightmares, we still hear it and wake up and have to remind ourselves he's dead and buried.

Eventually he got into Monroe Mister Promised To's car and they left, fast as the wind like. Leaving two wide strips of rubber on the street not so far from Roo's face, which was now bleeding so much that it made a kinda gluey-looking red trail further down the rain drain of the sloped curb like a giant dying slug made it and not a human being. Picking Roo up from the curb was like picking up our first dog after it died from being hit by a car, only lots worse cuz we felt more helpless when hearing Roo's breathing coming in deep gasps like it was all blocked up by stuff it shouldn't be blocked up by and we thought he was gonna die for sure.

Whether Raoul took Roo's teeth or not, we'll never really know cuz when we lifted Roo up there weren't any teeth to be seen anywhere except a few shards here and there to complement the bits still lodged in his gums. Maybe he swallowed them? We didn't know but we did know that Roo's wrecked face was the saddest and most disgusting thing we've ever seen ever and all that could be done at that point was call the ambulance and try not to puke and make the situation worse.

We guess it's pretty common to say 'it happened so fast' but it's so true in a crisis-type situation like that and as much as we rack our brains, we can't remember what looks people had on their faces or even who was on the grass that night, cuz it was just a blur of movement and we can't remember any sound but Roo's choking and the automatic lawn sprinklers across the street and truth be told, we only cared about making sure Roo was alright, at least as alright as he could be. Seriously, cuz we woulda never attacked Raoul de los Dios before, not with eight guys, but seeing Roo down like that, his face all crumpled small into the concrete like he got stuck in a trash compactor, we just lost it.

The only image apart from Roo that sticks in our heads from that night was Florence all silhouetted by the shape of the doorway, with light coming from the house behind her, shiny on her bare shoulders cuz they were hunched up and she was hugging her dressed-up self around the ribs but we couldn't see her face cuz we squinted real hard to try to make out what was going through her head at that moment but the porch light was too bright and she didn't move, we could just see her lit-through gold hair pushed up in the small wind, then Roo coughed his way to consciousness and started crying but it was like he wasn't crying at all, just tears pressed down over drying blood and no whimpers. There was a smell, though, and it's gross but it's true, when someone loses a lot of blood (and we mean a lot, not like a cut finger or anything but not like a slaughterhouse either cuz human blood is different) you can smell it, almost like liver mixed with seawater.

*　　*　　*

63

The ambulance came after what seemed like too long and we held Roo and wiped his face with a towel when blood dripped too much from the hole where his mouth shoulda been and when the medics finally showed up we heard one of them say, 'Jesus Christ in Heaven!' just like that when they saw that that-piece-of-shit-wearing-human-skin-Raoul had dislodged Roo's jaw completely from his skull and there were just two nasty sockets by his ears hanging out there looking empty and the only thing that held Roo's jaw to his head were the super-loose bits of skin where his sideburns woulda been. We were so angry and they almost didn't let us go with Roo cuz we were so worked up about everything but in the end, they did let us ride in the back and that was the first of two times that we ever rode in an ambulance with its lights and sirens on.

When we got to the hospital we were told to wait in the waiting room and read sports magazines while they performed emergency surgery on Roo, so we filled out forms sorta and made the toughest phone call ever to Roo's mom and we kept it really short like, 'please come to the hospital cuz Roo's been hurt but he will be okay,' though it must not have helped cuz she steamed through the emergency room doors and demanded to see her son five minutes later even though she lived nine minutes away. Her hair was still in curlers but it might as well have been on fire the way she was acting. It took her a while to calm down, the nurse had to reassure Mrs. Kickkick numerous times that Doctor Dinner was doing the surgery and he was the best in the city and the county and he'd be out real soon to tell them that everything was okay.

By far the worst part was when Roo's mom started inter-rogating us about what happened and as hard as we tried, we couldn't make it sound decent at all especially cuz we were so mad, though we were sure to keep telling her that he would be okay and didn't describe what his tongue looked like, all twisted over onto concrete bits and torn so that it didn't look real but more like movie make-up. She cried forever it seemed like when we told her and we even got her a cup of coffee but it didn't calm her down, she just kept repeating stuff like 'my beautiful boy' over and over again 'til it broke our hearts and we wanted to cry too.

It was like three in the morning when Doctor Dinner finally came out from behind the swinging doors that a bunch of gurneys – some with people on 'em and some not – were going in and out of and it was the first time we ever actually saw him in person and boy, did he have a reputation around town for being a sorta screwed up guy away from the hospital but inside it he was a genius and he always did a good job and that's why we were so happy to see him not looking super-upset cuz apparently he had a tendency to do that when he thought he failed.

He walked over all slow, then said that Roo would be okay and it was like a brief glimpse of paradise to see relief on Roo's mom's face cuz we were worrying more about her than us, if the truth be told. She was such a nice lady and we can't even imagine being parents and getting news like that one night, that they had reattached our kid's jaw fairly easily and the Doc thought that he could make a full recovery, but he'd be 'very badly scarred', and Doc Dinner kinda paused before saying, 'I am very sorry,' but made it clear that there was no other way.

The next day, when Roo was in seeing a dental specialist to see if he was a candidate for prosthetic teeth, Raoul was caught at the Taco Coleslaw Hamburger Hot Dog Apple. Some of the kids at the party had given a statement that Raoul did it and the cops caught him and cuffed him before he could finish eating his #8 captain combo of steak sandwich, bean burrito and jello but it wasn't real jello but the kind they made behind the counter with special apples mixed in. Later that day, he was booked for gross bodily harm or grievous or some other g-word.

We went to the trial and it was a fiasco and Raoul pleaded not guilty so the prosecution paraded eighteen witnesses (mercifully leaving Roo out) up to the stand who all identified him as the 'booter' or the 'bootist' depending on who was talking. And we really wanted to testify but couldn't cuz we told the truth that we didn't actually see him do it and we're glad we didn't cuz there are enough images that will never leave our heads from that night and we don't want two or three more, much less a movie.

They found his stupid smug face guilty but the judge said his hands were tied cuz Raoul was still a minor, so he only got remanded to a 'juvenile institution' up the highway in Upton and didn't get any real kinda sentence. We were really mad still but there was nothing we could do cuz 'justice had been served' and 'it's time to forgive' as Roo's mom said when she gave us a ride home and we weren't so sure we could forgive so we just stayed quiet. We found out later that just after the verdict, Raoul's dad, Mr. Fern-Micklewhite, disowned him and we aren't sure if it made Raoul worse, but it probably didn't help all that much considering.

That isn't the whole story though as much as we'd like it to be and we're awful ashamed to admit it and still feel guilty about it, but before the party even happened Raoul came up to us at school and suggested we show up at the party and 'make sure to bring Roo,' he said. Even after these years in between, we still feel like it's our fault and so if you're reading this right now, we're really, really sorry Roo and Mrs. Kickkick also. We didn't mean to, honest.

8

The Golden Ring was pretty much the only club in all of Barguss that is even worth mentioning. Sure, there was also the Iron Horse but that was a Country and Western bar type venue and the one and only time we ever went to that rat hole was the day that Autistik/Artistik played a secret show there under the band name of Jesse James and the Horny Outlaws. It would have been a classic show if not for them getting kicked out after one song, we think it was called 'Why Cowboys Suck (Each Other)' and apparently the homosexual implications didn't go over too well with the homophobe/bartender/owner 'Wild' Bill Hickock Cody Earp cuz he banned Thed Teldut and Thorpe Thorpe forever from his establishment after that night, even though it was just a joke intended to poke fun at their prejudices but they didn't seem to appreciate that too much.

Nicknames are pretty common with club owners in Barguss cuz The Golden Ring was owned by none other than 'Smarty' Marty Mindy. The guy was legendary as far as Barguss was concerned cuz before he got here in the early eighties, the only kind of music that ever came to town was usually the backup bands that rolled in to get good and drunk after the state fair at the Upton fairgrounds was over. Willie Nelson's backup band used to cause a hell of a lot of ruckus during those years apparently. They even have a plaque up in the Iron Horse with *a picture of those bastards in front of the Barguss water tower, well, at least part of it anyway cuz they appear to have pulled it down somehow and all that can be read of the word on the enormous tank that used to say Barguss are the letters B-A-R and all the mustachioed band members look really pleased with themselves. Our mama says the entire town didn't have water for a month after that 'damn prank'.*

Anyway, Smarty Marty brought in all kinds of new acts, the kind that inspired Thed Teldut during the time his mom used to work there and oftentimes there wasn't any daycare or even nightcare so he'd get to go with her and usually be made to sleep in the back room cot on club/concert nights when she could make big tips. It never really worked though cuz he could never actually get to sleep. Instead, he would just sneak out to the bar or peek through the vent at whoever was playing. The music was so darn loud anyway he could hear it through the walls in the back room. That, Thed says, is how he got introduced to the likes of The Talking Heads, Blondie, and Laurie Anderson. None of us are quite sure how Smarty Marty got those big acts to a pile like Barguss but he didn't earn the nickname for nothing that's for sure.

He and The Golden Ring went out of business briefly in 1988 only to reopen in 1989 'due to a shift in the tastes of musicalitude', that's how the Telegraph *quoted him but none of us had any idea what the heck it actually meant. Smarty Marty was always like that, making up words on the spot and we think sometimes not even he knew what they meant, but that was definitely one of his favorite pastimes. Well, that and young hookers, for which he did a brief stint in the Barguss County Jail for solicitation and 'intent with a minor' whatever that means. Word also had it that he was The Peteness's biggest cocaine client, well, before he got his throat cut and all.*

But Smarty Marty wasn't such a bad guy, he always had a night for local musicians and comedians at The Golden Ring,

*encouraging young talent in the general 'localitus maximus',
which we thought meant local area but you never could tell
with Smarty Marty. Even Florence Mink performed there
once, she did her Madonna song and dance thing that she
had performed at the school talent show again except it was
different cuz she was older and it wasn't cute but kinda sexy
instead.*

*It's actually a pretty funny story of how Smarty Marty
Mindy ended up in Barguss in the first place. He came from
New York City and he had been dating an on-the-verge-of-big-
time artist there, when all of a sudden, she demanded that he
marry her before she became ultra-famous, that way she would
know that she could trust him and she also demanded a golden
ring in the bargain. Long story short, Smarty Marty ran out
that night and never looked back, he just got on a random bus
and ended up in Barguss three and a half days later.*

*He named the club The Golden Ring on account of how he
said club life was 'the only thing he'd ever really be married
to', besides, he spent less on the down payment for the club
space than he would have for his wannabe fiancée's ring. At
least, that's what he said. He always wore a white tuxedo
coat with tails and a t-shirt with a white bow tie over his
long jungle shorts and hiking boots. The same outfit he was
wearing when he booked Thorpe Thorpe and Thed Teldut for
the third official evening of the localitus maximus all those
years ago.*

Tee Tee Ta Tee Two Too and The Golden Ring

It was their first show ever and we were there. We got in early
and the place wasn't as packed as we would have liked it to
be. The Golden Ring had a really strange decoration motif
and Smarty Marty had spent a lot of money to build the

venue stage like a bullring with the audience looking down on the performers cuz he wanted the name of the club to be 'consistamatent'. Apparently, he thought that was funny too but we never really got it.

The bar was in the front near the entrance and the ceiling was supported by these huge lumber beams that gave the place a feel of a log cabin, which was a bit strange considering the building had a giant roof like a carved-out oval to help the stage sound better. You actually had to walk past the bar to get back to the stage. The in-the-round bleacher seats sat about four hundred people and the seats encircled the stage, so the lights actually had to be hung from a trapeze-like structure that was secured to the roof.

Well, the crowd that night was well short of capacity, as it was mostly just school friends that had showed up on account of there was nothing else to do but when it was all said and done, even they had to admit that Thed Teldut and Thorpe Thorpe were pretty damned amazing. Their first show set the precedent, in some ways it set the standard that all shows thereafter would be judged by, cuz those of us that actually attended the first one still talk about it. It made them instant legends in Barguss and even surrounding regions owing to the fact that our word of mouth spread like wild fire.

That night, we waited forty minutes for the 'roadies' (we all knew it was Thorpe Thorpe and Thed Teldut dressed all in black with the word 'roadies' fixed in white tape across their backs but we laughed and watched) to set up one of the most elaborate sets we've ever seen, much less witnessed, inside a bullring designed to be a concert stage. On one side of the stage was a big blue mat and some Asian-looking paintings hung from the light fixture and on the other side was the set of a children's play. Thed later confessed they stole it from George Washington Elementary's fourth, fifth, and sixth grade pro-duction of Maurice Sendak's 'Where The Wild Things Are'.

When everything was set up, the 'roadies' disappeared and Smarty Marty came on the house speakers, rumbling in his low tone that 'tonight and tonight only, you will be treated to the most spectacular show this side of the feed lots, so settle down, buy a coke [only we laughed when he said that] and get reeeeeeeeeeeeeeeady, ladies and gentlemen, for the increeeeeeeeeeeeeeeeeeeeeeeeeeedible musicalataté stylings offff . . . Tee Tee um [and he must have been looking through the dimness at his card with the band name on it] am-a-lama hot Toddy To Desmond Tu-Tu!' Thorpe Thorpe once said that they almost didn't go on after that introduction but laughed about it afterwards and considered renaming the band if only the new name was just a bit shorter.

Anyway, after a warm up like that, the most anti-climactic entrance ever happened right before our eyes: head down, Thorpe Thorpe quietly emerged from the matador tunnel dressed as Peter Pan with his two-string bass slung over his shoulder so that the neck of it poked him in the backs of the knees while he walked all unsteadily. We all laughed but stopped immediately when he looked so shy, we felt bad for him. He had this ridiculous red feather sticking out of his green hat and the costume was at least one size too small. It was kinda sad really, so it didn't surprise any of us when he completely misjudged the length of the mic stand and smashed himself in the face with it when he went to grab it.

The crowd 'oooooed' in sympathy as Thorpe Thorpe crumpled to the floor, spilling blood all over the sand of the bullring stage so that it looked like a modernist sand painting and then it was dead silent in The Golden Ring, all forty-two of us refused to move and we could even hear Smarty Marty choking on his burrito near the bar area cuz he couldn't believe how badly the debut show had just gone wrong. It was not exactly a good thing that the mic was on the sand nearby Thorpe Thorpe's mouth cuz we could hear him painfully calling for a medic and we were sure he had broken his nose halfway off and it was a good thing that a pretty girl in an Emergency Medical Technician uniform came running down the matador tunnel to tend to him.

She turned him toward her, toward the tunnel, away from the crowd but we could still hear her words in the microphone, HER: 'Ohmigod!' HIM (*choking*): 'What? What?' HER: 'Nothing, it's just that . . . I'm going to have to try and pop this back in right here or you could lose a nostril!' A clamp of tension gripped the room upon the uttering of those words and all the Gee Street Girls put their hands to their faces, the ones that hadn't already anyway, and next thing we knew, there was a pop and Thorpe Thorpe screamed something terrible right into the mic and everyone jumped at least a foot in the air! Someone a few people to the left of us even screamed: 'Get an ambulance for the love of god!'

But then the bassline started, and we knew we'd been had. Thorpe Thorpe rocked back onto his heels and leapt into the air, executing a perfect 180-degree turn to face the audience and he was now wearing an Incan death mask! As he worked those two strings on the bass for all they were worth, he sprayed those of us in the front row with the fake blood from the tubing taped to his arm and concealed by the costume, before flipping up the mic stand with a deft flick of his foot and started singing 'Tastes Like Bloody Rubber Chicken' while the EMT (which we suddenly realized was Staceyleene in a blonde wig and smart-girl-type glasses and she wasn't wearing rollerskates so we didn't recognize her cuz we only ever saw her at Taco Coleslaw Hamburger Hot Dog Apple but we still felt kinda foolish) sang backing vocals into the same mic during the chorus. He had us. Right there, it didn't matter what they did later, we were eating out of the palm of his hand, but there was more, so much more.

After the song ended, Thorpe Thorpe suggested that

Staceyleene go find Thed Teldut and then he started casually talking to us in the audience, so coolly and calmly as if it were an audience of fifteen thousand all there to see him and that's when we knew they'd make it, but anyway he started talking to us about how the theme of the night was a costume party and just as he said that, a giant portable shower came waddling down the matador tunnel.

It was Thed and he was dressed just like Daniel LaRusso dressed for the Halloween party in *The Karate Kid*! The Gee Street Girls went nuts and started screaming, 'Daniel san! Daniel san!' But before they could sing a song or even introduce Thed properly, four ninjas emerged from the bar area and ran down the bleachers through the crowd screaming, 'Cobra Kai Rules!' before they sprang into the bullfighting ring, ready to attack! Thorpe Thorpe just kinda looked at us and said, 'uh oh,' into the mic and started playing a scratchy bass funk lick only on the neck of his bass.

Next thing we knew, Thed was fighting off all these ninjas by himself, single-handedly delivering punches through the shower curtain so that the ninjas never saw it coming, chopping one in the neck, delivering a nasty roundhouse to a midsection, and even punching one swiftly in the throat, Thed was kicking ass all over the Asian set on the stage and when it was down to him and the last ninja he did the crane kick from the movie and everybody just lost it they were so excited, but as Staceyleene dragged the unconscious ninjas off the stage and down the matador tunnel, we didn't have time to take a breath cuz Thed ripped off the shower curtain and revealed that he was dressed like Captain Hook!

From there, the show really took off and we won't even mention the monkey or the special guest appearance by the Principal Who Is Your Pal during the classroom set-up. Indeed, after that night, Thorpe Thorpe and Thed Teldut had cemented their legacies in the minds of everyone in the place and it took us less than a week to spread the word everywhere. When they headlined The Golden Ring two months later, the place was way over fire code with at least a thousand people packed in to watch them stage a brilliant gladiator battle with real archery, sword battling and fake ships.

After that infamous show (twelve people were arrested for impersonating police officers in a stage antic gone horribly wrong), they had some creative differences, ditching the name Tee Tee Ta Tee Two Too. They had a brief phase as Le Funke Deux, a pseudo-fictional band that had been formed by two brothers separated at birth, one had been raised in France and one had been raised in Quebec and one day they met and formed a formidable electronic duo. The novelty lasted for two months before they became Historico Future Co., which had some amazing shows with UFOs and pyramids but that didn't last either. It wasn't until they became Autistik/Artistik that they really hit it big.

9

Over fifty or so years ago in Barguss, an entirely new breed of cat was developed called the Barguss Blue. Actually, it's about the only type of cat you see around town at all except for the rich folks who try to be different with their Abyssinians or their Norwegian Forest Cats but the rest of us have pride cuz it put our tiny town on the global map. The Blue was bred by renowned Brazilian expat single-named veterinarian and long-time Barguss resident, Rozinho. It officially earned its breed status in the Cat Fanciers' Association Register of Pedigreed Cats on March 17, 1948. They have the best temperament of any cat we've ever seen on TV or otherwise and some can even be walked on a leash just like dogs and we know, we've seen it.

The bone structure of the Blue isn't all that different from a traditionally long and lean Blue Point Siamese, which was sorta the starting spot for the breed except the Barguss Blue's fur is black and it has furry hair tufts on its ears that are about an inch long each and the hairs actually part at the top like little bug feelers and it's really kinda cute. Just about everybody has a Blue around here, ours is named Mr. T but sometimes we call him B.A. Barracus or Clubber Lang as nicknames which is kinda ironic cuz he's a big scaredy cat. Thorpe Thorpe's is called the Fabulous Duke of Rounderhouse, which somehow *became Femur through the years and Thed's is really fat and called Pousenik Parable the IVth or Leon, whichever sprang off his tongue first. Most everybody's Blue has more than one name around here on account of them being pure bred.*

Annually, we have a contest for the prettiest and most talented young woman in all of Barguss. It's officially called the Barguss Blue Kitty Cat Queenship, though we mostly just shorten that ridiculously long title to Ms. Barguss Blue or even Ms. BB when we speak about the winner in common talk. It's kinda funny how lots of people here try and act like it's not a big deal but you can tell they really care about it when the time rolls around for the old Queen to hand over her title.

There are a few rules for the Queenship, though. Like, all participants must be female and over the age of eighteen or, if not, they must at least be high school graduates and they always give the award in the summer, just two weeks after the graduation, to one young woman in the class. This is important cuz there is always a college scholarship attached to the Queenship but the majority of Kitty Cat Queens use their scholarship money to attend the state beauty or fashion academies in Upton (one even went to trade school up there to become a welder) instead of going to real college. And it's not that we think we're better or anything like that but it just seems silly to us to waste that kind of money on being a 'beauty assistant' with an eye toward owning a salon one day rather than actually getting a degree diploma in bizness or something.

Now what was significant about the 1994 Barguss Blue Kitty Cat Queenship was the fact that one had not been given in 1993 due to the blimp incident. The mayor had decided it was best not to give one on account of the tragic deaths of Monroe Mister Promised To and Raoul de los Dios (but the real reason was pressure from Old Man Promised To who was a huge sponsor). So the mayor declared that all young women eligible to compete in 1993 would be able to compete in 1994, thus making the field 'twice as large and twice as competitive', he said, which we all thought was one giant joke simply cuz Florence was in the previous year's crop and she could pretty much mail it in.

In fact, lots of us didn't even bother voting cuz Florence almost won it the previous two years on write-in votes when she wasn't even old enough (much less graduated) to be eligible. Well, that was kinda funny cuz that opened the door for some unexpected cheating kinda competition from Lucy Trucey and her mom cuz they could never forget the talent show disqualification all those years ago.

It seemed like the smear campaign was a pretty calculated and coordinated one right from the start. Within one evening, three billboards (we only had five total) were taken over at strategic-type locations around town with large ads for Lucy to be the next Ms. BB. Lucy wasn't stupid, she and her mom knew that the majority of people in Barguss were working class and they'd probably vote for Florence anyway just cuz she was prettier but then Lucy decided to tug on some of those class strings when the billboards announced in big letters: 'Vote for someone like you, Not someone who thinks they're better than you.' And it was actually kinda funny cuz next to those words was a black and white picture of Florence sticking her nose in the air when she was crowned Prom Queen and a color picture of Lucy Trucey crying and looking all humble when she won the Homecoming Queen award during halftime of the big football game last year.

Honestly, none of us had expected anything like that to happen but we did kinda wonder where Lucy got all that money for those ads. Apparently, it went further than that, though, cuz the rumor was going around that Lucy was willing to buy votes. In fairness, we have to say that it was never proven that she actually did, but something fishy was

77

going on irregardless of what anyone could prove or disprove. After those billboards though, it was interesting how the town turned to view Florence's reaction. An interview ran in the Telegraph and Florence refused to comment on the signs and at the time we weren't so sure that it worked in her favor, showing she was above it in a way, seeing as how that was exactly what Lucy was alleging. But she did say one thing, 'I would only ask that the fair people of Barguss wait to cast their vote until after the talent competition.'

The actual crowning for the Queenship is really the culmination of a week of festivities devoted entirely to the competition. Former Queens come back to town and do seminars on dieting and eating disorders and how to apply the perfect 'face' of make-up and stupid stuff like that. Well, the residents of Barguss are allowed to vote at any time during the week for who they think should win, but most of us wait until after the talent competition on the Friday night to cast our votes and then the winner is announced in a big ceremony on Sunday after church gets out.

Whispers rolled through the crowd on that Friday night with some claiming that Lucy would win it going away on account of the votes accumulated during the week, while still others claimed that Florence would win it cuz she had a surprise performance planned for the talent portion or something. Honestly, we didn't much care at that point. See, we used to have a crush on Lucy and, well, Florence was Florence, and she always won everything anyway but mostly she pretty much deserved it. Cool and cloudy was what the evening was like but it didn't rain thankfully. Most of the town was spread out in the blocked off street and it was definitely the most people out together since the blimp incident (which the mayor made sure to touch on in his opening remarks before declaring the talent competition opened), sitting on their lawn chairs in front of the city council building, where a small stage had been erected.

Lucy was on first and she made her way from the contestant area (which was just a section of chairs out in front) to the stage and she sneered at Florence and we're pretty sure everybody saw it. Then Lucy launched into her exact same talent show performance from junior high except she sang it this time instead of lip-synching and we aren't exactly sure why but it made us feel bad inside cuz it was obvious she was trying too hard. She couldn't be done soon enough for our taste and judging by the overall reaction around us, for the crowd's taste either. After she finished, Lucy sashayed past Florence back to her seat and kinda shook her chest at her and we just didn't think that was very dignified or smart even, considering it contradicted the ads that had been put up, but Florence sat there silently, not batting an eyelid.

When Florence's turn came and she disappeared behind the big red stage curtain, we didn't know what to expect except . . . more Madonna maybe? That same sentiment of unsureness seemed to be buzzing around in the crowd too. Then the curtains swished open and we immediately understood why Thed and Thorpe had been so strange about saying they'd meet us at the talent show cuz they were actually up on stage with her and singing the medley from the most famous musical in our elementary school history: KIDS Incorporated! It was about a radio station run by a buncha kids and somehow Florence had managed to track down all the original stars of the musical, even a few who had moved away and to tell the truth, as simple and plain as it was, we've never seen so many faces light up at once in that crowd as they started clapping immediately and all right along with the song. The set was impeccable, just like how it used to be and the costumes were exactly the same only bigger and for just a moment, we were all transported back in time. It was magical and everyone knew who the winner would be that night and that announcing it on Sunday was just tradition and kinda putting off the inevitable.

79

Normally, the Queen's main duty is to preside over the Barguss Blue Cat Show hosted by the Prime Saddle Hotel every winter, but 1994 was different. That was the year that the producers and location scout brought the director in to check the town out and Florence Mink was the first person they saw while getting off the plane and she won their hearts with a wave of her hand (while still managing to hold onto her frightened Blue, Little Sweetheart Evangeline a.k.a. Sweety Bear or Lolita) and a great big smile from underneath the furry-hair-tufted cat-ear tiara that has come to be the symbol of the competition . . .

The Barguss Blue Kitty Cat Queen Welcomes Hollywood to Town

Mayor Yermo L. Nastich III wore bifocals and happened to have a crescent-shaped scar on the top of his bald head and nobody knew just how he got it, coulda been during a tour of duty in Viet Nam or even when he spent time in jail for his cocaine conviction prior to his current run as mayor. He was a small kinda guy but lifted weights a lot and he even won the lightweight division of the State Deadweight Open Championship twice with lifts of 278 lbs and 301 lbs. His secretary said he had the habit of carrying clean undershirts around with him in his briefcase, just for the fear that he might sweat too much. Mayor Nastich used to be a lawyer and even took it upon himself to negotiate the lump sum cash payment to the city of Barguss from Panazanc Film Partners, Inc. for the rights to the blimp incident.

Probably in less than one day, the amount of Barguss subscribers to *Daily Variety* went up like three thousand per cent but that's assuming that there was actually someone sub-scribed to it before the rights to the movie were sold in the first place. But not even *Variety* could tell us how much Panazanc really plopped down for the rights, all that was written was the really ambiguous 'middle six-figure sum paid out for the rights to a true story in backwoods America tentatively entitled *Roo Kickkick & the Big Bad Blimp*'. Apparently, Mayor Nastich had carved out a small percentage of the original payment to go to Roo cuz of 'naming rights' or something like that. All we know is that the timing couldn'tve been better cuz it helped Roo and his mom get out of their medical and dental debt and gave 'em a little money on the side too.

The subscriptions to *Variety* ended up coming in really handy though, when it became obvious that Panazanc had a directorial fiasco in their laps, which was odd cuz when it first sold it was one of the hottest properties in Hollywood, otherwise Panazanc wouldn't have gone to all that trouble and expense to outbid Warner Brothers for the rights. They turned around and handed the project to some hotshot young scriptwriter who said he saw it as a cross between *Pee-wee's Big Adventure* and *The Last Picture Show* and stars were even lining up around the block and the rumor mills and things were going crazy.

Supposedly, Johnny Depp had gotten into a shoving match with Christian Slater and Leonardo DiCaprio at the Viper Room over who could play Roo Kickkick better, while Julia Roberts was willing to dye her trademark ginger locks blonde in order to land the role of Florence Mink, and some cutting-edge-type casting director was considering musicians like Beck and Beastie Boy Adam Yauch for the roles of Thed Teldut and Thorpe Thorpe cuz they wanted a good 'soundtrack tie-in' or something, and so the rumors went (only to be repeatedly denied) as people got really excited about it around these parts even though some did voice concern about the way it would be portrayed and of course, nobody was louder than Old Man Promised To. But both the rumors and concerns faded quickly when it became apparent that Panazanc was having problems filling the director's chair as several big-name directors continually turned down the project.

First on Panazanc's wish list was Quentin Tarantino, the hottest director in Hollywood at the time and the funny thing was that he kinda strung Panazanc along for a while 'til he told them that he only directed his own original material that he wrote, and that was the all nice and official explanation but we're pretty sure that he pulled out cuz he thought Barguss was a backwater or something, that's what it said on the Internet anyway but we never really trusted the source. We always thought that was kinda funny actually, though we aren't exactly sure why. Next up was Martin Scorsese and he turned it down right quick and movie critic Milton Ryerson said it was cuz he didn't do 'real reality', and that was fine but then he did *Kundun* a few years later and that was based on a true story so we guess he just meant it if the project was wrong for him.

When a number of music video directors started turning the project down everyone knew something was wrong and people just assumed something was really wrong with the script or characters. There was even some guy named Jonze that must have at least thought about it cuz there was no news for like two weeks after he was linked to it but then he turned it down too and the film looked to be in serious trouble.

Just after that was when the mayor and the community took action to be more attractive to the production and to prospective directors. The city council actually partially subsidized a massage parlor (one director's earlier request cuz he said, we 'didn't have any culture') and then just as the hour was looking truly dark for finding a director, a famous Eastern European art house cinema darling popped up out of nowhere and signed on to the project to make his first English language film.

His previous films had won a number of awards all over the world and he immediately brought 'credibility to what appeared to be a sinking ship', said the *Telegraph*. Indeed, Krystof Zckwecy was our savior and it turned out that all Panazanc had to do was promise to build him a log cabin on the outskirts of Barguss to retire in cuz apparently all he wanted was 'to grow old and die in America' or something like that, which we thought was a kinda weird thing to say but nobody else seemed to take any notice of it and maybe that was cuz of his only partial grasp of the English language and they just figured he was trying to be funny but maybe they should've listened a little bit harder.

Anyway, we saw him for the first time when he arrived with the producers and the location scout on the old dirt airstrip just north of town. Krystof was in his sixties and looked like Albert Schweitzer with a bushy white moustache but with a green ponytail. He was wearing a leather vest and no shirt, which showed off the Guns N' Roses tattoo on his chest – 'Welcome to the Jungle Babby!' – except the word baby was misspelled and we think it was at that point that we all felt a little bit closer to Mr. Zckwecy cuz if anyone could understand us misspelling the word beautiful on the blimp, he could.

Sunglasses on, he stepped off the stairs and into the midst of the banner-waving three hundred and sixty or so people that had showed up to welcome them but he only had his sights set on Florence Mink, right from the get go. He advanced all cautiously and he took her hand in his before turning to the producers and saying, 'I think we found our star,' through his translator as our Kitty Cat Queen blushed and Lolita lurched and dug her claws into Florence's chest cuz she was so scared.

10

He just showed up really. Casting as far as we knew it hadn't even begun yet and this guy just rolls into town like a swan on a lake, cruising up Gee Street with his emerald green 1937 Super Charged Cord like he was driving right into town out of some history time warp. Nobody around here had ever seen a car that long or that gorgeous and he made sure to do several square-ish loops around town, following Gee to Hotblack all the way down to Zebulon Parkway then right up Feat and back onto Gee. He drove it slower than the speed limit in some places where people were and faster than the limit in others where there was nobody to stare on admiringly, but the cops on duty didn't even have the heart to pull him over, so they just rode behind and in front like a motorcade cuz if there's one thing that people here in Barguss appreciate, it's a classic car.

Whoever this guy was, we figured he must be mightly important cuz he had a striking-looking blonde girl sitting across from him in the passenger seat and she looked awfully familiar the way she would lean against the door and barely dangle the top of her forehead out the rolled down window so that her bangs would whip in the breeze as she clutched her long ivory cigarette holder with a lazy wrist. Yup, we'd been mesmerized all right. Some people actually followed the car over to the Prime Saddle Hotel on account of it being the best hotel in town and asked for autographs from the couple even though we had no idea who they were but they sure looked famous.

Well, it turned out that they were sorta famous after all. The girl was named Natalie Darling (we're pretty sure that it's just a stage name and not her real one) and she had been in two films, one with Mel Gibson and one with Arnold Schwarzenegger but hadn't had any starring roles just yet, although she assured anyone that would listen that she was 'up' for a number of roles in the biggest films. And the guy, well, he was just famous on account of the fact that he was the son of the great Western actor Roy L. Stevens and he had the same chiseled cheekbones and skin-taut chin too. The resemblance was amazing really and there was a part of us that almost wanted to ask him to say his father's immortal lines in The Great Trail Drive, 'Nope, that old tumbleweed sure don't look dead to me, Wyatt, it's just sleeping, and it's just like a message and the land is just like people and when it spreads its seeds and wakes up a month from now in a thousand different locations, well, old friend, that's when we'll know the true power of Geronimo,' but we kept our mouths shut cuz we thought he'd think we weren't cool on account of he must get that a lot.

Roman 'Herc' Stevens, everybody just assumed that Herc stood for Hercules on account of his imposing muscular-type figure but the funny thing is, it didn't. His dad used to call him his 'little Hercule Poirot' on account of how he always figured out the mysteries of the house like where the booze and cigarettes were hid at and sometimes he would feed the cigs to the family dog or bury them in the backyard cuz he didn't want his daddy smoking. Eventually, it just got shortened to Herc and all the efforts Herc made to save his dad ended up being in vain anyway cuz Roy L. died of lung and brain cancer at

the age of fifty-five. Herc wore a pompadour on his head like a
rogue shower cap and it was immediately obvious that he was
somewhat obsessed with Sal Mineo's Plato in Rebel Without A
Cause, *which kinda seemed a bit odd to us that he could quote*
dialogue from memory but we never said anything about it.

It just so happened that Herc and Natalie weren't in Barguss
to sightsee, but instead to get a jumpstart on their acting
careers, and the touching thing was that he wanted to be
just like his father . . .

The Horrible Return of Monroe Mister Promised To

Maybe that was a bad thing too cuz, as charismatic and heroic
as Roy L. Stevens was onscreen, he was known to be twice as
awful a person off it. He was the worst kinda drunk and a
peerless womanizer and Roman just happened to be his only
legitimate son through a marriage that later ended in divorce
back when divorces weren't so common but the rumors still
say that Ol' Roy must have had at least thirteen children by
different mothers all over the country including a secret baby
girl by a very well-known blonde bombshell of a starlet that
was much more famous than he ever was, so she kept it a
buried secret.

One day, long before they even started shooting the first
frame of film, Roman 'Herc' Stevens made himself the most
infamous newcomer to Barguss in less than three hours by
showing us that he was every bit like his father offscreen and
then some. It was a hot day and most everybody in Barguss that
didn't already have a job had been put to work building sets
for the film. Agghe Raine's jewelry store was being completely
rebuilt on the other side of town so that it looked like it came
straight out of *Breakfast at Tiffany's* and we all sorta thought
it was strange but didn't argue much.

And they were also building the stage and grandstand in the memorial park, not to mention actually reconstructing a blimp cuz the original one had fallen prey to Old Man Promised To's wrath and it had been burned up and its ashes were actually mixed in with the concrete that formed the base of the statue honoring his son. Although it was kinda funny watching them move the statue for the movie cuz it couldn't be there all in the way when they were shooting a re-enactment or something.

The movie people even added a few things that weren't there before too, like a new sign that said, 'Barguss: Home of the Biggest Blimp in the World' even though it wasn't technically true cuz some city in Belgium had that honor with its copper-lined dirigible that had been completely hand sewn with threaded copper and we have no idea how it stayed in the air but apparently it did. The sign made a couple of us uneasy though cuz we felt it made us look silly claiming that we had the biggest blimp in the whole wide world when even back before the incident we knew it wasn't the biggest in the world, we guess it just made us look arrogant.

While all this work was going on, Herc Stevens had managed to ditch Natalie in the room and finagle a lunch with Krystof Zckwecy in the hotel restaurant in order to have a talk with him about how much he wanted to portray Monroe Mister in the film. As the story goes, Krystof and his interpreter were impressed with Herc's bravado but they said they weren't so sure that he was tough enough to play the role. You see, Krystof had envisioned the character as a cross between Harry Hamlin's Perseus in *Clash of the Titans* and Paul Newman's 'Fast' Eddie Felsen in *The Hustler* and that if Herc could 'prove' that he could do that, then the part was his. So the last bit just kinda hung in the air and Herc got Krystof's point once it had been translated and it all went downhill from there.

Of course, Herc had been a welcome visitor a few days before he set to making the town feel his disdain for it. He vandalized two signs in broad daylight, spat in the street in front of people as they were walking and even urinated on the bronze city seal embedded in the concrete sign out in front of the courthouse on Gee but it didn't stop there and everything that Herc did was worse than Monroe Mister Promised To (apart from the horrible accidents with Jo Mary Jo and Maria) and as much as we are ashamed to admit it, we almost wanted him not to be dead instead.

From the courthouse, Herc made his way to the Taco Coleslaw Hamburger Hot Dog Apple and ordered table service on the best meal in the whole place (the #17), a super-deluxe combo: sneaky beef taco with all the trimmings and the quarter pound buffalo burger with whole mustard seed coleslaw on the side not to mention the ballpark slam hot dog topped off with chili and cheese and a great big caramel apple straight from the Barguss All-Purpose Apple Factory for dessert. Well, Herc ate all that while complaining pretty loudly that it was the worst food he ever ate and then walked right out the door without paying cuz he said, 'nobody should have to pay for that shit!'

Then he made his way down to Paulson's Cocktails and started in on one of the worst drunk tears we ever heard of, before or since. Apparently, the bartender stopped serving him after his thirteenth shot of vodka in a half hour. Indeed, it wasn't too long before Herc challenged the entire bar to a pool contest at $500 a game but that didn't last too long cuz he refused to pay up after losing the first game on an eight-ball scratch to a strangely sober Hasselzwell Smol. A fight would have erupted if not for Herc's projectile vomit splattering everyone within a ten-foot radius with a hideous mixture of the #17 and enough vodka to kill small household pets, so the bartender had to settle for just throwing him out.

Only problem was Herc landed on his feet and made his way down to The Golden Ring and got there just in time to take advantage of their happy hour 'two beers for one' special. By then the police were only one step behind him, just as they had been most of the late afternoon and they had gotten to Paulson's and were filling out another report of obscenity and battery and this time drunk and disorderly conduct to go with the previous ones from the Taco Coleslaw Hamburger Hot Dog Apple and the courthouse.

Well, Hasselzwell Smol had gone home to take a shower and change into a clean undershirt before making a few calls and finding out that Herc was at The Golden Ring. By the time Hasselzwell showed up with a few of his buddies though, Herc was all passed out on the table and Old Smol decided to wake him up with a pitcher of water and demand his five hundred bucks for winning at pool. Of course, there was only one thing in the whole world that truly ticked off Roman 'Herc' Stevens, son of famous Western actor Roy L. Stevens, and that was someone getting his pompadour wet on purpose. Sad to say, those guys never knew what hit 'em. By the time the cops finally showed up, Hasselzwell and two of his buddies had busted jaws and heads and a bloodied Herc Stevens was leaning casually against the bar trying to talk the frightened barmaid into going home with him.

Smart as she was pretty, Natalie Darling didn't stick around to deal with the fallout from Herc's awfulness, nor did she even try to bail him out of jail. In fact, she left that night to go back to Hollywood cuz it had become crystal clear to her during her late lunch with Krystof that the part of Florence Mink had already been won and so she might as well go find another job back in California, which must have been good for her cuz as soon as she got back she landed a role in an Eddie Murphy movie.

Well, the Barguss P.D. released Roman 'Herc' Stevens from jail 'on his own recognizance' the next morning due to the urgent request of the producers of *Roo Kickkick & the Big Bad Blimp* and there's actually a sorta famous picture now that shows Zeke and Norville Brundleby (who are the brothers that actually own Panazanc and had taken a personal producing interest in the film) shaking Herc's hand on the steps of the police station to tell him that he just nailed the part of Monroe Mister, almost as if his behavior was just an audition and that kinda stung cuz there were some people actually hurt on account of him and in movies that's not supposed to happen and anyway we thought some of his behavior was more befitting a combination of Raoul de los Dios *and* Monroe Mister Promised To but that might just be us.

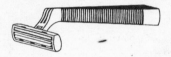

I I

Two weeks later there was a big 'open casting session' that
was supposed to be just for locals but a buncha people from
Upton and even as far away as West Haynesworth (ninety-two
miles away on a good day depending on weather and highway
conditions and maybe even flooding) showed up to try for a
place in the movie, which we didn't think was very fair at all.
'Course our opinion didn't matter that much and it mattered
even less when 2,672 people stood in line to be interviewed for
roughly 500 slots, checked for 'photogenicity' (whatever that
means) and then, if they passed, got issued wardrobe or got
issued a permit saying that they had been certified to provide
their own wardrobe after they got shot with a polaroid and
the picture was filed.

They held the big session on a Saturday starting at 5:30 a.m.,
which was maybe good for a lot of people that worked regular
weekly hours but not us cuz we had to skip work back then
just to get to the grand ballroom in the Prime Saddle Hotel in
time to get in the big giant line that stretched all the way out the
ugly knobbed dining room dome that looked like a blown-up
golf ball, except it had glass windows that reflected the light
in a million different directions. At first, we were behind some
idiots with Upton High Wrestling sweaters and we couldn't
help resenting them being in Barguss. Last time they were here

they swept the meet and Barguss High didn't get a single point in the competition.

But then we saw the Gee Street Girls and moved up in the line past a few people that were obviously from out of town cuz they were complaining about driving and being tired and stretching their backs. A few people even said something about us moving up but when we asked them where they were from and told them we were from Barguss they acted like they didn't hear us and looked up at the golf ball dining room roof like they were inspecting it or something. 'Course the Gee Street Girls were always so prepared and we couldn't help but tell 'em we thought it was funny how they brought lawn chairs and everything so they didn't have stand up like us.

Well, we guess the sad thing was it didn't take long for the movie people to turn us all down (the Girls were flat told they couldn't even play themselves), all on account of how we didn't look 'folksy cool enough' for their tastes, which Lily and Luanne Lukash objected to in unison saying that they 'had been born and raised in Barguss' and how could they not look like they were a part of Barguss? They 'were authentic, damnit!' But it fell on deaf ears or worse, just got laughed off. We didn't care too much about being turned down cuz if we made it we'd probably have had to quit our jobs anyway which maybe we would have done, but Candy, Mandy, Brandy, Luanne, and Lily were so mad that they said they were going to make their own movie about what Barguss was really about. We really liked that idea and we told them we'd help even though we thought at the time that nothing would come of it, but maybe we should have given them a little more credit. They really were kinda mad. Mad as we've ever seen 'em. Anyway, seemed like within the next coupla weeks the movie casting people rounded out the cast pretty well after Florence Mink and Roman 'Herc' Stevens had been lined up.

J. Bartholomew How got cast as Roo Kickkick. We're

pretty sure you remember him cuz he was already kinda famous before he got cast in the lead role. He was forever on the covers of pretty boy magazines like Tiger Beat *and* Bop *and* Star! *and stuff like that. He was the good-but-funny-witty-and-rough-around-the-edges-but-really-cute-and-doughy-eyed teenager in that one sitcom and unfortunately the name of it escapes us at the moment but we're pretty sure the name of it starts with a G or maybe a U. Anyway, what we always remembered about J. Bartholomew was that he had this really weird haircut where he parted it in the middle but his hair was sorta long and so light and thin that it kinda floated in the breeze even when there was no breeze and most of the time his hair just kinda looked like wings glued on his head. He was pretty quiet and mostly forgettable except he always picked his nails with a switchblade after the actor who played Raoul de los Dios had given him one . . .*

Madalick 'E.P.' Pinchone had sleepy eyelids that somehow drooped when he smiled (which wasn't all that often) and a nose and jaw of someone who knew how to take a few knocks. The E.P. stood for 'El Peleador', which we think means 'The Fighter' in Spanish but his nickname in English was 'One Punch' Pinchone so it's doubtful a whole lot was lost in our translation. Madalick was a former gang member and supposed leader of the L.A. gang Los Angelos Miraculosos, but he had recently turned his attention to acting after getting some screen time in a documentary about gangs called For My Family *and it was about gangs all over America basically being like families for the gang members which was nothing new but apparently (sorry, we never saw it) Madalick was a revelation in the film cuz he took the film crew into his room and showed them his oil/acrylic and mixed media paintings and everyone was all surprised that a 'gangbanger' could be so brilliant and artistic. After that, he got some gallery shows and a buncha roles in TV cop shows playing hardcore criminals but* Roo

93

Kickkick & the Big Bad Blimp *was definitely his big break. Although his ethnicity wasn't one hundred per cent certain on account of him never knowing his mama, we still thought it was kinda racist to cast him as Raoul de los Dios just cuz he could speak Spanish and he was brown-skinned and really didn't look anything like MacJohnson but that was before we knew that the filmmakers had a plan and that was just after we met . . .*

Fyodor Dearnt Rheeves, who played Thorpe Thorpe, for the first time. To the casting director's bitter disappointment, Beck had turned down the role of Thorpe Thorpe so that he could 'focus on a new album'. Fyodor, on the other hand, wasn't such a bad second place but you could never tell from the casting director's sour face. FDR happened to be the lead singer of the underground band called ReDeck that was a cultish-type favorite among its fans almost like Fugazi really, cuz they had never signed a major label deal and said they never would, so it was a big coup to get him to go solo and play the role of Thorpe and not even be considered hypocritical cuz he was just acting and wouldn't be doing music cuz Autistik/Artistik would be doing the score anyway. It was a common misconception that he had been named after the great Russian author, Fyodor Dostoevsky, and one that he addressed in one of ReDeck's most famous angry teen anthems 'Rhyme and Punishment': 'People always come up and say, hey you're named after that guy / that's when I have to stop them right there, man, don't you even try.' As it turns out, Fyodor's mother was a theatre-with-an-'re'-type of historian who happened to be really into the Russian 'theatre' in particular and she actually named him after the First Russian Theater Actor, Fyodor Grigoryevich Volkov, at least that's what Thed says cuz they used to hang out a lot together, him, Thorpe Thorpe, and the guy that played . . .

Thed Teldut: Mr. Link 'Doober' Stubbs. Link was an edgy

rock/hip-hop/electronic producer before he got cast in the movie cuz he was a friend of the casting director and we guess that was about the time we began wondering if you really needed a nickname to be considered for casting in the film cuz it was getting kinda ridiculous and then we thought maybe if the Gee Street Girls had told them who they were they might've gotten cast due to the fact that they had a collective nickname. But anyway, Link was really cool and knew everything there was to know about music, you could ask him anything, like . . . what year did Miles Davis's Bitches Brew *come out? And he'd never even have to look it up or second guess or anything, he'd just say 'August 19th, 1969, boys,' and then blow a smoke ring from his rosewood pipe before going off on how great the album cover was and how Abdul Mati Klarwein was the artist that did the cover and he did Santana's* Abraxas *too and how Link thought he was one of the best artists ever and he even suggested to the producers that they pick a Mati work of art for the movie poster. We think Link owned more vinyl records than anyone in the history of the world cuz his brother used to work at Capitol Records and got records for free and would give Link boxes and boxes for birthdays and holidays and sometimes, for no good reason at all.*

Well, it wasn't exactly the biggest chunk of casting but probably the funniest bit was how they cast Doctor Dinner. Eventually it was Morloine Harrison Westleycake that got the role as Doctor Dinner. He used to be a soap opera star but he was all notorious cuz he got addicted to speed and busted for it in an infamous police chase that ended up on the regional news and it was kinda funny that Morloine didn't look anything like Doctor Dinner and was about twenty years older and forty pounds heavier. But the funniest thing was how the producers tried to cast a dead guy in the role first.

The word goes that they tried to get Orson Welles to do it cuz if he did Transformers: The Movie, *he'd do* Roo Kickkick & the Big Bad Blimp *in a heartbeat. Only problem was they didn't realize he was dead, which is silly cuz he used to be a huge star and we have no idea how they could forget something like that. So they got in touch with his estate and tried to get his image rights from them so they could reanimate him with computers like a buncha other old dead stars who had been in vacuum commercials and what not. In their minds, it must have been like some wonderful cameo that was gonna happen when a portly Orson Welles barged through the operating room doors of Barguss General after seven straight hours of surgery and screamed 'Damnit! Face facts! I've performed a miracle to save the boy's face!' at the hysterical and crying Mrs. Kickkick.*

It never happened though. The Welles Estate never gave permission for his likeness to be used. The producers seemed pretty disappointed at that though, and even a scheduled dinner party hosted by the real Doctor Dinner didn't seem to cheer them up, but it probably should've cuz Ol' Doc was always regarded as one of the biggest weirdos in the whole town and he couldn'tve picked a better way to show everybody once and for all than the night of that dinner party . . .

Doctor Dinner Lives Up to His Ill Reputation

Lawrence O. Dinner, M.D., was the best surgeon in all of Barguss and you already know that but it didn't always used to be that way. Actually, Lawrence O. used to be Larry L. Dartbine, M.D., distinguished graduate of the University of Chicago medical program and practicing maxilofacial, oral, and orthopedic surgery out of a tiny Seattle suburb called Wallaby or Wendelby, something like that. Yes indeed, the

Doc was a valued member of the community: he headed up his local Neighborhood Watch program and always made sure to press full charges on any burglar stupid enough to get near the gated community. He also chaired the Welcome Committee for newly arriving residents in their neighborhood and was a regular great guy all around cuz everybody said so. Even then, he was famous for his lavish dinner parties that included nine courses and generally some exotically rare breed of Spanish-type sherry or thirty-year-old French wine.

There was only one problem with the kind Dr. Dartbine and that was his sexual compulsion disorder. Once, during his darkest hour, he actually left a back surgery-in-progress where he was inserting a rod into an elderly patient's spine. Word has it that the Doc just swept back from the body, mumbled something about needing a break, ripped off his gloves and exited the room only to come back later and find that the nurses had called the head physician at the hospital to come down and finish the surgery while he had been gone.

Dr. Dartbine's license to practice medicine was revoked that day and when the allegations became public in the local paper that Dr. Dartbine had spent that hour away from surgery worshipping a prostitute's feet with the aid of real melted butter and coconut oil, his debutante wife served him with divorce papers. Larry L. Dartbine left Seattle in disgrace and one month later, Lawrence O. Dinner, M.D. arrived in Upton, then moved down to Barguss when someone recognized him on the street.

Nobody in Barguss recognized him though and we certainly weren't in any sort of position to turn away a highly qualified doctor just cuz he had a few problems. As a favor, the Washington State Medical Board only pulled his license there, which allowed him to practice medicine in another state and that was great news for us. In fact, the summer he showed up we had a rash of scoliosis cases among the young and the doctor's help was needed immediately. As we all came to find out, the Doc was a foot fetishist of the highest order, which was kinda funny cuz we figured he'd be a podiatrist or whatever that foot doctor is called if that was the case, but the Doc said he 'never could concentrate if that were his specialty', so that answered that.

As for the big dinner party for the Hollywood types at his house, it was pretty obvious that Old Man Promised To had put him up to it cuz he wanted to meet all the movie people and especially the writer and tell him his version of the story so that he and his son's legacy were intact or something. Old Man Promised To may have been a lot of things but nobody ever accused him of being dumb and he knew that if he didn't make a favorable impression on the Hollywood types, then he and his son would be remembered badly by everyone who ever saw the film.

Funny thing was, in all the years that Doc Dinner lived in Barguss and that was probably like twelve or thirteen, he'd only thrown six dinner parties but just those few were enough to earn the Doc a rep as a class-A pervert. But to tell you the truth though, that was never really a big thing to us folks in Barguss cuz he always did his job real well and never screwed up again while doing surgery, so we figured that getting a real hard-on for somebody's feet wasn't the worst thing in the world. Don't get us wrong now, it's weird as hell but we just don't see a whole lot of harm to anybody in paying a woman to dip her toes in chocolate pudding for you to lick off as opposed to the mayhem Monroe Mister Promised To, Zeeda, Raoul de los Dios, and hell, even Roman, used to wreak on us. Well, as far as we knew, none of those Hollywood people had any idea that the Doc was a bit weird, but they sure found out that night and it gave us a story to tell for years and years.

The Doc's house was on rich people hill overlooking the city and he lived alone, not having remarried after the divorce fiasco with his first wife and that isn't to say there hasn't been sufficient interest from the female population though, even Mrs. Kickkick went out on a date with him once but she said she couldn't continue when he asked to sip champagne from her work boots. Though it was kinda silly how many women were impressed, or at least super-curious, about the foot fetish tag the Doc had on him. We even heard the Gee Street Girls say that they kinda liked the idea of having their toes sucked and the look in their eyes showed they'd probably already had that experience anyway and probably with Roo but mostly we joked with Thed and Thorpe that they just wanted to be worshipped more than anything else, even if it was only for their feet and not their whole bodies or their minds or souls or anything else like that.

Well, there are only like twenty other houses on rich people hill (all spaced out, of course) but the Doc's house is different cuz it's all done up in a Japanese motif with paper windows and sliding doors and everything. We've never been there but Florence told us all about it afterward and she really liked it. Actually, Florence and her dad were the first two guests to arrive that night. As was customary with Japanese tradition, Doctor Dinner asked them to remove their shoes and then just kinda sat there staring and we think it's funny how the Doc probably decided to do his whole house like that so people would have to take off their shoes and knowing him, that's completely on the list of possibilities.

Florence and her dad were taken into the dining room and instead of being greeted with a typical American large wooden dining room table for everybody, they were told to sit at one of four small tables set up. Each one was a Japanese table but they all had pits beneath them so that the guests could put their feet down instead of having to sit on their knees. The next guest was the screenwriter and Doc Dinner sat him at the table opposite Florence and her dad and they had to have a stilted conversation about Florence's lines in the new script from across the room.

After him was Krystof Zckwecy and Donny Barn who both showed up pretty stinking drunk already and singing old eighties tunes like 'Tenderness' by General Public except Krystof insisted on singing it in his best basso vibrato and Donny was singing all in scratchy falsetto, so it must have sounded weird to hear them coming up the steps with their arms over each other's shoulders supporting themselves. Those two had been pretty much inseparable since they met at the Prime Saddle steak night and shared stories about being outsiders in the U.S.

Old Man Promised To showed up next and he was sat next to the screenwriter in order that he could weave his oily Lionel Barrymore-type charm on the young man with the glasses and squinty eyes for most of the evening. Then came Norville Cline with Dr. Nancy of all people, and they were both seated with the screenwriter and Old Man Promised To. Everybody knew Norville was married but we guess Dr. Nancy didn't care on account of it being so long since someone actually paid attention to her. She still looked good for a fifty-year-old, we mean, even Thed Teldut said once that he'd 'bang her' if he ever got the chance.

The Fern-Micklewhites happened to be in town that week and they made an appearance and truth be told, they'd made more appearances since Raoul died and we can only guess that was cuz they felt his death cleansed their family name and they didn't have to worry about him screwing up any-more and reflecting badly on them, besides, mostly older folks just give them pity that their crazy son died. They got seated next to Krystof and Donny who were reciting Gary Cooper as Marshal Will Kane and James Millican as Herb Baker dialogue from *High Noon* back and forth by that point. And it was that scene where Marshal Kane tried to get a whole buncha people up in a posse but everyone was all scared and then he had to explain to Herb that he couldn't get anybody, and so Herb (who really only wanted to help if everyone else did) got all scared about facing Miller and backed out on Will at the last second and said it was like suicide. That's one of our favorite scenes ever.

Anyway, the Fern-Micklewhites were all transfixed and looked back and forth from face to face during the recitation and they didn't quite know what to make of it (cuz they'd never seen *High Noon* before, they didn't like movies much) so when Donny and Krystof lapsed into a sad sorta silence, they eagerly turned around at the sound of the door to see a coupla more people coming in.

The party rounded out with Roman 'Herc' Stevens and J. Bart How showing up and getting seated at Florence and her dad's table. Supposedly Madalick, Link and Fyodor were all invited but they had bizness to 'tie up' in Los Angeles and they wouldn't be on set for another coupla days. So Doc Dinner had a table all to himself and the guests thought that was pretty bizarre cuz they were all sitting four to a table. It was at the point that the Doc came out and put fifty-year-old bottles of cognac on each table and Donny and Krystof must have drooled or something cuz all of a sudden they were wiping their mouths with napkins.

Doctor Dinner was dressed in a man's Japanese-type robe and he made a big speech to those gathered that this was a 'special dinner consisting of very rare ingredients' such as oysters that grew off 'the northernmost coast of the northernmost island of Japan in La Perouse Strait' or some such and they could only be harvested every three years when the ice melted and other exotic stuff like that cuz he mentioned kangaroo meat too and even well-aged truffles from France and all other kinds of 'delicacies' we didn't even know existed, he said he'd serve 'all that and more' to his guests that night if they'd just be patient.

After that, he opened the kitchen door behind him and seven young women filed out from behind it only for Doctor Dinner to close the door with a slam behind them so none of his guests could see into the kitchen. Four of the girls were nakeder than the day they were born and were quite hairless all over and the other three just had on tight white t-shirts and teeny tiny white shorts and Doctor Dinner made this big speech about how the girls were from the 'farthest reaches of the globe' and not to worry about their cleanliness cuz he had shaved them and bathed them himself and stuff like that but right when they entered the room it was obvious to the Barguss residents that they were just the dancers at Dixie's Gypsy Den all made up to look Japanese or something and somehow, whether it was just embarrassment or plain old not wanting to show unsophistication in front of the out-of-towners, nobody said anything about it as the naked girls removed the cognac and laid down flat across each of the four tables with their back skin making squeaky sounds on the polished wood as they shifted into a comfortable position.

Doc piped up that he'd 'seen this in Tokyo once' and 'it's very erotic'. He must not have been paying attention to the looks on the people's faces though cuz he turned up this pipe and stringed instrument music on the stereo and sat down at his table with one of the girls that was wearing a t-shirt and really, really short shorts and Florence said it was actually Tandy Jenkins and we all went to high school together and we thought that was kinda gross cuz the Doc is like forty something.

Anyway, the other two girls went back into the kitchen and got the oysters and laid them out on each of the girls' stomachs and handed chopsticks to all the people that were gonna eat and only Dr. Nancy decided not to eat after mumbling something about being a vegetarian. Florence's dad removed his sweating palm from her knee under the table and took up some chopsticks and was the first one to try the oysters while J. Bart and Roman just kinda prodded the girl with one chopstick each to see if they could get a reaction from her but were disappointed when they couldn't.

A table over, Krystof and Donny had collapsed on each other's shoulders again and were just laughing their darn heads off as the Fern-Micklewhites picked the bits of oysters off the girl's tummy just like it was the most normal thing in the world. They even 'mmmmed' in unison at the quality of the seafood the Doc had had flown in. Old Man Promised To was chatting about himself in the most glowing way to the listening screenwriter, who couldn't take his eyes from the woman's concealed bare crotch cuz her legs were shut and Norville, well, Florence says Dr. Nancy saw him tuck his lumber into his waistband so no one would notice he was so turned on by the exotic food presentation.

Meanwhile, Doc was in his own little world as he got Tandy to stand up on his table in a bucket of water as he washed and shaved her legs and it was kinda like dinner and a show cuz the Ol' Doc did the same with the other two girls wearing shorts and it was obvious to most of the people there that the Doc had spent a long time planning the whole thing and some felt compelled to at least put up with it, so they wouldn't hurt his feelings.

Apparently, the night ended with Roman, J. Bart and the screenwriter each taking home one of the 'table girls' as they had been dubbed and without doubt had their ways with them. Old Man Promised To had left earlier than them after securing a deal to pay for the screenwriter's sister's lung surgery and kidney dialysis in return for a 'fairer' portrayal of him and his son in the script. Dr. Nancy gave her card to Tandy cuz she had caught sight of some split ends and thought that Tandy was obviously a Summer color family and not a Winter one. Norville Cline made sure to take what was left of their table cognac bottle and escorted Dr. Nancy to his Aston Martin outside. Florence's dad walked her home and didn't say anything, just had an odd little smile on his face. Donny and Krystof passed out underneath their table sometime after free styling gibberish to the Japanese music that sounded kinda like Kajagoogoo filtered through a kitten's voice box. Ever the last to leave, the Fern-Micklewhites thanked the Doc for his 'unique' party and took home some of the leftover kangaroo meat after the doctor's firm insisting. Tandy and the other girls stayed the night with the Doc and we don't know about you, but we almost don't want to know what else went on in the house on rich people hill that evening.

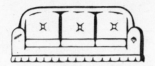

12

Angry probably isn't even the right word to describe the Gee
Street Girls after the casting session where we all got rejected.
Parts of their faces were going bright red in patches, like their
ears and just under their eyes and they went off together
whispering in their low voices that we knew not to get too
near cuz there could be wrath involved. But as crazy mad
as they were, we thought for sure they'd never make good
on that promise to make their own movie so we were surprised
as hell when our phone rang and instead of hearing a 'hello'
or a 'how are you?' all we heard was 'do you remember The
Vinny 'n' Mookie Show?'

First off, everyone our age in Barguss remembers that show,
it's like the only local classic there is on television cuz they still
show reruns of the old shows on the local public access channel
8 and the truth is those episodes are already around ten years
old. It might even sound silly but they're pretty much treated
as sacred texts in our high school video and media classes but
maybe we're getting too far ahead of ourselves there. Basically,
The Vinny 'n' Mookie Show was a show filled with stupid
stunts and pranks before there were any other shows like it
on TV.

It just started as two guys with a camcorder, they were both
raised up in Barguss but not born here and they played the

characters of Vinny and Mookie who were basically two pretty stupid but pretty lovable cousins from out on the East Coast somewheres cuz they always had good accents and furrowed their brows and flared their nostrils a lot as they drove around Barguss doing the craziest things. The shows now, they were pure genius. There was that one where they took their retarded friend out to the park and told him the sand volleyball court was a giant sandbox and watched him eventually treat it like a catbox was too much man, we recorded it and rewound that part over and over and another show was about dreams and career aspirations and basically it was an interview with Vinny's other cousin Minty who was a pimp up in Upton and Vinny was drilling him on how he could be one too and it was called 'Pimpreneureal Tips for the So Inclined'. But the real guys behind it actually did even crazier things in real life.

Raw Mike Tall was the guy that played Mookie and he was known to always carry a knife around with him and whether that was actually true or a rumor just so people wouldn't mess with him, we'll never know. Although one guy did get his ear carved off one night by a masked attacker and this was way before Raoul was old enough to pull any of that stuff so everyone just assumed it was Raw Mike and started calling him Van Gogh and he never seemed to mind. We think he moved north to Upton after the show collapsed and that happened when . . .

Dance LeRoy finally got arrested. He played Vinny in the show and supposedly he was the one who had 'borrowed' his dad's camcorder and taken it out on nightly missions to film the show and later edit it in the high school basement before putting it in an unmarked envelope and sending it on to channel 8. As legend has it, he went to great lengths to create the character of Vinny, rejecting something like two hundred wigs before settling on the right one for the character and even went out and got a monogrammed sport suit that said

'Vinny' all in cursive over the heart in light blue, all this for the character that frequently screwed up while pulling off stunts like stealing from the Taco Coleslaw Hamburger Hot Dog Apple drive-thru and then running his old Cadillac into the side of the building (there's still a chunk of concrete missing). But the real Dance was a relatively smooth character, that is, until he got caught. In a desperate effort to outdo his friends for most outrageous driver's license photo, Dance showed up at the Department of Motor Vehicles as Vinny with the wig and all, had his photo taken and was promptly booked for fraud. His parents packed him off to military school in California (that wasn't his only 'infraction', though, he'd been vandalizing the local army base with his urine for months) and no one here has heard from Dance since, although we occasionally get the creepy feeling on our necks when watching something oddly similar to The Vinny 'n' Mookie Show on TV that Dance is somehow behind it.

All that flashed through our minds when Lily, Brandy and Mandy said, 'do you remember The Vinny 'n' Mookie Show?' We met four-fifths of them out on Gee Street two hours later where Luanne brandished a brand new camcorder and said her dad had actually said she could use it but she wanted it to be just like the show, so she said she didn't need it and then she snuck back into his closet and weighed the handy carrier bag down with the exact weight of rocks so he'd never be able to tell. 'It's gotta be au-ten-tic,' she said, 'just like Dance and Raw.' It was at that moment that a car came speeding around the corner of Hotblack, pointing its brights right at us as it sped up the curb and stopped hard.

With a half-scream, Mandy Mulryne told us to get in fast as we could. Turned out she had hotwired her cousin's car but that was after she took the license plates off with a rusty screwdriver and with us all piled in, she made an illegal U-turn that put the Lukash sisters' butts in our laps and we didn't complain at all cuz it was kinda cramped in a good way with seven people in an old brown sedan. Luanne scrambled into the front seat and began recording as Candy and Lily plopped wigs on our heads and started applying glue to our upper lips and before we knew it we had huge moustaches tickling our cheeks and chins. The girls did most of the talking to the camera, they were all dressed up like disco girls which was good cuz we kinda went stiff as cardboard when it got pointed at us.

That was all well and good despite the fact that nobody had told us where we were going just yet, but when we crossed the double yellow line on Gee and skidded up rich people hill, we had a pretty good idea. Mandy turned off the lights as soon as we got to the neighborhood then swung the car around and parked 'for a fast get away', she said as she pulled ropes from underneath the front couchy-type seat. Lily grabbed the keys from Mandy and opened the trunk to pull out a dolly handcart with little difficulty. Luanne fixed a light on top of the camera and we shuffled up the street toward the Promised Tos' mansion as quietly as we could.

Mandy picked the gate's lock and we were standing around dumbly as she picked the fourth garage's lock too and opened it to reveal the missing statue of Monroe Mister Promised To! It had been taken down by the movie people for 'continuity' they said, and so it had resided in Old Man Promised To's fourth garage until it could be returned to its pedestal at the memorial park. Luanne had the camera right on us, as we must have smiled at the thought of stealing the life-size statue. There was only one problem, it was heavier than we ever thought it'd be, must've been like 300 lbs at least. The handcart wasn't gonna do us any good, so we snuck to the back of the garage and popped the gardener's riding lawnmower into neutral and eased it over to the statue that looked so weird at night with the bright light from the camera shining *on it almost like a real person turned to stone from looking at the gorgon Medusa.*

We were able to tip the statue onto the lawnmower, crushing the seat and frame it seemed like, but it gave us enough lift to be able to push it down the slopey driveway and you know, we really can't be blamed for it getting away from us and taking off through the gate and picking up enough speed to jump the lip of the pavement and crash down the hill and maybe if the girls had helped more we could really have stolen it instead of having to bury it where it lay: right at the foot of rich people hill. Somehow, nobody had heard us make that terrific noise in the middle of the night and somehow, no one even drove by as we shoveled the statue and the busted-up lawnmower into the ground right by the crooked tree that stood by the sign that announced: 'Grosvenor Acres'. When we were done with digging that hole big enough to fit both bits of evidence in it, we covered up the slight mound with brush and tumbleweeds and carved 'MMPT' into the tree so we'd always know.

Funny thing was, while we were out all night making Barguss history, we had no idea that Florence and Roo were falling in love across town . . . well, sorta.

The Incredible, Almost Unbelievable, Eight-Hour Courtship of Miss Florence by Mister Roo

Of course, it didn't really take eight hours exactly, it was probably everything kinda building up and up over years and years inside Florence but the bizarre path it took that night led straight into Roo's arms, minus a coupla excursionary-type detours that weren't exactly planned but happened nonetheless, probably cuz Florence was feeling pretty crazy then.

It was less than a week after Doctor Dinner's dinner that it happened. Filming had finally started and had actually gone late that day and Florence wasn't in the scene but she 'was required on set' to be fitted for costumes and practice her lines and 'glean, glean, glean', as Norville Cline said. Apparently, Krystof had spent the entire day screaming at Madalick that he 'was not in the feeling of the evil', cuz it was the scene where Agghe Raine got stomped and they ended up just re-casting the part with a veteran stuntman as Agghe after the actor guy complained about being hit so much so they fired him, cuz really, all they had to do was put a pair of glasses on the guy that had an optical thingy that stuck out of the right eye for looking at diamonds and *voilà*! The stunt man was Agghe.

Sorta sad how it didn't really take any acting ability at all cuz he just had to say, upon hearing the jingling bells on the door, 'may I help you?' without looking up from a diamond inspection and when he finally did look up, he caught a fierce one right in the chops. They reshot that one take fifty-seven times and well, fake Agghe basically got kicked all up and down the set for hours and hours. So by the time Florence was allowed to go, she was dead tired of rejecting about seven hundred different types of spoons to wear in her hair and sick of watching Madalick go to work on the stuntman. By the time the scene wrapped, the stuntman had one broken rib and a grade-two concussion, 'for the realism!' Krystof had barked.

11:41 P.M.: IT STARTS.
Florence showed up on Roo's doorstep crying the biggest tears he'd ever seen and only wearing her night shirt and pajama bottoms that Roo would never have recognized as Monroe Mister's old silk pair, but they were, navy blue with gold trim and only slightly frayed at the bottom cuffs where she would drag them on the carpet cuz they were too long for her. Words came out all unintelligible cuz she was gasping and coughing and crying all while trying to talk and eventually she squeezed out a high-pitched whine that she 'just didn't know where to

go'. As it happens, a pretty girl doing a thing like that can break a guy's heart in two seconds flat.

Less than a minute later, Roo had Florence comfortably wrapped in an afghan his grandma had made him before she died and barricaded behind three pillows and an ottoman cushion on the couch. Then he put a cup of hot tea in her hand and sat across from her and didn't say anything, just kinda sat there with that blank look he was always so good at cuz it made people tell him their problems.

That must've been when the whole awful story came pouring out: the trauma of Monroe Mister's death and the stress of working on the movie and how playing herself was giving her a complex cuz she didn't really know who she was anymore and finally, at the bottommost layer, all the awfulness her dad ever did to her. At this point, Florence had jettisoned the cushion and pillows and was only half wrapped in the afghan and Roo had eased closer to her and was rubbing her shoulder and she was making eyes at him and . . . well, if this were a movie, it'd be the scene that every romantic comedy has where the distanced couple all lean into each other to lock their lips together and find out if it's for real but of course they get interrupted cuz it always happens that way cuz if it weren't for obstacles, the lovers would never appreciate their love, right? Right. So there's this knock at the door that startles Roo and Florence.

MUST'VE BEEN AROUND 1:30 A.M.: THREE KNOCKS AT THE DOOR, ALL SLOW-LIKE: *PLONK*, PAUSE, *PLONK*, PAUSE, *PLONK*, AND IT MADE A SOUND LIKE *PLONK* CUZ IT WAS CHEAP-TYPE WOOD.
Roo, as curious as Florence (we like to imagine that at this point, Florence irrationally thinks it's the ghost of Monroe Mister come to claim her but says nothing of it), reluctantly left his seat and probably cursed himself quietly for being so

close and yet so far away. Asking who it was, Roo got no response and since he lived in one of those houses that was built by trusting builders and had no peephole, he just had to open the door.

Outside were two figures with Asian features holding hands and Roo was just as astonished as Florence, who nearly fell off the couch cuz she was leaning over so far to see out the front door. 'Brother!' they both said and smiled in unison, looked at each other, smiled again and then waited patiently to be invited in. But Roo though, he just stood there with no idea of what to make of it and he'd be lying if he ever told anyone that the thought of slamming the door in their faces didn't occur to him. He had no choice but to invite them in. It wasn't too long before he found out who they were cuz they each handed him a letter.

Shusaku Kikukiku a.k.a. DJ Dirty Elvis was from Okinawa, Japan, and had only recently moved to Osaka via Tokyo to live with his cousin and pursue his career as a trance and deep house DJ and it was a rather short time (less than a month) before fame embraced him. At the time of his trip to visit Roo, he was the #1 DJ in all of Asia due to his chart-smashing debut album *Unbreakable Chi*. In fact, 'Shoe', as everyone would later call him, was still quite stoned from flying in from Amsterdam after a world DJ conference and taking a late bus into Barguss from Upton. Unlike Fyodor, he actually was named after a famous author, Shusaku Endo, cuz his mother had read *Deep River* like sixteen times in a row after Lt. Lem Kickkick had left her pregnant with him.

Laura Mon Alzar was born in Manila proper but raised in the Quezon City suburb and even though she was not yet eleven, she was really, really pretty and had already been awarded the First Runner Up slot in the junior competitive version of the Binibining Pilipinas Pageant the year before. She wanted to be a doctor when she grew up and she was the best soccer player in her whole school. Under the coach's system, she played withdrawn striker and routinely popped balls into the net from twenty yards away. She had the oddest habit of wrapping/knotting crayons up in her hair and we woulda thought that she and Florence would have gotten on well right away cuz of that but Roo didn't notice that Florence bristled at the attention he gave his new guests.

It turned out that they were both in Barguss for a one-month cultural stay to meet their half-brother. Apparently it had all been coordinated by Mrs. Kickkick, right down to Shusaku picking up Laura in Manila and then taking her to Amsterdam with him cuz she wasn't old enough to travel alone internationally, or any other way really. We guess there had been some resistance from Laura's mom but Mrs. Kickkick eventually convinced her it was okay and it probably helped that Shusaku was so famous and had all kinds of money and her little girl flew first class with him everywhere they went.

When they both stepped into the light of the room and were better able to see Roo's face, they gasped at his scars and he really didn't pay attention cuz he was used to being stared at and he was just trying to digest the new information that he wasn't an only child cuz it was like his world was shifting and so many things were happening at once. So after he let Laura feel the scars on his face, he led them back to his room and prepared the bed for Laura and a cot for Shoe and it couldn'tve taken him more than twenty minutes to do that and be all polite even though he was distracted and told 'em he'd see them in the morning and went back into the front room.

But no one was there. Not used to being ignored, much less at a time of such crisis, Florence had up and left. When Roo came back all he saw was the afghan crumpled into the couch with Florence's negative space still shaping it and stuff. He grabbed his coat and ran out to his car. The very same car that he had bought from Hasselzwell Smol four months previously, the 1976 Volvo 244DL (navy blue with sunroof) and proceeded down Gee to look for Florence with his brights on.

PROBABLY 2:49 A.M.: PRIME SADDLE HOTEL LOBBY BAR.

We're pretty sure that Florence didn't have the tightest grip on reality at that point in time so it really was no surprise that she showed up at the cast's HQ, the Whistle Bar in the lobby of the Prime Saddle, a bit dazed. Most people we talked to that were there that night said Florence looked kinda 'entranced' as she walked right up to Roman 'Herc' Stevens's pompadour with the Christopher Reeve-type Superman curl on his widow's peak (he hadn't really bothered to get out of costume since the shooting had wrapped for the day). He and Madalick were skol-ing tequila and listening to each other's rambling stories about the opposite sides of the tracks when Florence walked right in, kissed Roman full on the mouth and said, 'come to bed, Monroe.'

We guess Roman did like most men would do in that situation, he rolled with it, content to be Monroe Mister if it meant time alone with Florence Mink in a bevy of all different naked kinds of positions. So he role-played and filed it in his head under 'field work', then pressed the elevator button to take Florence up to his room.

She came down about three hours later and it wasn't due to the fact that he was good or anything but more cuz he was so drunk and sloppy that she fell asleep and woke up when Madalick crashed into the wrong door in the hallway and nearly started a fight with a startled J. Bart How, who, judging by Madalick's screaming laughter, had answered the door in a pair of ducky PJs with attached slipper feet. Madalick must've felt bad or something about the door mix-up the next morning cuz that was when he gave J. Bart the switchblade. Just to say sorry.

ABOUT THREE HOURS LATER: 5:32 A.M.
Hungry and exhausted, Florence walked up Gee Street. We know cuz we saw her on our way home to be dropped off by the Girls. We were sitting in the back trying to get the dirt out from underneath our fingernails so our mama wouldn't yell or have cause to suspect us when the distress signal went out later that day as it certainly would cuz we all knew how bad Old Man Promised To would freak when he found the statue of his dead only son missing but we stopped picking at our nails when we saw Florence shuffling toward the Taco Coleslaw Hamburger Hot Dog Apple.

'Damn,' Brandy said all disgusted and yet happy, 'Florence looks like something ate her and spit her back out,' and then all the girls laughed cuz as much as they liked and admired Florence and followed her every fashion move (nearly), they never really liked her as a person and we guess that was primarily cuz they knew Roo would choose Florence over any one of them any day of the week but after that, the girls all went quiet and we cruised along in silence, except for when Mandy hit a squirrel crossing the road by Thed's house. We didn't stop to bury it.

But there was something so porcupine about Florence that night that makes us think about seeing her like that again and again and maybe that was what kept us going in the car cuz even though it looked as if she needed some help, there was something all prickly about her that said, 'don't come near me,' but not in so many words just in body language. Now we aren't the smartest people in the world, but we're pretty sure we can see low points in other people like it's written across their faces and that was the lowest we've ever seen Florence before or since. The lowest of the low, we swear.

We all know how it feels after a long hard night to experience the beautiful relief of knowing that the Taco Coleslaw Hamburger Hot Dog Apple is open '25 hours a day' just like the sign says out front in purple heated neon. And it had to be with the very same relief just multiplied by like ten when Florence was struggling with what to order and Roo came up behind her and put his hands on her shoulders and told the high school kid working the place alone that she'd have an applesauce and a strawberry milkshake, her favorites.

ROUGHLY LIKE 7:40 A.M.: THE DEAL IS SEALED.
As an advisor for the film, Roo had a key to the locked up set and he and Florence ended up back in the Raine jewelry store cuz they knew they'd be alone and nobody would be around cuz like most people that worked on the movie, they couldn't wait to be away from it when the day was over. Florence sat on fake Agghe's desk and swung her feet cuz they dangled off the edge and Roo trudged around underneath the stage lights that weren't turned on. It must've been so obvious to Florence that he was nervous when he even walked over to one of the fake walls and tested it with his weight and it almost tipped over and crashed into the boom equipment, but it didn't.

Florence patted the desk and Roo went over and sat next to her and she put her head on his shoulder and just started crying again right away, bigger tears than before and all Roo could do was hold her there as she let it out in gulps of air that she'd 'been struck by the ghost of Monroe Mister', and apologized for her night with Roman and apologized for being her father's daughter and apologized for burdening him with all of her sad details and then she just thanked him, looked up and kissed his cheek and then his lips too and somehow it lasted. Happened all fast too, not like the movies at all, no dramatic tension, no build-up of music or anything but chokey-type breathing and 'just bang', cuz that's what Roo told us later and we smiled at the time but we got kinda jealous cuz, back then, we'd never had a 'just bang' moment in our whole lives and we wanted one pretty bad too.

Well, she moved in with him that next day, not at all worried about sharing the apartment with four other people, including Roo's two newly discovered half-siblings, but for that kinda extended moment that early morning she was just kissing Roo's reconstructed lips with her pristine ones and testing his prosthetic teeth with a playful tongue tip, and using both her index fingers to trace his smiley scars up to his ears then back again to his mouth and she didn't even need to say that for years she had wondered about what it was actually like to kiss Roo's broken-and-whole-again face and what it would feel like and would it be good?

13

'Course Roo and Florence didn't know we saw them kissing that night (how could we tell them that we were worried about Florence looking like she did, so when Mandy dropped us off, we backtracked to Gee Street and saw Roo and Florence at the Taco Coleslaw Hamburger Hot Dog Apple, so we hid and then kinda followed them to the studio just cuz we were curious what would happen?) and we didn't say anything about it either, especially not even when we all went to the Iron Horse a few nights later to play some pool. We should probably tell you that it isn't the Iron Horse anymore, don't get us wrong, it's still a Western-type bar but now it's a restaurant too, specializing in rare steaks and overcooked potatoes and beans but now it's called the Hitching Post & Horse Shack and the novelty is that there is a hitching post inside the bar with old merry-go-round horses tied up to it as some sorta joke.

We think they just decided to redecorate when they bought the horses dirt cheap from the county fair cuz it had debts to clear and had to sell almost everything at auction. In fact, we think Doc Dinner still has the 'Test Your Strength' thingy where you try to ring the bell by slamming the hammer down but it's still kinda weird that he doesn't ever use it, it just sits in his backyard and we had a sneaking suspicion that maybe the next scene that the Gee Street Girls were filming would consist of us sneaking up there and ringing the bell at night trying to wake his ass up.

Well, we met Florence and Roo and his new siblings and it was kinda exciting to meet new people from so far away but to still have them be related to Roo, so they were oddly familiar looking. We liked both Shoe and Laura immediately cuz there's just something about those Kickkicks you can't quite put your finger on but is so invisible and so likeable about them just being who they are. Shoe was really talkative that night and we asked him all kinds of questions about Japan and ended up with an acid trip sorta history lesson from Admiral Perry on to the emperors and geishas and the bombs and stuff and by the end of it all, we were pretty sure that Shoe was one of the most interesting guys we've met, ever.

Laura, well, she's about the cutest little girl we ever did see and that excludes Florence of course, cuz she's just Florence. We did get a pronunciation lesson though on account of how we pronounced her name just as if it were a typical American one, kinda like Lowra, 'low' like not so high, with an 'o' sound in the middle. But she got all upset and said that instead, we should pronounce it with an 'ow!' in the middle like you just hurt your hand. So we did it a few times 'til it was satisfactory and she smiled a big smile in appreciation. Super-cute kid that Laura, and a hell of a pool player too. She's picked it up in less than two games, a real natural.

Anyway, Thed and Thorpe showed up a bit later with Link and Fyodor cuz they'd all been hanging out nonstop nowadays, what with Link and Fyodor mimicking their every move so that they could play them on the big screen, or so they said anyway but really, we think they all liked hanging out together just cuz they really were kinda similar people whose lives all revolved around music and stuff related to it. Seemed like all they ever talked about was musical trivia anyway.

We already had a coupla games of pool going on opposite

tables when Roman and some big white dude we'd never seen before walked in. We didn't really pay much attention to him (actually we kinda looked away and started racking up the balls for a new game) cuz we just figured he was one of Roman's big-time Hollywood friends out for a weekend of Barguss slumming and if it's one thing we learned about those types of guys and girls it's that they love to be recognized but hate not being normal at the same time, almost like it's some kinda paradox. Besides, in a weird way, it was getting normal in Barguss to see famous friends of famous friends coming out to visit if they didn't have their own movie to do, they'd just fly to Barguss for a weekend. One time, we saw Winona Ryder hanging out with Roman at Paulson's Cocktails and we were gonna go up and say hello but he saw us and gave us a look that we should leave her alone so we did.

Anyway like we said, they're slumming it. They have to be. We haven't got anything super-fancy in Barguss and mostly we mind our own bizness so that's probably why there've been so many sightings of famous people lately cuz word must spread pretty fast around those types of people that they won't get hassled for autographs around here or have to hole up in their hotel or anything to avoid deranged fans.

So after Roman got a beer, he sauntered over and asked if he and the big white guy could join in and play on our table cuz we just whooped Link and Thed something fierce on eight ball and we said 'sure' but it got mighty uncomfortable when the white guy got all close and stood right next to us and it wasn't until that moment when we finally looked at him that we got a flash of something and it was that this big white dude looked just exactly like Raoul de los Dios with curly red hair and freckles and everything!

It wasn't until he said something that we actually realized who it was and the shock of it all was pretty good cuz even a few inches away the make-up was some of the best we've ever seen. It was none other than Madalick Pinchone, still in costume as Raoul de los Dios and it was so damned convincing we had to jump around for a bit and pull on his hair and rub his cheeks until he threatened to stab us in the spleen and it was then that we knew the casting director had done an amazing job. For the transformation, Madalick had shaved his paperclip-thin moustache right off and put green contacts in his brown eyes and his thick dark hair had been shortened, straightened, then permed and dyed orange-ish red and then, on top of all that, he had make-up on his face that made him look white, with freckles and everything but with that same scary look in his eyes, even behind the contacts it was the same look Raoul used to shoot at us. It was amazing.

Halfway through the pool game, Roman and Madalick were killing us but the real fact was we weren't even concentrating, we couldn't get over the transformation and mostly it gave us a cold feeling to look at him cuz he was almost exactly the same height as Raoul and it made that layer just underneath our skin colder than the freezer in winter and it was really like Raoul was alive again and in some ways, we couldn't think of anything more disturbing. It wasn't until they sunk the fifteen ball and had only one more before the eight ball that we looked around to see what other people's reactions were.

Roo had a kinda sad smile on his face as he looked at Madalick taking a shot and we exchanged glances and he just shook his head and whistled low like he couldn't believe the likeness was so uncanny. Florence completely ignored Madalick though and instead of pool, played those paddycake kinda hand games with Laura. Thed and Thorpe were whispering to each other and we had a feeling they were discussing a song and didn't really seem to notice Madalick but we figured they'd been on the set earlier and had already seen him. On the whole, it seemed like most everybody was taking it a lot better than us but we guarantee if Candy, Mandy, Brandy,

Luanne and Lily had been there they'd all have jumped right out of their skins from the fright.

In scanning the Hitching Post eating area though, we did notice Krystof and Donny Barn were at a corner booth splitting time telling stories about their old countries again, Donny and his amber waves of Alberta wheat fields and Krystof and his hammers and sickles and commie-type stuff that almost killed him as an artist. Sometimes they'd look all conspiratory, hunched over a bottle and two dirty shot glasses (that was the only way they drank, bought a bottle and split it fifty-fifty), lowering their voices and throwing looks at anyone who came near them, even if it was to go and use the bathroom down the hallway from their table.

This wasn't anything out of the ordinary though cuz everybody knew Krystof and Donny had become really good friends. 'Two crazy foreigners, they need each other,' everyone always seemed to say. In fact, it wasn't out of the ordinary to see stuff like Krystof touring around in Roman's borrowed Cord on Gee Street with Donny on his motorbike right alongside and them pointing up at the stars and screaming about astronomy and the comparative geniuses of Heinrich Wilhelm Olbers and his famous 'Why is the night sky dark?' paradox versus Johann Bode and the no-longer-controversial Bode's Law.

But there was something about their communication that night at the Hitching Post that made sure we couldn't take our eyes away from them talking about whatever they were talking about cuz we couldn't hear what they were saying but we could read their body languages and it looked really serious and then they just kinda relaxed, completely too. Just sorta sagged in their chairs and had smiles on. Exactly at that point, Roman snapped the eight ball right into the corner pocket by our fingers, Krystof gashed up the palm of his hand with a used steak knife and Donny did the same and they clasped hands and didn't say anything. Just after that, Krystof got up and *left and Donny went to the bathroom and we couldn't ever figure out just why but it sure looked like they'd made a pact of some type or another.*

Our Savior Krystof Makes a Large Popping Sound

Halfway through the production and the producers were feeling great about everything related to the film, mostly cuz it was ahead of schedule and under budget somehow (most filmy-type people attribute it to Krystof's habitually independent way of making movies under a former Communist regime) but beyond that, all the little things seemed to be going right and maybe if the producers chalked that one up to providence, we local people chalked it up to perseverance. As it turned out, we were the ones forfeiting our Saturday and Sunday nights to help sew the new blimp or construct a new set. Krystof was one of the few that appreciated us, he was always really thankful, even to people who didn't help, he'd walk up to them and say 'thanks you,' and sometimes they'd ask why, and he'd say 'for sharing your town.'

He was gracious always and the people of Barguss really got to liking him, even if his methods weren't the most orthodox at times and a lot of people actually said that maybe the reason that Krystof was being so nice and grateful was 'because he'd have to live here among us' and for the most part, that was pretty much true. At the moment, Krystof was living at the Prime Saddle with the rest of the crew but they were just in the process of pouring the foundation for his cabin on the outskirts of town (which we thought was kinda weird cuz the cabins we knew of didn't really have foundations, but then we were told it was a 'luxury' cabin and all we could do was nod).

But the producers did like Krystof for other reasons too. For one, he was really great with the young actors, well, maybe 'really great' isn't quite right cuz he was really hard on 'em, but as difficult as he could be and he could be very difficult (this one time he threw a half-hour-long screaming tantrum on a stack of packing crates all in Hungarian or Polish or whatever and when he was done, calmly got up and ordered a hot green tea then went back to work like nothing had ever happened), he was dragging some very fine performances out of his actors though (in particular the ones with the least experience, like Florence and Madalick), at least that's what everybody said.

In fact, they'd been shooting the big finale-type blimp scene in the memorial park for a week and we'd gotten to be there everyday but it's really boring and really not worth telling about cuz more than anything we sat around for hours and hours just to get up and stand around for fifteen minutes after they'd moved the camera. We really didn't think they needed the whole town there but they did and it ended up shutting down all of Barguss for four days to relive the blimp scene all over again but really we were just bodies cuz all of the extras that got cast from Upton and West Haynesworth got to be up in front and get their faces in the picture. The rest of us were just one big mass of a crowd packed in between the grandstand and the bandstand except there was only one tree where the bandstand was a coupla years ago when it actually happened. The other tree had gotten diseased and was cut down the year before.

The fourth day really wasn't supposed to be any big deal cuz all of the action shots of Roo and Raoul on the blimp had been taken care of and all the band shots of the concert and the crowd shots and the city council shots and the MarMartuchys' shots too, all that had been done in the previous days. Krystof just wanted one big sweeping crane shot from one side of the park to the other, from the city council, through the crowd, up to the band, then up the tree and straight up the rope to the blimp where Roo was hanging and Raoul had already plummeted and nailed Monroe Mister Promised To. It sure sounded like a heck of a shot and the crew guys and gals had been setting the whole thing up since 3 a.m. that morning and by the time we got there, everything was ready.

Before they started shooting we caught up with Roo but he was kinda downcast cuz he'd just been told that he couldn't have a cameo if only for the simple fact that his real scars made J. Bart's make-up look really fake so he couldn't ever be allowed into the frame. The producers told him he'd just have to be satisfied with an advisor credit and that was it. We sorta shot the shit for awhile before Roo told us he had a weird feeling about Krystof and we asked why and he said he just couldn't explain but he'd seen him and he was kinda walking funny and he smelled really weird. That caught us off guard. 'He smelled weird?' we asked and he said, 'yeah,' and we asked how he smelled and he said he couldn't explain it and just when we were gonna ask more questions we got told we needed to 'return to our positions' cuz they were ready to shoot and we parted from Roo with some uneasy glances going both ways.

We kept our eyes peeled for the next two hours as they shot the giant crane shot over and over, like at least five times but everything seemed to be going fine. Krystof was the only one up on the crane cuz he liked to shoot certain parts of the movie himself and he'd actually taught the cinematographer lady a thing or two. Well, after he finished the sixth shot and the camera was all extended at the top of the crane which was maybe fifty feet up in the air, Krystof stood up and pulled out a bullhorn and we all figured that we were done shooting for the day. We mean, they had actually shot the ending with Roo consoling Florence the day before and this was the last shot needed for the end of the movie.

'Thanks you all for coming,' we'll always remember Krystof

saying that and the way it echoed and stuff and how high up he was, then he turned and took the film magazine off the camera and tossed it to two assistants way down below who caught it with a stretched-out blanket, 'and I just have one more thing to say . . .' If words could actually hang in the air, his kinda did as a few hundred people and all the residents of Barguss listened intently for that one last thing he had to say and from where we were standing (so far away and all) we didn't actually see him flick the lighter open cuz it was broad daylight and all that but we definitely saw him touch it to his shirtsleeve and it was in that instant that his whole body caught fire!

People went crazy, some got really quiet and covered their mouths and couldn't believe what they were seeing, others started screaming, others ran away while we just sorta stood there and looked at the human fireball from eighty yards and we've seen some pretty bad things in our times but that was probably the worst of all of them and especially the eerie way that he sat down in the chair behind the camera like he was all calm about it and he kinda looked like he was just nodding his head forward a lot as we ran closer.

You've probably heard campfires crackle on quiet nights, well, it was like that only a lot louder when human flesh is involved and to this day it's the pops that his body made when it was being all eaten up that still stick in our memory. Running past people who were running away and some still too shocked to do anything but sit, we stepped on a few people and they yelped but we kept running and dodging and got close enough to see three crewmen cranking the crane down by hand cuz we guess Krystof had jammed the raising and lowering mechanism before he lit himself and we even heard Norville Cline screaming, 'Save the camera! Save the camera!'

When they finally got him down and ripped him out of the seat, part of him actually stayed in it and it was then we knew it was too late for Krystof, the bullhorn fused to what was left of his hand skin. We guess the good news was they saved the camera anyway, we're sure Norville was very proud.

A funeral service was held at the cabin site and Donny Barn read out the suicide note that Krystof L. Zckwecy had given him the night before and made him promise not to open it, 'except in emergency'. Donny read it pretty loud and clear and there was a big quote from Yukio Mishima's *Sun and Steel* in the middle: 'Of late, I have come to sense within myself an accumulation of all kinds of things that cannot find adequate expression via an objective artistic form such as the film.' Krystof changed it a little though cuz apparently Mishima said the 'novel' instead of 'film' but anyway, it goes on later: 'as I pondered the nature of that "I", I was driven to the conclusion that the "I" in question corresponded precisely with the physical space that I occupied. What I was seeking, in short, was a language of the body . . .' It went on but we forget it all, it was mostly meant to be this string of logic for his suicide being his 'last great artistic endeavor', for 'what can be more artistic than orchestrating one's own death?' or something and it was pretty disturbing to think of it that way we thought but we were standing next to Shoe as he nodded his head solemnly like it made all the sense in the world. Roo was helping Laura color a picture of the cabin's foundation with a skull and crossbones drawing inside it like a pirate flag almost. Everyone else seemed to be listening pretty hard and Florence was crying under her black veil.

As funerals go, it seemed like the classiest one we've ever been to and we didn't say anything when they laid the coffin down in the foundation where the guests' bathroom plumbing would have gone had Krystof not died. It fit perfectly. Shoe whispered something about it being a lot like Dalí in his museum in Spain, and Thorpe Thorpe shuddered even though he was a coupla people away. We didn't tell anybody but we did kinda wonder about the logic of putting the charred body in the big new silk-lined silver coffin when it was pretty obvious that he'd probably rather've been cremated seeing as how he tried to do it when he was still alive and all but we certainly kept that to ourselves.

The film's set building crew took a one week hiatus from the film and set to helping the construction guys finish building the cabin so they could turn it into a museum for Krystof and his career. Aside from that, the movie pretty much shut down for awhile as no one was quite sure what would happen with it and some people had even started spreading the rumor that it would be abandoned. That wasn't the case however, the producers started working overtime to get the production going again. Really everyone thought that Norville and Zeke didn't much care that their director was dead but more like they were just upset he'd left them in such a lurch. They didn't even shed a tear and we know cuz the director search started again that afternoon just after the funeral. And who can blame them really? It was a horrible position to be put in by an employee when so much money was riding on one project but when we thought more about it, maybe they shoulda been a little bit better prepared for this kinda thing from Krystof cuz one of the first things he ever said was that he wanted 'to grow old and die in America', but we guess he just ended up doing it a lot sooner than everybody thought, at least the dying part anyway.

We're not exactly sure if it was happenstance or planning, but the Gee Street Girls released part one of their 'Barguss Miniseries' on the local channel 8 public access that evening and supposedly, it was really, really good, a kinda Ken Burns style with the camera all panning over photographs and Lily narrated it. She had the best voice, sorta husky but sexy and always made us pay attention but with the funeral and all we weren't able to see it that night, but the girls did promise us that if it'd got a good response then it'd be rerun sooner or later.

14

With the producers scrambling all around for a new director, we suddenly had a lot of time on our hands, everyone did. In a way, life kinda became normal again but with just a few additions. Roman (having finally convinced us he wasn't such a bad guy, he was just trying to win his part), Madalick, Link, and Fyodor pretty much hung out with us and Thed and Thorpe and Roo and Shoe full-time now. We'd play basketball at the old junior high in the afternoons cuz it still has the best outdoor courts in town. Madalick had a mean inside game on account of how he used his elbows like they might fall off at any moment and Roman could really pass (like between his legs and everything) and knock down the occasional awkward jumper, while Link and Fyodor were pretty much useless except for fouling.

It was kinda frustrating sometimes though cuz we only had nine players and we'd played a few days four on four with one person sitting out (Shoe always refused to play and would never say why, and when we pressed him, he feigned ignorance of English, which we thought was funny cuz it seemed like he spoke better than we did but we let him be anyway) but that was before Roman got the bright idea to call the screenwriter to join us. At first, he turned us down cuz he 'had work to do, gentlemen', but after another day or two he must've gone *a little stir crazy at the Prime Saddle and agreed to meet us at the park but only if he could catch a ride with Roman in his Cord.*

Turns out the writer's name was Clue Brush and this, like it was for just about everyone we guess, was his first time working on a motion picture. He'd done a lot of television comedy writing but nothing too big really, mostly The Simpsons *and* Saturday Night Live *and stuff like that. Clue was from Maryland originally but his parents had up and moved to L.A. when he was in junior high. His dad was an oil company vice president and his mom was a housewife so when they got to California, Clue went to Thousand Oaks High School for Sons and Daughters of the Rich and Talented (T.O.H.S.S.D.R.T., 'toes dirt' for short) and after overcoming cocaine addiction during his sophomore year, he graduated with honors and led the water polo team to a state championship then went on to UCLA film school with no significant problems. Clue was a pretty bright guy, just had a really obnoxious laugh that kinda made us question why we liked him so much but only while he was laughing and drawing the attention of everyone within a fifty-foot radius. He always caught shit cuz of his first name though and mostly people just quoted snidey remarks from the movie at him or just settled for calling him 'Colonel Mustard' or 'Professor Plum' on account of the board game. He hated that.*

Most night after basketball, we'd all go to Paulson's or the Hitching Post and Horse Shack and Link and Clue would get beers for everyone cuz they were old enough and the bartender usually looked the other way for a twenty-dollar bill and an autograph for his sister in Biloxi or wherever. We guess you could say we all became friends cuz we spent so much time together hanging out and waiting for the production to start back up again and no one was sure when that would be exactly. Turned out, the producers had split up and Zeke had gone to Los Angeles and Norville had gone to New York City to recruit a new director.

A lot of stories got told those nights when there was nothing else to do, but by far the best one ever was told by Thorpe Thorpe the night before they found a new director for the movie and he even titled it and everything, just stood up on the chair and said (with plenty of Thorpey-type dramatic pauses for embellishment's sake), 'ladies and gentlemen, please, gather around, this very true story is called . . .

. . . Journey to the Center of Thed Teldut!'

And right when he said that, there was some laughter and even one girl over by the pool tables screamed with glee and we saw Thed going all red through the cheeks but his eyes were expectant and we could tell he had no idea what was gonna come out of Thorpe's mouth and so he clenched a napkin hard and finished his beer pretending that he didn't care but . . . stop right there. We aren't quite ready to tell Thorpe's story just yet. If this were a film it would be a freeze frame like in *Goodfellas* but Henry Hill keeps talking in voice-over anyway even though the image doesn't move.

There are a few things you need to know about Beau and Thorpe Thorpe to understand the upcoming story a little better. See, Thorpe and Beau never really knew their father, all they did know about him was his last name was Thorpe and as for how they felt about him, there really isn't a much better way for saying they hated his guts for leaving them. For that matter, Thorpe wasn't too keen on his mom either for cursing him with a redundant name that was (for eight or nine years) the running joke of our class in school. Mostly people just called him 'Echo Boy' and they'd make a cup with their hands over their mouths and act like they were shouting over a cliff or a great big canyon with their voices: 'Thorpe, Thorpe, Thorpe, Thorpe . . .' and then laughing like banshees or howler monkeys or maybe something in between.

Honestly, the boys weren't too keen on their mother either and that's cuz the day that Thorpe stood up and blessed the junior high talent show with the best and most vulgar performance ever, his mom snuck out ('for a smoke' she said) and never came back, left without a word but we didn't know that 'til later. The boys searched for her for a week but after that, gave up hope and all of a sudden, Beau had to get a job to make some money cuz they had a house payment and had to eat and that really made Beau grow up quick cuz he was just short of eighteen at the time and almost able to take legal custody of his brother if he could prove he could support him.

The first few months in the Thorpe house were an absolute disaster with dishes everywhere and no cleaning being done and it took a visit from the social worker to get them to start cleaning up on a regular basis. Beau got a night job at the Cooper Market just so he could keep going to high school and hopefully graduate, but by Christmas he was having trouble making ends meet and that's when he approached Sassa Medusa Belle about a part-time job as a 'courier'. Well, Sassa always did have a heart so she said yes right away and offered him the least dangerous route cuz she knew his circumstances.

By February, Beau had dropped out of school and passed his GED high school equivalency test. He'd quit his job at the Cooper Market and pretty much worked for Sassa full-time. But like most pre-teens, Thorpe didn't appreciate all that his brother was doing to support the both of 'em and the fights at home increased in intensity and with no parents/referees around, the boys made more than a coupla trips to the emergency room together, which brought the social worker back to the house and a suggestion that the boys split their living space in half with Thorpe taking the basement and Beau taking the ground floor. That solved a lot of problems cuz the basement had a private entrance with stairs leading down to it at the side of the house and a bathroom and everything, so they pretty much had to get together for meals but sometimes they didn't even do that.

Beau became fiercely proud of the fact that he was sixteen months away from paying off the mortgage on the house, all cuz of his hard work but then, one night, The Peteness paid him a little visit. He brought two thugs with him and made an ultimatum that Sassa should stay out of dealing drugs in Krakatowa Proper, the yuppie housing community on the north end of town that was Beau's run, built mostly for people commuting to Upton and their fancy jobs. After the ultimatum, the thugs pounded the message into Beau and Thorpe heard the whole thing downstairs through the vent and had to drag Beau to Barguss General (cuz Thorpe wasn't old enough to drive yet), a full twelve blocks, to have him saved before Beau bled too much internally.

It really was a close call though and after he healed, Beau Thorpe got a shotgun to 'protect his property' and to make double sure that The Peteness didn't walk into his house again, he walked uninvited into The Peteness's house (on Sassa's 'behest') real late one night and took care of the competition as quietly as possible. That wasn't much more than rumor for a real long time but the truth has leaked out over the years and nobody around this town has messed with Beau Thorpe since, that's for sure.

Okay, much better, now just imagine we're back at the Hitching Post and the images start moving again and you're watching Thorpe Thorpe's slow-motion mouth in a 'rosebud'-type close-up as he hushes the anxious-looking audience and says (one more time for those in the corners of the bar who didn't hear):

'. . . ZEE BON JOURNÉ (and he pronounces it all in a phony French accent that's pretty funny and people laugh a little too loudly of course) to zee CENT-AIR of MISSYOUR (and he turns and points right at him just to embarrass Thed cuz we all know who he is and then Thorpe's voice gets even louder) THEDALOMOOSE TELDOOT!'

By then, Thorpe had put a creaky chair on top of the table we were all sitting at and Shoe poured him a fresh beer with too much head on it so it slushed over the side as he handed it to him and then Thorpe Thorpe thanked Shoe and began, all slow-like. He started with some kind words for Staceyleene (who was nowhere to be found that night so we figured she'd be working the late shift over at the Taco Coleslaw Hamburger Hot Dog Apple and we figured he must really be over the moon for her if he talked so nice about her in public when she wasn't there) and he blabbed about how the night he spent with her was the best of his life cuz it was the night he lost his virginity and then the guys in the place grinned and the girls all giggled at the same time.

We weren't real sure where he was going with this just yet, on account of how he'd only been talking about himself and he continued to, saying how he took the long walk home from Staceyleene's dad's house after sneaking out the window and blowing kisses to her through the glass pane and by that time we wanted to hear how this story concerned Thed, cuz he was really starting to look antsy and we sorta felt sorry for him. Thorpe went into detail about the walk home . . . well, not every detail, he'd actually told us this part already and one of the grossest and funniest details to us was how Thorpe Thorpe took Staceyleene's stained sheets with him on the way out and dropped 'em in the dumpster by the Taco Coleslaw Hamburger Hot Dog Apple but he didn't tell that to the group of course.

He talked about how he had the re-release of Bowie's *Hunky Dory* on his beat up old yellow walkman and he had listened to 'Changes' appropriately enough before he and Staceyleene did their thing and he must've stopped it the night before cuz when he turned it on the next morning it started playing 'Oh! You Pretty Things' while he skipped fast back to his house on the piano part (he liked it so much, he rewound it twice) and we're guessing he was describing everything in detail cuz he wanted us to believe that his world even *looked* different after losing his virginity but we didn't exactly know much about that back then cuz we hadn't 'crossed that bridge yet', as Mrs. Kickkick would say.

When Thorpe entered the house in order to get a quick snack before taking a nap cuz he 'didn't get much sleep', he said with a wink and it was followed by more giggles but all the giggles and even smiles stopped when Thorpe described how weird it was that Bowie sang the opening line of the song just as he saw Thed's motionless body lying in the middle of his living room floor. He said he stopped cold and could barely move and had a bad feeling all over, even down in his toes and he forgot to close the door behind him when he noticed a yellow piece of paper on Thed's chest kinda fluttering in the breeze from 'the open portal', which was really just the door but that's what he called it, all dramatic and everything.

Indeed, there was a sticky note attached to Thed's chest, it said: 'Might be dead. Looks that way. Please don't take to hospital around here. If still dead when we get back, will bury him. DON'T CALL POLICE! Sorry.' It was signed 'Your Big Bro, Beau' and underneath the fast signature that Thorpe was pretty sure only he could read was this: 'P.S. Please feed Beau Junior and . . .' next to those words was a childish drawing of a spider indicating that the tarantula should be fed too. Thorpe Thorpe paused there and a hush fell over everyone listening, we could even hear breathing though it was mostly Thed's and in a way, it was oddly reassuring considering the tale being told.

Explaining that he was so in shock and he didn't know what to do, Thorpe actually fed Beau Junior and the tarantula before walking back to Thed's stiff bluish body and smile with dried saliva stains at the corners of the mouth and Thorpe knew that wasn't any good at all. So he read the note again and paid particular attention to the line, 'Please don't take to hospital around here,' cuz it was the 'around here' that stuck in his mind and he didn't want his best friend in the whole wide world to die, so without thinking too clearly he picked Thed up and banged out the door back first just as the music ran up the wires leading to his headphones and Bowie screamed/sang the song title bit of the chorus and Thorpe was able to lug Thed over to his car, stuff him into the passenger seat, belt him in all tight, then start the engine and reverse into the road so fast that gravel flew out onto the asphalt before the car's back end did.

Thorpe drained his beer, leaned back in his chair and began describing to the patrons of the Hitching Post how he was in shock and didn't notice that he needed to fill up on gas 'til he was a third of the way to Vegas. At the gas station, he called Beau at Sassa's place to explain what he had done in his state of shock and was surprised to hear that Beau was quite happy that Thed's body was no longer in the house and he told Thorpe to give him the number of the payphone he was on so he could call him back. One minute later, Thorpe got a call from Beau telling him to take Thed to a doctor that Sassa had recommended in Las Vegas cuz 'he'd keep everything quiet if it needed to be kept quiet, you know what I'm sayin'?' Thorpe agreed and next thing he knew he was back on the highway, trekking fast toward Nevada.

By this point, most people were on the edge of their seats, not quite believing what they were hearing. Somehow it just seemed too silly to believe, even in Barguss some tales can be too tall, blimp or no. That's what a lot of the faces looked like anyway, mouths cocked open, halfway between disbelief and utter excitement. So far, three people had bought Thorpe a drink to keep him going with the story so the bartender wasn't too worried as long as people kept forking money into the till. But when we looked at Thed though, his arms were crossed over his chest, all high and with his elbows sticking out and we could tell he didn't believe a word of it or at least, didn't want to anyway.

Back to the story, Thorpe said he was getting bored of driving by himself and having to change radio stations every thirty minutes cuz he was losing the signals and so he turned it off and started talking to Thed about everything under the sun. He spilled his guts about a few new songs and how he had really honestly fantasized about having sex with Linnelisse before she went back to Scandinavia and how if Beau found out, well, he'd probably shoot him in the leg so he'd 'always remember', and he talked about how amazing his night was with Staceyleene and how he was real sure he loved her and wanted to marry her even though he occasionally had thoughts for other girls but never followed through on them and did that make him a bad boyfriend? Then he talked to Thed about how his favorite part of Staceyleene's body was her forehead, right at the temple, like right where she pulled her hair back tight into a ponytail and it was just on account of how he loved the smell of her skin in those two spots more than the rest of her spots cuz, for some reason, it excited his hormones or something and just then, the garish lights of Vegas showed themselves just over the hill, lighting up the whole night.

'Best conversation I ever had with ol' Thed, what a good listener he was!' Thorpe's comments got huge laughs from everyone there and it made Thed turn a Rudolph-nose shade of red we'd never seen before and for the few people sitting close enough to see it, made them laugh even harder. Roo was smiling quietly in the corner and he had his arm around Florence Mink who was playing some kind of word game on little scraps of beer coasters with Laura. Thorpe took a deep breath and surveyed the crowd before continuing.

He found the doctor's office without too many problems but it was in the shadiest part of town, literally. There were only a few lights around and Thorpe said that made him really uneasy in a city that prided itself on the amount of lights per square foot it had on twenty-four hours a day. Well, Thorpe and the doctor were able to drag Thed into the office and Thorpe said it looked like something out of the first *Batman* movie, like when the Joker gets his face redone in some dirty old surgery room. When the doctor examined Thed he did say that he found a faint heartbeat and faint breathing but they were both so low that they were almost imperceptible and he pointed to how Thed's chest didn't appear to be moving up or down.

Thorpe got into how the doctor told him that Thed was kinda 'in a state of hibernation', and that it was possible he'd slip out of it in the next coupla days but the doctor couldn't guarantee that Thed would have full brain activity cuz it completely depended on his brain getting enough oxygen. Then the doc said something funny, he recommended getting Thed outside, 'maybe taking in a show,' while they were in Vegas cuz maybe a little activity would get more oxygen circulating in Thed's system. Thorpe must have looked confused, so the doctor reassured him, 'don't worry, he'll snap out of it at some point.' When the doctor received his $50 for his services, he let Thorpe take an old spare wheelchair for an extra twenty bucks so that he could move Thed around more easily.

Well, Thorpe knew a genuine opportunity when he saw one (even if it was a bit suspect) so he drove straight to the strip and found the hotel that Wayne Newton was performing at (we think it was the Stardust), then hauled Thed out of the passenger seat and into the wheelchair before proceeding to the ticket office to buy seats for that night's show. Thorpe explained in the most solemn way to the lady seated in the high-backed red chair behind the ticket window that his friend had a 'very rare nerve disease called *hydroplaxia nervosa*, that affects the brain,' and the last thing he wanted before he died was to be in the front row at a Wayne Newton concert and maybe even sing 'Little Green Apples' or something with him, 'if it wasn't too much trouble'. It was the most blatant lie that Thorpe Thorpe ever told and what was even funnier was that it worked.

'Can he sing like that?' was all the ticket lady asked in a loose Southern accent, all leaned forward in her seat and inspecting Thed, 'he looks catatonic.' Thorpe was quick to respond while smoothing Thed's hair down with his left hand, 'Oh no, no, don't worry, he can sing, he's just resting right now.' With that, the ticket lady made one phone call direct to Wayne's private line and explained the situation to Wayne's personal assistant on the other end of the phone and Thorpe stifled his laughter when she tried to pronounce *hydroplaxia nervosa*, instead calling it *gohydraplaxica religiosa*.

Upon hanging the phone up with a big smile and a flurry of 'yes sir's, she turned to Thorpe: 'Mr. Newton is a very, very generous man and he'd be happy to grant your request,' and with that, the ticket lady slipped two tickets underneath the glass and smiled a pathetic smile at the both of them. Thorpe said he started crying and making a big scene about thanking her before moving on to play the slots for an hour 'til they could take their seats in the Wayne-a-torium.

Before going in, Thorpe had found a man willing to part with his Polaroid camera for $40 cuz it only had four shots left on the roll, so Thorpe paid for it with a fraction of his winnings. They lingered near the slot machines long enough for Thorpe to see an old woman hit the jackpot and keel over, only to see the people around her start grabbing her winnings. On that note, Thorpe pushed Thed's wheelchair into the Wayne-a-torium and a man in a nice black suit escorted them to the very front of the theater, just a bit to the left, so Thed's wheelchair could sit squarely in the aisle. Then two more men brought out a ramp to put over the stairs to the stage and Thorpe really started getting excited cuz the only thing that could mean was that they would wheel Thed up there at some point.

Thorpe stopped telling the story for a moment when he noticed that Thed had relaxed in his chair and was taking a leisurely sip of beer. Thorpe mentioned something about Thed looking awfully relaxed and Thed responded that it was cuz 'it couldn't possibly be true', and that knowing that made him feel better. Thorpe just kinda nodded and got back to the story and his audience that was almost visibly ready to laugh, hard.

'Wayne didn't disappoint at all!' Thorpe launched right back into it. He told of how Wayne opened the concert in a super-sharp-looking black tuxedo and got the crowd all riled up with 'Danke Schoen' and then worked his way through his biggest hits like 'Bill Bailey' and 'Red Roses for a Blue Lady' and Wayne even went out in the crowd with red roses and *gave* 'em to all the ladies wearing blue dresses (and a few to those who weren't too, just cuz they looked pouty) and then did 'Dreams of the Everyday Housewife' and 'Little Green Apples' and he even sang a real special song, that no one was expecting, when he hauled off on 'Home is Where I Wanna Be on Christmas' from that episode of *Bonanza* he did so darn long ago and the crowd ate it up but that was how he finished his set and went off stage and Thorpe got kinda down in the mouth and was sure Wayne had reneged on the deal, that was, until Wayne came back out for the encore and told the audience how they were 'in for a real treat this evening', cuz one of his 'most special friends' was gonna come up on stage with him and help him sing 'Daddy Don't You Walk So Fast' and then motioned to Thorpe to wheel Thed up on stage and as much as Thorpe has been on stage in his life he said he got all nervous wheeling Thed up there.

'This is Mr. Thed and he's going to be helping me out tonight, aren't ya Thed?' Wayne's enthusiasm was infectious and Thorpe almost felt bad as he subdued the laughter deep inside of himself when Thed didn't respond, so Thorpe reached down and pushed back and forth on Thed's neck, forcing him to nod. Wayne dug it so he kicked the band right into the tune and started singing and after the first stanza when Thed was obviously not singing, Wayne decided to prompt Thed with something like, 'take it, Thed!'

Well, the band kept playing but Thed didn't make a sound, even with Thorpe holding his microphone and everything and Thorpe could tell the crowd was getting nervous but Wayne was all calm and cool as he jumped back in for the second stanza and he kept looking over at Thed for him to join in and it was obvious that the crowd had a sorta disappointed/sympathizing look in their collective eyes. It was then that Thorpe took over. He leaned in close to Thed and it must've looked like he was trying to coax him to sing but instead he did a tidy little trick of ventriloquism and started singing the next stanza with Wayne in the most beautiful falsetto that the 1,142 people packed into the Wayne-a-torium that night had ever heard.

Wayne's cheeks were bulging and it looked like he had tears in his eyes from where Thorpe was craftily singing for Thed and it seemed like everyone in the audience that could stand was standing and clapping and cheering and the ladies with the blue dresses and the red flowers were all sobbing and so, so thankful for being there in the theater that night when the last few words of the song bounced around the theater and they could almost hear the exclamation points and it ended all dramatically with the band winding down and Wayne waving his arms and moving over to Thed and giving him a big hug and Thorpe took a picture from behind them with the Polaroid so that he got a piece of the crowd in the picture too and then meekly pushed Thed offstage to the loud, loud cheering of the crowd.

After the show, Wayne was being real generous and he invited them backstage to his private dressing room, shut the door behind them, locked it, and then gave Thorpe Thorpe a real stern talking-to just as Thorpe was getting comfortable with the thought that he had gotten away with the whole darn thing. As it turned out, Wayne had known all along that something wasn't quite right, from the second Thed got wheeled up on stage. He also knew Thorpe was faking singing for Thed and he didn't know what was wrong with Thed but he suspected something was going on. 'That Wayne sure was astute,' Thorpe said. Apparently, the only thing that saved Thorpe's butt from the cops (and Thed's too supposedly, but really, we're pretty sure Wayne was just teachin' Thorpe a lesson) was the fact that it was such a good performance (that, and Thorpe's tearful plea that he was in a band too and it had been his lifelong dream to sing with Wayne). Still a little angry but certainly not heartless, Wayne decided to give Thorpe some solid advice: he said that there was no substitute for 'showmanship' (and he commended Thorpe for that) but that Thorpe still needed to trust the audience, not lie to them.

Anyway, just before Wayne pushed them out the door with a pat on the back and an order not to return anytime soon, he presented them with an autographed picture that had this message written in an elegant hand: 'Dear Thed, Please Get Better Soon So We Can Do It Again! With Love, Wayne'.

Thorpe said he drove Thed straight back to his house and the whole way he was sure Thed was gonna wake up cuz he was showing signs of it, what with his color returning and his chest moving and so Thorpe raced back to the house determined to keep the secret and he just barely made it too. By the time Thorpe pushed open the front door, Thed was mumbling little nonsense words and so Thorpe laid him on the floor back in Barguss just as he'd been before, but without the sticky note on his chest. Then he went over to Staceyleene's for the night and just waited and waited 'til the right time to tell everyone the 'whole sordid story'.

Meanwhile, back at the Hitching Post, we didn't think the laughter would ever stop. One guy we've never even seen before (must've been an extra from Upton or somewheres) was hanging from the rafters and barking like some damn dog. Every person in the place just lost it when Thorpe Thorpe was describing how Wayne Newton's face looked when he tried to prompt Thed to sing but Thed wasn't singing and that made us think that sometimes there isn't anything much funnier than silence but we guess it depends on the situation.

In fact, even Thed laughed when he heard it but it was so obvious he didn't believe it and so Thorpe shushed everybody and told Thed to stand up and then asked him if he didn't believe it and Thed said, 'no, of course not,' and then Thorpe untucked the back of his shirt and pulled out a framed photo that he had stashed in the waistline of his jeans and he held it aloft and showed it to the whole audience before dropping it in Thed's open hands and it was none other than the very picture that Wayne Newton signed for him and inside it, behind the glass but in front of the picture was the Polaroid of the back of a comatose-looking Thed getting a sideways hug from Wayne and in the background was a blurry middle-and-old-aged crowd going crazy. Upon seeing it, Thed's jaw about hit the floor it flew open so fast.

There was a brief moment of silence as people looked from Thed to the picture and back to Thorpe Thorpe with this huge grin on his face and then the whole place erupted in screams and the loudest, hoarsest laughter you ever heard. Folks like Madalick were screaming bad stuff like, 'Oh shit! Oh shit!' cuz they just couldn't believe it and Roman had his head all buried in his arms on the table and he was just shaking all over.

At the height of it, some joker had gone over to the jukebox and put in a few quarters so it would play 'Daddy, Don't You Walk So Fast' and just about everybody in the place hopped up and started dancing on everything, the tables, the bar, the pool tables, the chairs, way too fast for the beat and well, pretty much everybody except for us and Thed was doing it. He just looked completely stunned and his face was all-over white when he turned to us and said that 'seeing pictures that you have no way of remembering being in is almost like feeling you aren't alone in your body and someone else stole your face and legs for a while and went walking around doing crazy things,' but we could barely hear him over all that racket and the image that really stuck in our minds from that night was just him clutching the picture frame all tight to his chest like a little kid, kinda like he was just testing to see if it was really real or not, if it was solid.

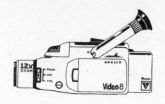

15

By the time Norville and Zeke got back from their dual trips to opposite parts of the country in search of a 'viable and experienced' director, the news about Krystof's bizarre death had already broken in the national media and so just about everybody in the relatively superstitious entertainment business turned down the job pronto cuz they all said that it was cursed or something. It was probably the worst when the evening news with Dan Rather ran this scathing take on the movie industry 'lacking a moral center', and even showed ('if you have small children in the room please have them look away, what you are about to see is very disturbing,' Dan said) some bootleg footage of Krystof burning himself all up and we asked around but no one we know had any idea how those news guys got a hold of that video footage.

The next day, there were news crews everywhere just like they'd grown outta the ground and they were all asking nasty questions about Krystof like, 'did he ever molest children?' and we just couldn't understand what kind of conclusions they were trying to draw besides just being general scaremongers. It got kinda bad with five national news crews tracking down everyone they could find in the street for their comments on 'Mr. Zckwecy' and they always pronounced it wrong, like Zak-kwe-see. Anyway, Norville and Zeke decided they needed to do something quickly so they had Mayor Yermo call a town meeting on the steps of the city hall so they could talk to the Bargussians (that's what we're called) and the media people all together.

It happened at noon and the media were there at eleven, setting up and stuff so they could get camera angles and be in sight of the speakers to ask questions. Most of the shops closed at about ten minutes of twelve, and everyone who cared made their way to city hall. The day was pretty warm and there were no clouds in the sky for some reason so it was just kinda hazy. To us, the set-up for press conference/town meeting didn't look that much different from the Barguss Blue Kitty Cat Queenship Contest but we didn't say anything of course. Most of the cast stood up on the stage behind Norville, who stood at a podium, and Mayor Yermo stood off to the side wearing his ceremonial robe and when the clock on the bank across the street struck twelve, Norville started talking.

To be honest, we aren't much for speeches but Norville's was something else. He seemed so sincere when talking about his sadness that Krystof had decided to end his own life and even read a bit of the suicide note and explained to the media that it was Krystof's 'last act as a passionate artist' and nothing more. We still didn't understand why it was his last act as an artist but the way Norville said it, it did make an odd kind of sense, 'the body as canvas' and 'making a bold statement' and all that. He went on to say that the cast, crew, and town were greatly saddened by Krystof's death cuz we all thought we had a fantastic movie on our hands (when he used we to include all of us we sorta got a good shiver on account of how nice it was to be included) but he said that now the cast, crew and town had a 'higher purpose' and that was pulling together 'as a family' and finishing what was started, making a great film to honor Krystof with (in addition to the Krystof Zckwecy Memorial Museum that he made sure to say Panazanc Film

Partners, Inc. was honored to pay for). Not that we'd ever cry at something like that but we did need to hide our eyes from the sun a bit. And you really had to give it to him, cuz Norville was as smooth as they ever came.

'Course he quickly took advantage of the stunned silence from the media to introduce each member of the cast. That Norville sure was smart too, recognizing all that free publicity just sitting right in front of him. After announcing the cast, he gave a very brief plot outline and probably one of the taglines that the marketing people had dreamed up: 'Sometimes there's nowhere to go but up.' Once recovered, a few members of the media (one was a particularly good and smart-looking lady in a really nice purple dressy suit with thin little glasses and her hair up) asked some questions but Norville deflected them by saying that he needed to thank Mayor Yermo for the wonderful atmosphere for filming and then he dropped the biggest bomb of them all: 'and I'd also like to announce, right here, for the first time, our new director and screenwriter, Mr. Clue Brush!'

That decision was kinda like a coup, promoting from within and all, not to mention that writer/directors were just beginning to be the rage in Hollywood at that time. We were just as surprised as Clue looked though when he stepped up to the podium, which was kinda funny cuz he had a speech prepared and everything and he certainly said all the right things about 'protecting the ultimate integrity of Mr. Krystof's final work' and that since the second half of the movie had been completely filmed by Krystof, he was going to focus on the beginning and essentially tell Barguss's story in two chapters instead of one, which was met with pretty wild applause (kinda led by us), so much so that some of the camera media people turned around to film us for the news. He also said he'd done some rewriting to focus on some of the characters' backgrounds and we didn't know it at the time but it essentially included all the 'research' *he'd done by hanging out with us and the new script would definitely include Thorpe's story about strapping the catatonic Thed into the car and going to see Wayne Newton but he didn't say that at the time.*

After all that, they answered a few media-type questions and dodged the ones about Krystof being 'insane' or 'deluded' and the media left pretty well happy cuz they got what they wanted, a scoop with the exclusive announcement of Clue as the new director and a bit of a sideshow entertainment/explanation from Norville. We guess pretty much everybody went home happy that day which was good cuz Clue wasn't wasting any time, they started filming again the next day at 4:30 a.m. and everybody needed their sleep, so that's the beginning of how . . .

The Production Gets a Clue

Well, something else started that morning too, and it was the search for the missing statue. Maybe it'd been put off by Krystof's death and funeral, not to mention the media frenzy. In fact, it kinda seemed like Old Man Promised To actually waited 'til a few things died down to announce that the statue of his son had been stolen from his garage. Considering we did it nearly three weeks before he finally announced it, we thought it was funny it took him so long. We guess when you have that many garages you don't exactly notice things right away.

Irregardless, as soon as the media people left, the Barguss Police Department organized two teams: a search team that started searching the whole citywide area and an investigative team. They just questioned a few people about it, like us and Roo and especially Shoe and Laura which we didn't think was so nice. They obviously didn't have anything to do with it at all but just cuz they weren't from around here they got it worse than most of us. We had to laugh about that one but only based on the fact that Shoe and Laura wouldn't have anything against Monroe Mister Promised To if they'd never been here while he was alive, which made just about every long-term Barguss resident our age a suspect.

They didn't find the statue that day or the next, when shooting started. They were mostly filming scenes that set up a love triangle between Monroe Mister and Roo and Florence, so we stayed away from the set for a while. Besides, it was more amusing to watch the cops hassle Beau Thorpe about the statue he knew nothing about. We got a call from Mandy later that night and she said they hadn't even been questioned about the statue and then she laughed real hard through the phone so it sorta hurt our ears. She told us to meet them down on Gee Street to talk about it.

We got there a little late and they had already ordered and got their dinner from the Taco Coleslaw Hamburger Hot Dog Apple and they were re-telling the story of how Thorpe had dragged Thed out to Vegas to see if he was dead. Staceyleene was in uniform and standing out there with 'em, laughing right along and it was obvious she was shirking her duties but nobody really cared cuz she'd been working there for like three years and was practically an assistant manager.

When Staceyleene saw us, she told us to tell Thorpe that she'd love to go to Vegas with them when the production took off for a few days and we had no idea what she was talking about but we told her we'd pass it on. Lily explained to us that Clue had decided to completely turn the production on its head and include more local stories, so they were actually gonna film the Wayne Newton stuff in Las Vegas cuz Clue's brother used to work for Wayne and they already got him to sign on and do the movie so the production was going to move to Vegas after they finished filming in Barguss.

But the really awesome part, they said, was that new characters were being written into the script like Beau Thorpe (Scott Baio was mentioned as a career-resurrecting possibility) and Sassa and The Peteness and they were especially excited about The Peteness for some reason and we had to ask only to have them gush that Brad Pitt was 'interested' in the part as a cameo cuz he had just finished filming *Legends of the Fall* or something and basically the Gee Street Girls had worshipped him ever since *Johnny Suede*. But that was all just gossip, what had been confirmed was that they weren't actually going to stage Roo getting his scar as it had been written in the original script cuz it was just Raoul and Roo in some ditch but Clue had rewritten it to be more factual and include the party. And the best part, the girls said, 'was that they'd be casting you soon, all cuz you guys took Roo to the hospital that night!' They all kinda screamed at that but our cheeks just got real hot at the thought of having people play us, so we told 'em we just didn't want to talk about it at all and went over to the Taco Coleslaw Hamburger Hot Dog Apple and ordered the #12 apple pork piggy platter and told Staceyleene to bring it on out to us when it was done.

We must've looked real down cuz when we got back the gals all tried to cheer us up by telling us they were going to film the car accident with Maria as 'motivation for Raoul' (turned out, Clue had nixed the deal with Old Man Promised To cuz getting promoted to Director gave him a bump in salary and he was more than able to take care of his sister's medical needs and he found he just wanted to tell as much of the truth as he could about Barguss in half a movie), and even Luanne and Lily hung on us a little and talked crap about us being famous too, but really, it just made us uncomfortable and not really want to talk about it.

Then they all got real, real quiet and we knew something was up. Staceyleene brought our food and that kinda broke the awkward silence, which we didn't want to ask the girls about and they sure weren't gonna tell until we asked, so getting the #12 pork and apple skewers braised with caramel and barbecue sauce was a perfect interruption for them to have more small talk with Staceyleene so we could eat our food without having to talk or listen. The parking lot lights came on and the lights in the stores across Gee turned out for the night and people were pretty much going home when Staceyleene headed back to the restaurant for the dinner rush and Brandy waited until she was out of earshot before saying, 'okay! I'm dying, guess what we did?'

At that moment, it really didn't matter if we guessed or not, so we just kept eating and waited for them to just up and tell it. 'We sold that video clip of Krystof lighting up to the news people and we got tons of money to finish making the documentary!' They all seemed really excited about it and as for us, well, we were just shocked. Not entirely surprised mind you, but shocked and stuff. Anyway, due to the fact that we were quiet and just eating our food and still kinda feeling strange about Clue making us characters in the movie and didn't give them all kinds of attention about what they did, they got bored and told us we 'sucked' and then left for home.

Of course, they neglected to tell us that they'd edited the footage of us robbing the statue and created a *Vinny 'n' Mookie Show* entitled 'The Statue of Limitations'. Then again, if we'd known, we'd have asked them what they intended to do with the footage but we wouldn't find out 'til later that getting them mad at us probably wasn't the best idea in the whole world. So we just sat there and watched the mountains behind the bank's clock tower go from darkish navy blue to total black and then walked home as the stars were coming out and all kinds of stuff weighing down our minds.

On the way back we ran into Shoe and gave him what was left of our #12 and he seemed really thankful. He listened to our problems with what was going on with the movie and how we were always fine about our friends being famous and stuff like that but really, we never wanted to be dragged into it but he was a great listener and he just said that if people were being cast to act out what really happened, we shouldn't have to worry about becoming famous or not cuz on the big screen we'd just be two forgettable characters, a 'Rozenkurantsu to Girudensutarun,' he said and we didn't completely understand but we got the gist. Before we left, he told us he was playing a special DJ set for Laura's eleventh birthday at the Hitching Post in a coupla nights and we should definitely come and bring Laura an 'American present', then he smiled and left and we always admired how he was so easygoing. We really liked Shoe, and we knew we'd miss him when he left in a week.

The search for the statue wasn't exactly called off a few days later but the power was transferred from the police department to a number of volunteers who had been deputized by Mayor Yermo (he was bowing to pressure from certain people like Donny Barn in the citizenry who suggested we leave the kid 'buried', which told us he really knew what happened with the statue but no one else caught on, thankfully), who suddenly didn't like how the city was paying for the search with tax dollars and it was one of his rare shining moments of standing up to Old Man Promised To. Of course, they never found the statue on account of the fact that the Gee Street Girls volunteered for the search team and managed to comb rich people hill thirteen times without finding the statue (or the mower), go figure.

Bitter and defeated both by Clue deciding not to take it easy on him or his son in the script and also by not finding the statue, Old Man Promised To decided to commission an even bigger statue from the same company in Upton. Supposedly it was gonna be like twenty-eight feet high or something. The rumors went around pretty quickly and certain people made

sure to get a word in to Mayor Yermo that they would never
let a statue like that sit in the memorial park (due to its size) but
Old Man Promised To was oblivious to all that, he just missed
his son and by all accounts was going a bit crazy. Besides, we
all knew how he had Mayor Yermo in his pocket. Yup, it sure
looked like the armies were gathering on the horizon and a
battle was shaping up down the road.

But that was all in the background and only talked about
on the phone or in the barbershop, what ended up being front
and center one week later was an exclusive on channel 8 public
access: the first *Vinny 'n' Mookie Show* in over eleven years.
It was even announced and hyped up on the local radio waves
and before anybody knew it, 'The Statue of Limitations' was
airing in everyone's living room, showing the statue getting
stolen by two guys in wigs and 'staches and then running it
out of Old Man Promised To's on a riding mower and then
us burying it in a dark brown mound of dirt with the words
'somewhere in the Arizona desert' written in white funky type
at the bottom and we figured it'd fool no one cuz Barguss is
way far from Arizona. We have to be honest here, by the
time it was over, our hearts were beating too darn fast and
we were scared to leave the house cuz we were sure someone
had recognized us, had put two and two together real easy and
would be banging down our door any minute to throw us in
jail for trespassing or statutory kidnapping or something truly
horrible and we'd never see our friends again or even make it
to Laura's special surprise birthday party.

16

We didn't go out at all the next day (couldn't even pick up the phone) and believe it or not, there was no knock on the door whatsoever. By the day after that, we had gotten several phone calls from the Gee Street Girls that basically consisted of several of them laughing in chorus (mostly Candy, Brandy, and Mandy) before suggesting that we buy a paper, only for the words to be followed by the phone slamming down on our ears. So after one too many of those aggravating calls, we decided to exit our cave, go get a copy of the Telegraph and try and figure out exactly what was going on since the 'new' Vinny 'n' Mookie Show got aired on channel 8.

We got a real funny feeling when the paper flopped open on the kitchen table and we saw the big front-page headline: ' "Dig Him Up!" Is Father's Earnest Plea' and just under that in bold type before the story started, it said, 'Promised To Urges State to Form Common Bond with Arizona to Search for Stolen Statue.' It was probably at that point when we realized the Gals weren't laughing at us but instead were laughing at how many people we'd been able to fool and as it turned out, by the bottom of the article, it'd been mentioned that Arizona authorities had recently formed a special civilian task force to start searching 'the videotape evidence of the show' for clues regarding the statue and its burial location. We couldn't help but think that was insane cuz searching for a six-foot statue in the thousands of miles of Arizona desert was way far beyond searching for a needle in a haystack and that was discounting the fact that the statue wasn't even in Arizona and we just had to wonder how they could possibly be so stupid.

On the next page was an article about how Old Man Promised To was calling for the extradition of Mr. Dance D. LeRoy III and Mr. Raw Mike Tall back to Barguss so they could be asked where the statue had been hidden and also tried 'for what they did to my son' exclamation point. Well the oddest thing about both articles to us was that nobody questioned Old Man Promised To's attachment to the statue and how we couldn't really tell the difference between him talking about the statue and his son's real body, which was long gone and buried and we figured he was really losing it if he couldn't tell the difference between the two.

The phone rang again just then and we hesitated a bit before picking it up, even though we kinda knew it was the Gee Street Girls, we just wished that it was Luanne and Lily instead of all five of 'em but that's just cuz we think the Lukashes are a teensy bit nicer but you'll never hear us tell anyone that cuz it would get right back to the Mulrynes and they'd do something else like maybe even tell the cops we committed the statue crime just to get us back. On the third ring, we answered and it was Luanne and Lily and Mandy all on separate phones over at one of their houses. We talked briefly about how stupid everyone was for thinking it was the cast from the original Vinny 'n' Mookie that did it and then we talked about the poor people in Arizona who would eventually be scouring the desert for a non-existent statue when it was at the foot of the hill that the owner lived on and we laughed a lot but still felt kinda uneasy like we weren't completely safe just yet (but we didn't tell them that, no way) and then Lily said Roman had been seen at the Prime Saddle with Gwyneth Paltrow or someone 'who looked so much like her it was scary', and then Luanne gossiped about how we might not have to worry about any further investigation into the 'stupid statue' cuz she had heard from Staceyleene who heard from Thorpe who heard from his brother Beau who heard from Sassa on the city council that the Jo family had been making noises about filing a civil law suit against Old Man Promised To cuz new evidence had been uncovered in their daughter's death and that something that big could have the power to make the silly statue investigation go away entirely but it might take a little while due to the courts being so slow. Of course, Luanne's uncle is a lawyer and he said that the case probably wouldn't hold up without an eyewitness, so then Lily said that the Jo family were just 'sabre-rattling' to get a reaction from Promised To, cuz they were still really angry but they hadn't actually filed the suit yet. As far as the witness thing though, it was kinda funny to us how no one mentioned Zeeda MarMartuchy, but then again, nobody had much mentioned Zeeda since he'd been committed to the state mental facility in West Haynesworth a year after the accident.

We said goodbye to the girls and they told us to turn on the national news channel before giggling and hanging up and so we popped the power on the TV and there it was, a helicopter shot flying over downtown Barguss with the headline hovering on the bottom of the screen: 'Missing Statue: More Real-Life Movie Drama or Big Hoax?' Then they showed police criminal sketches of the alleged 'perpetrators' and we got cold shivers in our stomachs and didn't want to eat breakfast at all, so we turned off the TV for good cuz we just couldn't look at it anymore.

It was after that when we felt super-bad and guilty that the cops were gonna go after Dance LeRoy and Raw Mike Tall in their homes when they obviously didn't do anything and we sorta had trouble believing that anyone would mistake

us for those two just cuz we had wigs and fake moustaches
on in the dark. And for at least a little while, we thought
about what would happen if they tracked 'em down and they
denied everything and had great alibis and stuff and then the
cops would come right back and start looking for us, the real
people who did it. The whole darn thing was just getting way
blown out of proportion and we kinda wished the Girls had
never aired the show in the first place.

Just then we got that knock on the front door that we'd
been so scared of and we froze, the thought of not answering
it popped into our heads and the thought of jumping the back
fence did too after we'd already leapt at the initial knock and
all and then we got real quiet and snuck over to the door to
look out through the peephole and see who was there, only
to be able to breathe a big sigh of relief between us and open
the door for Shoe. He always had a big smile on his face and
we invited him in but he suggested we should really get going
cuz we really needed to get supplies for . . .

Laura's Great American Surprise Birthday Party

It was raining like hell outside and it was a good thing we all
managed to fit under Shoe's umbrella as he explained how
the original plan had been for us to set up a big tent in
the memorial park cuz Laura loved circus-y stuff like that.
Apparently Roo and Florence had taken her to the zoo in
Upton on account of a new exhibit featuring really rare
mountain goats from Lhasa or something that they had going
on there. The rain was creating puddles all over Hotblack
road as we crossed it and had to jump over a pothole that
had filled all the way up and was overflowing down into the
storm drains.

Our destination was a fake Scottish bargain store called

MacValue's and it had a big mascot wearing a kilt standing out in front and waving his big puffy hands around and trying to get people to come in. Shoe took us to the entrance of the store and said with a hushed voice that the man in the suit scared him. Couldn't blame him really. 'Hamish of the Clan MacValue' was a bit of a scary mascot with his highland broadsword that was known to 'slash prices', not to mention his huge white eyes with tiny black pupils and large red moustache that looked like old movie theater carpet pasted onto the upper lip of a Charlie Brown-headed costume.

Once inside, we split up to cover all the items on the list. But we got held up when we were forced to have a ten-minute-long conversation in the paper goods section with our old second grade teacher, Mrs. Druabotte (who had recently retired at the age of seventy-six), when we were too slow to avoid her completely by ducking down the wrought iron aisle. It was actually kinda funny how she kept confusing us for a different set of twins she must've taught five years before us and kept asking us how Massachusetts was and we couldn't really tell her we weren't the people she was thinking of but she wouldn't hear of it, she just kept telling us how funny we were, always kidding around.

So finally we went on about how Massachusetts was too cold in the winter for our wives and dogs and we all wanted to move to California and build computers and her eyes got a great glow about them when we told her it was completely due to her that we were successful in life. It was a good thing that we were in the paper goods section cuz we had to get a box of tissues and offer it to her for those big tears rolling down her face. After grabbing a few things down from the top shelf for her, we went about looking for the rest of the things on the list and ran into Shoe while looking for balloons.

He didn't say anything about us being so slow and he didn't

even look upset at all. Shoe was always great and easygoing about stuff like that. So of course, he helped us grab the flowers and the candies and everything else on the list, including renting the helium dispenser. We never really said anything to him about it, but we really admired Shoe and not just cuz he was a world famous DJ and so down-to-earth and cool about stuff but just how he always managed to navigate around so easily in a foreign country, always seemed so capable. Maybe that's on account of how we knew if we ever had to travel to Japan we'd be in the deepest pile of crap ever . . . we wouldn't even be able to read anything or speak to anybody. Yup, we were really glad that Roo had such a great brother, even if he was only half.

We got to the Hitching Post at about five o'clock and some people were already there setting up. In fact, the bartender and Thorpe Thorpe were putting the finishing touches on an indoor tent that crowded up against the walls and ceiling and colored everything with alternating lines of red and white, but it was great and we had the sense we were really just in a tent and not inside at all, that is, 'til we had to go use the bathrooms. But what was even greater than the tent was that Thed, Link and Fyodor had managed to assemble a kid's swing set inside as well. Everyone knew that Laura loved swinging on the swings and we knew she'd probably be disappointed when Roo and Florence told her that she couldn't swing on her birthday cuz it was raining outside. It was all mighty impressive and we were glad to be of help.

All the balloons had been filled with helium, the tables had been set up with tablecloths even, and the two-layer chocolate cake had been delivered by the time Roman showed up with the karaoke machine. Then the guests started arriving at about six and Laura was due in with Roo and Florence at seven fifteen. Most of the guests were crew and cast from the movie and Clue showed up too, we figured he definitely had a soft spot for Laura cuz he fired a little girl extra in the Taco Coleslaw Hamburger Hot Dog Apple scene and put Laura in instead. Sure, everybody liked Laura and Shoe, and Roo really wanted to give her a nice going-away present but we think it was such a big deal cuz we hadn't had a party in a real long time and it was a nice excuse to forget about statues and TV crews and lawsuits and Promised Tos.

Mrs. Kickkick was able to get the night off of work and it was really good to see her. We hadn't been able to talk to her in a long time (mostly due to work and the movie and stuff) and even though we didn't say much, our eyes met and lots of stuff was communicated without needing to open our mouths. We always liked that about Mrs. Kickkick, no matter what. While we were hanging the banner that said 'A Very Happy 11th, Laura!' Mrs. Kickkick told us that Roo and Florence were keeping the surprise intact by not saying anything. It just so happened that that night of the week had been a usual going-out night for all of us: Roo, Shoe, Florence, Laura, J. Bart, Madalick, Roman, Thorpe, Link, Clue, Fyodor, Thed, and the Gee Street Girls.

In fact, it was the usual second night of our thrice-weekly pool nights, which was something Laura always looked forward to cuz she had managed to turn into one hell of a shark. In her three weeks in Barguss, she took enough money off of J. Bart and Roman to buy her family a new house and dining room set back home in the Philippines, she was *that* good, but we also thought Roman kinda let her win sometimes on account of how cute she was when she won and so awful when she lost, that most of the time he let her win so she'd be pleasant to him. She sure was a sneaky one, that Laura.

Well, Roman took off at six thirty to go pick up Madalick, J. Bart, and the Gwyneth Paltrow look-alike and he promised he'd be back in plenty of time to see Laura's face light up with surprise and he stayed true to his word too, which ended up being a huge relief due to the fact that when he walked back in the door with everybody, he was holding a sign that the bartender had been stupid enough to hang outside: 'closed for private party.' That really would've spoiled the surprise. At seven ten we turned out the lights but nobody got quiet, in fact the Gee Street Girls started giggling and laughing and Candy even started telling a ghost story before she got hushed by Clue and somebody next to him. We could hear the rain plinking on the wooden roof and everyone waited for the door to open.

At seven eighteen, Roo yanked the door open and we caught him talking about it still raining and maybe the power had gone out on this grid or something and he finished with a 'hello?' to a seemingly empty bar. That was when someone flicked the lights on and everybody yelled, 'SURPRISE!' and Laura nearly fell over from the shock but she had the biggest smile on her face that we ever saw from her and we wondered if it was bigger even than Roo's but only for a second cuz the band started playing 'Happy Birthday Bop' on the stage set up underneath the tent and the crowd parted so Roo could scoot Laura to the front where the guys had all dressed up like animals from the zoo that Laura had just been to.

Everyone sang along to 'happy, happy, happy, birthday girl!' as Thorpe Thorpe (Lhasan Mountain Goat) was screeching vocals in unison with Thed Teldut (Siberian Tiger) while Fyodor (Tuscan Tree Ape) was ripping up a pair of drums as Link (Rare Nigerian Blood Red Flamingo, supposedly) was slightly off to the side of the stage and hunched over the Delta Systems™ Hot Box Synthing Module. Basically, Thed's Neolix® Super Jam 550 portable guitar/keyboard and 808, the vocals, the drum beats and Thorpe's bass all got filtered through the Hot Box so that Link had complete control of how the music was coming out so he could fade up and down and put it through filters and everything, kinda like 'Mad Professor and everybody else is a crazy three-headed, six-armed Lee "Scratch" Perry', at least that's how Link had explained it to us earlier. Shoe looked super-intrigued by the Hot Box Module but the rest of us were just enjoying the music and looking up at the roof of the tent and it was like not being in Barguss at all, but somewhere bigger and cooler.

The band finished the song and promptly switched instruments, Tree Ape Fyodor took Goat Thorpe's bass and moved up to vocals while the Goat took over the drums and Laura just clapped and clapped while the band said, 'thank you, thank you, we're all here tonight because it is a special young lady's birthday, so everyone, please give her a hug and a great big present,' then they launched right into one of Fyodor's band ReDeck's biggest hits, 'I Wanna Be With You (Put Your Whole Soul In A Bottle)' except it was a wicked remix with Link cutting up the drum beats and spitting them out in a random order with the bass as rhythm track morphing into the beat and then on the second part of the song Fyodor's voice got tweaked so it sounded like a girl was singing it and a really pretty girl too.

When they finished that song, Florence led Laura over to a small throne (actually just a lawn chair spray-painted gold, but that night it was a throne) set up on top of a table (we got the idea from Thorpe) and the cake came out with eleven big candles on it and everyone 'oohed' and 'aahed' as the cake made its way up to Laura's level. Mrs. Kickkick was just over her shoulder and she must've whispered something funny cuz Laura laughed and gave her a big hug and it made us happy just to see it.

The band seemed impatient though and they started playing an impromptu song called 'Blow 'Em Out' and they were obviously referring to the candles, so Laura took a real deep breath and blew them all out at once and was greeted by cheers and Thorpe Thorpe announcing that the 'party has officially started, the bar is open, please wait nicely for your cake,' and then they played a cover version of Luis Arcaraz's instrumental version of 'Laura' and it was all slow and sweet with a few machine beeps in it and Mrs. Kickkick gave Laura a big hug and even cried at the end. It was at that point that the band started packing up to the sound of some 'boos' from people who didn't want them to stop but Link told everyone that Laura's brothers wanted to sing her a song and Roman rolled the karaoke machine onstage and the people got really excited again.

When everyone had their cake and the stage lights had been adjusted (and some turned off cuz the tent was getting too hot) Roo and Shoe stepped up on opposite sides of the stage and the music came in and it was Rosemary Clooney's version of Johnny Mercer and David Raskin's 'Laura' (but they changed it a little so the pronunciation was right) and people started hooting and hollering when the duet began and Clue took Laura's hand and started dancing with her around the tiny empty dance floor. And it was pretty much obvious that everyone was fixated on how graceful little Laura was, and it seemed that time must've sped up while everyone was watching her twirl cuz before we knew it, Roo and Shoe were crooning the last lyrics in a halting falsetto harmony that brought the house down and made Mrs. Kickkick have to go to the bathroom to get tissues.

After that, Laura was offered a microphone and she got up on stage and she brought the house down again with her sultry gospel-y version of Ella Fitzgerald's 'Bewitched, Bothered, & Bewildered', and even though we thought she was too young to sing as sexy as she did, we still enjoyed it. In fact, it turned out that it was that song that had guaranteed her the First Runner Up slot in the junior competitive version of the Binibining Pilipinas Pageant when she sung it for her talent portion. After Laura came down from the stage it was open mic time and anybody could go up and sing.

Madalick immediately jumped on stage with one glove on, a dirty old hat tipped forward over his eyes and an open balloon with a pinched-off opening for him to suck helium through at the appropriate time. 'Uh oh!' J. Bart said and pointed and next thing we knew, Madalick was ripping through an ultra high version of 'Billy Jean' and doing his best Michael Jackson hip thrusts all over the stage. Well, Roman couldn't be outdone, so he got up there with Thed Teldut (who was still wearing his Tiger costume) and sang Buck Owens' 'A Tiger By The Tail' and did this weird modern dance with Thed while pulling at his tail until it nearly came off. A few more people got their shots at karaoke but nobody else was as good as those first few songs so we went off in the corner to have some cake and talk to people.

It turned out that the eerily good Gwyneth Paltrow look-alike was actually Gwyneth Paltrow but as silly as the possibility seemed when it came to Barguss, we were pretty used to meeting all of Roman and J. Bart's famous friends back then. Apparently, she really liked hanging out with Roman cuz he understood what it was like to have famous parents and what not. We didn't bring it up or anything but we listened when she talked about some new film she had just finished shooting and it had a number instead of a letter in the title and it took us a while to understand that, or at least fake like we did. She said she was having a great time but by then we wanted to talk to someone else so we thanked her for coming and got up to go talk to Clue just as Brandy came by with the camcorder. The Gee Street Girls were taping everything at that point and we didn't want to be party to them annoying some movie star.

We couldn't even have a decent basketball conversation with Clue. He was so hung up on telling us that he actually wanted us to play ourselves in the movie and we really wanted to say no but he begged and begged, so we couldn't break his heart like that and we ended up telling him that we would at least think about it. Even though we didn't want to tell him that we were scared that we would do it all wrong and mess everything up but he said we really didn't have any lines and all we had to do was be in the crowd shot at Tee Tee Ta Tee Two Too's first show and of course the big scene when Roo gets curbed. We didn't bother telling him that we didn't exactly feel like reliving the most horrific helpless moment in our entire lives over again but we knew he wouldn't take no for an answer so we sorta slid away when he went to grab another beer.

That was just as Shoe took the stage as DJ Dirty Elvis and he had this really great sequined jumpsuit on and his long black hair combed up into this hilarious pompadour, real close to Roman's actually. He also had a huge pair of sunglasses on and rings choking his fingers and he did a few flying kicks on stage and the audience just ate it up mostly cuz they were pretty drunk by then but when Shoe got behind the turntables with his fake sideburns that looked like dog's hair, he was all bizness.

No one in the room had ever heard his music, so we were all real curious as to what it would be like. It began slowly, with a humming old man (at least it sounded like it) repeated over and over until it started to form a beat: hum-hmm-hum-hum-hum-hmm, kinda like that and then this wicked drum beat drops in almost like the old guy is just breathing in some park cuz we can hear bird sounds too and maybe wind going through the trees: snare-snap-snare-snare-snare-snap. And even though the humming/hmming continues, we hear the old guy's voice as the music builds up and drum beats get faster and faster and this electronic sound like a jet going by gets louder and louder and the words come out like 'watashi . . . watashi . . . wa . . . ta . . . shi . . . no . . . watashi no . . . chi' and it almost sounds so nonchalant as the music builds and builds to this great crescendo where you can hear all sorts of people's voices, the old guy's and a woman's and a little girl's and a robot's and it just says 'watashi tachi no chi' (we think) over and over and everybody was dancing like crazy and we even danced with Gwyneth for part of the song and she was a really good dancer, at least, we thought so, but don't take our word for it, we're pretty uncoordinated.

Shoe's performance went down as legendary. Most of us in Barguss had never heard dance music like that before but the coolest part of his set was in the end when he mixed a bit of haunting piano into an electronic storm it sounded like and we almost thought it'd be too much but it wasn't, it was light and sweet and it faded perfectly into some flute and string kinda opera song and for some reason (and even now we aren't exactly sure how), it really worked: underneath the white and red tent, looking around at people's red sweating faces and some of them had smiles and some had confused looks like they were trying to place the music as they stopped dancing and just listened with their heads cocked upwards and it was so beautiful and we felt even more strongly that we weren't in Barguss but somewhere Europeanly romantic and far away, though we did see Roman out of the corner of our eyes finally heading for one of the windows in order to open it cuz it really was getting unbearably hot when we thought about it instead of the music and so he threw open the window when that opera singer hit the highest note and the breeze rushed in and it was like being in the movie for a split second and we couldn't help but look around for the Gee Street Girls and if they were filming cuz we felt like we were being watched somehow but it didn't matter as the crispy air brought a total mood change to everyone gathered inside the Hitching Post that night, from a kinda agitated excitement to relief and a hint of happy tiredness.

We found out later from Shoe that the music he played at the end was Maria Callas singing 'Près Des Ramparts De Séville' from the opera *Carmen* but as soon as he told us, we almost didn't wanna know, we almost just wanted it to be magic when Roman threw open that window and the cool air came in as the voices rose and it seemed like everything red turned blue and everyone at the party turned to look out at the night sky to see that it was no longer raining and just all smiled at the very same time.

17

It's pretty hard to describe what odd senses the human body can experience when thrust into a nearly picture perfect representation of its own past. Like for instance, when we got to *The Golden Ring* and saw Smarty Marty all in make-up to look about five years younger (he was gonna play himself too) and wearing that exact same awful white suit coat with tails he wore the day of Thed and Thorpe's first localitus maximus we got feverish and the real weird thing was that seeing the stage set-up and Clue aligning the camera for the first shot actually made us feel better like we weren't actually living our lives again but then it made us feel nervous and a bit worse cuz we'd have to be in the movie.

We've heard some people say that that's their version of hell, living a certain part of their lives over and over again. Donny Barn always says stuff like that. More so lately too, he just hadn't been the same since Krystof died. He didn't go out in public much and he hardly ever rode his motorcycle on the highway or even around town. 'Course they've already made a movie about something similar and that's the Bill Murray movie called Groundhog Day, *kinda funny how the movies have already covered that base. Thorpe always says that movies 'play out the collective imagination of the society they're created in', but we think that's a load of crap. If it's* anything we learned from hanging around the movie, it's that only a handful of people get to put their perspectives in movies, not everybody, but we didn't tell Thorpe that. We just nodded.

Before we told anyone we were there, we walked around the bar area trying to think about the advice Clue gave us to 'just live your lives over again so I can get it on film . . . just lose yourselves in it and feel what you felt back then . . . and don't look at the camera!' So we kinda skulked around the corners and stayed out of the light and just watched as they set up lights all over the place but in such a way that it sorta looked natural, given the surroundings. Fyodor and Link were sitting at the bar drinking beers when we cruised by and asked them how they were doing.

They said they were tired already and shooting hadn't even started, so we talked a little bit about how they felt 'performing' in the movie cuz it would be their second performance after the blimp scene that got shot when Krystof was still alive and they said that with Krystof gone it almost did feel like it was their first time performing together like it was so much more raw and not as slick and then they went out of their way to say that they weren't calling Clue a bad director, it was just that his style was so different from Krystof's on account of how it was Clue's first directing effort and Krystof had done a buncha movies. Before we left, they told us to 'loosen up' and 'just enjoy it'.

Walking to the front lip of the bullring stage, we had to tell Clue that we were there and ready when he was. Clue had a big smile on his face as he jumped down from the small platform erected on the far side of the bullring sand. He told us that he had an idea about how the audience would be introduced to The Golden Ring and it would be a Scorsese-type shot where the camera followed us out of our car, in through the front door past the bar and down into the ring to get seats at the very front. Our only line of dialogue was, 'hey, what're you doing out here? They're gonna start in like five minutes,' and we were to say it to two guys smoking outside but the best part was that Clue got Thorpe Thorpe and Thed Teldut to play those two guys, so there was this weird thing going on where we were telling the actual guys that their characters were gonna start. Well, we can't really explain so well, it kinda messed with our heads really.

Clue got the Gee Street Girls to sit in and be themselves as extras too, which they'd been waiting for forever so they were really happy and even went out of their way to recreate the signs (that were supposed to be funny serious but stupid at the same time and making fun of the whole rock and roll thing) they held up at the first concert: 'Thed = The Godhead' and 'Thorpe Thorpe Rocks Our Socks!' and of course there was also '6T 4EVA!' which was always our favorite. Even Roo and Shoe got to be in the crowd, though Clue did make Roo wear a big black turtleneck scarf-type thing sorta like Orko had in the He-Man and the Masters of the Universe cartoon that played on TV all the time when we were kids, just so that no one watching the movie could see his scars.

Anyway, we did the shot seven times in three hours and it was kinda different each time. We didn't exactly get the dialogue right the first coupla of times cuz Thed kept making us laugh and we also had to do it again when the camera operator got the focus pulling wrong and one time the cinematographer underexposed the film or something so we had to do the walk again. After that, we just sat around as they filmed Fyodor Thorpe smashing himself and Link Thed fighting the ninjas which was a fun scene to shoot but we hoped we weren't smiling too much and looking stupid. All in all though, we sat around a lot and we never thought filmmaking could be so boring, but of course that was before our next night of shooting where . . .

Roo Kickkick Loses His Whole Face Again, Sorta

We got the shakes when we showed up at Florence's house the next night and we can't quite say if it was the way it was lit or the way people were dressed and clumped in small groups talking low or what it was exactly. Maybe it was something invisible, something about that very curb and the heinousness committed upon it, that made our lips pucker tight around our teeth and be thankful that it wasn't us, all mixed in with the sad guilt in our bellies that we coulda prevented it somehow. Sorry really, more than anything else, that's how we felt in our toes with them all scrunched up against the ends of our sneakers and reminding us of that night, just so damn sorry that it ever even happened.

Of all the people to surprise us outta that little reverie, Florence had snuck up behind us while we must've been staring at the curb and she put a reassuring hand on our shoulders and didn't say anything, didn't even raise her eyes up but we didn't need any words to know that she felt some measure of that guilt and pain too. We'd never spoken to her about it, or anybody else for that matter. It was like as soon as Roo's face was fixed and he was gonna be okay, it stopped being a topic of discussion (not like it ever was) but it just stopped being anything period. No one really talked about it, no one close mentioned it around Roo, almost like we were going back to being normal and so even though everyone was so enamored with Roo's face, they never mentioned the scars in conversation in front of him, never stared at them either, or at least tried real hard not to cuz they were just his 'smile' and his 'pearly whites'.

The closest anyone ever got to mentioning his scars was saying 'what lovely cheekbones' he had and we're pretty sure that was Dr. Nancy who said that, just trying to con him into a cocoa butter facial or something else expensive. Kinda funny how something terrible happens and then everyone feels like they can't really talk about it and no matter how much they think about it they never go and say anything cuz maybe they're too polite or they're just plain scared they're gonna hurt somebody's feelings, namely whoever it happened to.

So there we were with Florence, standing just outside the house where it all happened and come to think of it, we hadn't been back since it went off and for a moment, we wondered, how many people had? How many people came back and stared at the bloodstains on the concrete and gossiped about what happened and even acted it out with their bodies and words. And we were standing not twenty yards from a buncha people who were putting time and money into recreating something that we honestly wished never even occurred, that sometimes we wish it could be wiped away and Roo could be normal again and not have problems with Temporo Mandibular Joint Syndrome and his deviated septum and the three facial surgeries he's had since the first one to clean bone and teeth chips out of his nasal cavities and sinuses and throat and the three tongue surgeries he's had in addition to innumerable trips to the speech therapist in Upton to ensure he can say the letters 't' and 'd' correctly. So yeah, if some stupid magic genie ever offered to take that all away and return things to the way they were before, we'd do it. And we wouldn't even have to think about it. It's not even a question but 'that doesn't change the present', as our mama always says, so best to keep moving on. Florence offered us a tissue, holding the whole box out to us, but we refused and wiped our faces on our shirtsleeves, turning away so she couldn't see.

To be honest, the first few hours were a blur and we were still kinda in shock if such a thing is even possible to experience three years after the fact but really, we just walked through the scenes that Clue had us in. 1, Us and J. Bart as Roo, ringing the doorbell. 2, Us and J. Bart Roo at the door, entering the party. 3, Us and J. Bart Roo walking inside. 4, Us in the backyard with Link as Thed acting crazy drunk. 5, Us taking care of Link Thed. And then, after all the close-ups and at 2:36 in the morning, we were supposed to film the big scene. Clue wanted at least one shot to be from our perspective, just like The Golden Ring scene and he fully intended to shoot the scene all from hand-held with him following us out to discover what was being done to J. Bart Roo. The real Roo was nowhere to be seen and we didn't blame him at all.

Clue left us a few minutes 'to prepare' while he got the handheld camera ready. He was actually going to shoot it himself and really he just wanted us to 'react' to what we saw and 'go from there'. When he said 'action!' and pushed us forward through the door, it would be silly to say that we were even half prepared for what we were about to see and it really didn't matter how many times we'd seen it in nightmares played over and over except we were too slow or our punches carried no weight in the dream world and we could never stop it.

Seeing Raoul like that all leaned over Roo and yelling at him, our ears started ringing and we couldn't hear a thing he was saying, just couldn't keep the instincts at bay that we were saying that this was real and happening all over again and next thing we knew we were all over Raoul and probably the weirdest thing was no sense of déjà vu and people say we're lying when we say that but it was as if it were happening all over again, for the first time. Raoul managed to drop back and push away, then the fast blue car pulled up with Monroe Mister hanging out the driver's side window and they were gone up the street fast as lightning.

Pulling Roo up made us realize that it was only J. Bart and our surprised reaction must've worked well cuz when Clue cut he said it was amazing and he was really happy with it but he made us do it again anyway but not before Madalick came over and told us not to be so rough and we had to go and apologize and tell him that we really got lost there and we were sorry. We think he understood cuz he kinda nodded and shuffled off back to his position.

The second time we did it wasn't as good though and Clue even said so but he said it was insurance for the first shot. After that, he took a few close-ups and then we did a scene where the ambulance drove up and we were denied access to it (which didn't really happen in real life) but that was supposedly so Clue could write this really heart-rending and not quite true scene at the hospital with Doctor Dinner and Mrs. Kickkick.

That was the last of the filming that we were involved in and it was a good thing too cuz by the time we got home that night, even though we hadn't eaten anything in about sixteen hours, we couldn't touch a thing in the fridge and we couldn't go right to sleep either cuz it felt exactly like the night it happened, when we got home at four in the morning from the hospital but just had to watch TV to calm down. Except this time when we turned on the TV, it was still on the national news channel and they happened to be running some late-night lawyer-type talk show but it was the topic ('Promised To Civil Suit') that made us stop cold cuz as soon as we saw it, we knew the rumor was true and that the Jo family had filed the law suit anyway (and without the benefit of an eyewitness apparently). The anchors were going on and on about small-time politics and had to mention the movie a number of times of course, but none of that really interested us, what interested us was the thought that even from beyond the grave there'd be justice for everything the Promised Tos ever did and especially justice for the Jos cuz Jo Mary was a great girl who just made really bad choices with guys, but maybe that's kinda obvious.

18

When it came time for Shoe and Laura to leave and go back to their side of the world, they couldn't have known then what would happen after they flew to Manila where Shoe would rent a car and drive them to Quezon City from the airport and drop off Laura with her mother in the tiny hillside house with brown roof tiles within shouting distance of the Ninoy Aquino Parks & Wildlife Center so she could go back to school and take more dance and piano classes and grow up a beautiful and smart young lady and eventually win the real Binibining Pilipinas Pageant, but that would be long after Shoe drove back to the airport and flew to Tokyo and took the train to Osaka where he lived cuz he had left Okinawa to go to university in Tokyo and had never gone back to the island and after dropping out of school had left Tokyo too on account of he thought it was way too crowded and too crazy but he said he still went there about three or four times a month to record and do shows but when he got home he said he was going to record a new album about 'being half-Japanese in America', and we all smiled cuz we didn't really know what it meant but little did Shoe know at that point that on a chance trip to the Nanzen-ji Temple in Kyoto to record the sound of birds for his new record he would meet an amazing young singer named Moira, who was an Irish tourist separated from her group, and well, they would get to talking and eventually he told her what he did and she had heard of him and 'loved his music' and she would be 'honored to sing for him' and twelve months later they were married, and his new album Terminal Gravity *topped the world charts and they had a one-month-old baby that they named Ryuichi after Ryuichi Sakamoto who was Shoe's idol, but they called him 'Ru-kun' or just plain 'Ru' for short.*

But anyway, the morning (super-early too) they left it was just them and Roo (driving, of course) and Florence and us all piled into the 1976 Volvo 244DL (navy blue with sunroof) after throwing Shoe and Laura's bags in the back and we took the highway north so we could get to the airport on time for their flight to Manila. Actually, they had a few more bags than usual cuz Roo had a going-away party at his house the night before and everyone came and brought real nice presents for the both of them.

Roman brought a nice necklace for Laura and a silver watch for Shoe while Link brought a Dynatrix Automatic Reverb Producer (one of the last ones ever made that still worked cuz Dynatrix had a big product recall in 1987 on account of how the units kept catching fire but the unit that Shoe got had a small shield attached to protect the user should it ever go up in flames) for Shoe to use in his music and Link must've known that Shoe's face was gonna light up when he saw it and everyone got a chuckle out of seeing that. Madalick gave Shoe a utility knife with his nickname engraved on it and he also gave Laura a small painting of her that he had made on a paper bag the night before. Everyone agreed that it was amazing too. The Gee Street Girls all combined on a really nice dress for Laura that they had to drive up to Upton to get and when Laura opened the package she started crying cuz it was so beautiful. Clue brought Laura a really nice camera and some rare records for Shoe. Thorpe Thorpe and Thed gave

Shoe a tape of some new beats they had made in Thorpe's basement room and they also gave him their first CD, two guitar picks, a key from Thed's broken Neolix® Super Jam 550 portable guitar/keyboard (cuz he had just bought the 650 and dismantled the old one for parts) and strung it up on a snapped gut bucket string like a necklace. Shoe put it on right away and looked really proud. Fyodor straggled in late and presented Shoe with some pressings of ReDeck's three albums, all on vinyl. We're sure that by the end of the night, Shoe and Laura had more than they could carry back to their countries but they looked so happy irregardless. J. Bart didn't make it but no one really noticed.

Goodbyes were said that night and there were some tears too (mostly from the girls but we did see Clue wipe his eyes a few times), we were all sorta sad in that car on the way to Upton early the next morning but nobody said anything about it cuz it would either make it real or spoil the moment of watching the sun come up over the mountains and hit the undersides of the clouds so that it made an optical illusion of everything expanding. We got Shoe and Laura to talk a little bit about what they missed and were glad to be going back to but that conversation died well before the airport and so Roo put in a tape and it was A Tribe Called Quest's Midnight Marauders and Shoe surprised us by knowing almost every word to 'Lyrics To Go' just as we pulled up to the airport parking gate that spat out the ticket to be displayed on the dash.

Us and Shoe and Roo carried the bags up to the check-in while Florence and Laura walked behind, swinging their hands in lazy movements like pendulums except they weren't really paying attention it seemed, that or trying not to cry too much. Roo put his arms around Florence and leaned against a pillar and we just kinda shuffled around and checked the monitors to make sure the flight was leaving on time. They were gonna fly to Los Angeles first and then on to Manila and it looked to be on schedule. Shoe and Laura got back with their boarding passes and we knew that was pretty much it, even though they said we were all welcome to visit them and we said they could come back anytime. Just after that and a couple of hugs, we gave Shoe a pair of bowling shoes that we stole from the Downtown Alley on Gee cuz he said he thought they were great and would be fashionable in Japan and we thought it would be a funny way for him to remember his nickname (not like a knife or anything). Then we turned to Laura and gave her some hair bands and two small spoons with the state seal on the handles and a little purse that said 'Princess' on it.

At first, she just looked confused and it was then we turned to see that Florence had tears in her eyes and she got down on her knees and gathered Laura's hair up in two piggy-tail lumps on the sides of her head and then inserted the spoons through the hair bands so that they hung down from the pigtails by her ears and were all shiny. Then Shoe took Laura's hand in his and they both said, 'goodbye brother,' at the same time and Roo just said, 'goodbye brother, goodbye sister,' and shook Shoe's hand and gave Laura another kiss on the cheek and we all watched as they walked down the great big hallway where the fluorescent overhead lights would hit Laura's spoons and reflect back at us as she bounced up and down and waved from far away while still walking toward the security checkpoint and that was when we sorta learned the hard way that . . .

Sometimes Saying Goodbyes Is Hard To Do

Everyone was leaving us, sure seemed like it anyway. The day after our trip to Upton, the Barguss shoot wrapped and the crew started packing up all their equipment and trucks to move on to Vegas and then back to Hollywood to do post-production on the film like adding noises to it and stuff like that. The last day of shooting was real anticlimactic actually, Clue just rigged up a pickup truck to carry a camera in the bed that shot over the cab and filmed them driving into Barguss from the freeway and down Hotblack to Gee then straight back onto the highway as if they were going to go north.

We didn't have time to have a party that night cuz Clue was real close to running over budget and they needed to be in Vegas and filming by morning. He had saved some money by not casting much more than Krystof already had but he had spent an excruciatingly long time on a high school graduation scene that he said he could never get quite right. Florence said he was forever mumbling something about *Less Than Zero*'s graduation scene at the beginning of the movie being the best 'transitional scene' in eighties cinema and he was 'just trying to capture something like it'.

So us and a buncha extras had to sit in the town's only football stadium for three days while he filmed the cap tossing and diplomas getting handed out. That was by far the most boring time yet and we all got sunburned too so that delayed filming a little while cuz the make-up person couldn't quite make J. Bart look normal on account of how his skin 'was fairer than an Englishman's ass', or something of the like. Roman says J. Bart had to take baths in aloe for two days before it got any better but the best part was he had a weird burn all around his mortar board shadow, sorta etched into his skin.

Mostly we tried hard to believe that everyone wasn't leaving. Even when the production had the Barguss wrap lunch (they couldn't have a wrap party due to the fact that the movie wasn't really done yet) it seemed like we'd known most of these people for a long time and we really liked a lot of 'em. We played one last game of pool with Clue and Link over lunch. They both said we were welcome in L.A. anytime but we're not sure exactly how much they meant it. Fyodor had to say goodbye too, since he was the only other actor required to make the trip to Vegas with the production even though he had a nasty bout of the flu and would eventually end up giving Wayne the exact same illness by accident. There really wasn't any time to rest in show business, just about never it would seem, that is, unless you're awfully sunburned and look too different from the day before we guess.

Everyone else was free to do what they wanted, pretty much. J. Bart took a private plane outta the Barguss airport not long after lunch cuz he had to be back in Hollywood to audition for a new film. Madalick and Roman were planning on heading back in his Cord the next morning. They had both landed roles in the new Jerry Bruckheimer movie so they had to go back and start working with personal trainers as quickly as possible to be fit for their roles. Things were definitely winding down.

But that night, us and the remaining cast members and of course Thorpe and Thed and the Gee Street Girls and Roo and Florence all got really hammered on vodka and lemon soda at the Hitching Post and to be honest, we don't really remember much beyond that. Vague memories of pretending to be werewolves and trying to scare Beau into shooting at us with his shotgun and us harassing Donny Barn as he was out taking a walk with his cat (which was odd cuz we hadn't seen him in weeks and didn't even know he had a cat, much less a Barguss Blue named Gwendolyn Hammerstairs, Queen of Renova-on-the-Lake or just plain Kiwi for her everyday name), all that survives, though we are pretty unproud of those memories considering.

We woke up the next morning on our backs in the weedy lot behind the Taco Coleslaw Hamburger Hot Dog Apple. From there, breakfast was pretty much taken care of when we found a whole buncha extra money in our pockets (mostly folded or crumpled dollar bills), where it came from, we had no idea and that was a little scary but lucky too cuz we split the #3 eggs and fried apple combo breakfast burrito meal which is just plain huge.

After we got our bearings, we headed down to the Prime Saddle to say goodbye to Madalick and Roman, who were packing up the Cord as we strolled up. Both doors were open and Madalick was kinda hanging over the front seat wedging some stuff down underneath it. We weren't all that surprised to see Roo and Florence there but we were surprised to see the Volv all packed up and with Thed and Thorpe's hairy butts hanging out the passenger windows, front seat and back seat. They leapt out to chide us about how we shot craps with Donny Barn (apparently using squarish rocks with penned-in numbers on them though we can't picture it) in the street and managed to win $37 before pissing in the storm drain and giving him and Kiwi time to get away. We made a sheepish type of mental note to thank Donny for breakfast next time we saw him.

Then Thorpe said they were all having a caravan trip out to Los Angeles where they'd swing through Vegas and pick up Link and Fyodor before hitting California. Turned out Roo and Florence were going too. Florence wanted 'to strike while the iron was hot' and get some more acting work right away but basically, she wanted to get the hell out of Barguss and this was finally her chance to do it. As it turned out, Roman had offered them the guesthouse on his dad's converted ranch in the hills and they took him up on it. Thorpe and Thed had to go just cuz they were needed in Hollywood to start working on the score cuz it would be needed once the movie was edited.

We said our goodbyes, a bit disconcerted that the Gee Street Girls weren't around, but we were informed that they had already said their still-drunken goodbyes and had adjourned to the Prime Saddle pool area to 'get some sun' and we'd never admit that our pulses raced a bit at the thought of seeing the

Lukash gals in swimsuits again. The last time we ever saw that beautiful sight was in eighth grade when Oliver Martin Rivelo had a birthday pool party (the one where no one would admit to pooping in the public pool in the memorial park and we aren't sure but we kinda think it was Thed) for his fourteenth birthday and the girls wore matching one-piece purple bathing suits with a spider tie in the back up near the neck that showed off their muscular shoulders.

Can't really explain why that particular detail of their bodies ever turned us on so much. The Lukash family had always been one that spawned fine athletes. In fact, their father used to play pro baseball (set-up and relief pitcher) in Mexico and Luanne and Lily both played ice hockey (goaltender and defenseman though sometimes Lily played leftwing in a pinch) and their older brother Lucien (or Luc for short but everyone called him Duck due to a hunting accident he had when he was ten) got third place when everyone but the top three fell down in the 1,000-meter run during the state track meet in his senior year of high school. Duck was four and five years, respectively, older than his sisters. Lily was the younger one and the shy one too, Luanne was ten months older and had a whole lot redder hair but they both had blue/gray sets of eyes that sure were something to look at when it wasn't too dark outside.

The cars pulled up the highway ramp together with the Cord in the lead and we're pretty sure Roman wouldn'tve had it any other way. The cars kinda looked like ladybugs look when you're young and trying to burn them with a magnifying glass (except much smaller) and the sun glinting off the glossy parts on the wings or the back windows. Well, the movie was gone and we just had to wait for the final product. Our friends new and old had pretty much gone with it and at that moment in the parking lot with only one untied shoe between us (the spoils of a drunken night out), we tried not to feel as alone as we'd felt since our dad left for Minnesota all those years ago and didn't come back. That feeling didn't really last too long though.

It so happened that the production moved on to Vegas to shoot the Thed and Thorpe with Wayne Newton scene the same week that a few members of the national news media drove their broadcasting vans back into Barguss. Turned out to be perfect timing for the big civil suit concerning Old Man Promised To and the Jo family. Apparently, Zeeda MarMartuchy had given a statement about the facts of the case after all. We guess he felt pretty guilty and partially responsible for Jo Mary's death and was only just now coming forward to help justice be served as best it could. We really did admire Zeeda, we'd heard that he had an awful time of it after the accident with terrible nightmares and hallucinations and seeing specters and ghosts and stuff like that. Really, we don't even want to think about how nasty that mental institution was either. The whole thing must've messed him up pretty bad. Maybe he just needed to 'unburden his tired old soul', as our mama says, before he could get any better mentally.

But that day that we said our goodbyes, the blacktop was starting to get pretty near the temperature of the earth's core so we decided to check out the pool area and hopped inside to the air-conditioned plushy red-carpeted lobby of the Prime Saddle as the Cord and the Volv disappeared over the last highway rise to Upton. They'd be heading west once they got that far, and we really tried hard not to think about all the fun and ridiculousness we'd be missing out on by not going but all that kinda faded when we re-emerged into the sun on the hotel pool deck and saw Luanne and Lily three-quarters reclining and shielding their eyes with their female forearms that had just the right amount of blonde hairs on them while the Mulryne sisters proceeded to push the portable bar into the deep end of the pool despite the loud yelling of the short Alabaman barkeep and Candy got it all on tape.

19

The good news and the bad news was that the first day of civil court case #19954b, Jo versus Promised To, started off with a bang. And not just the bang of the gavel on the wooden drink coaster thingy on the judge's bench, or the bang of the state seal as it slipped from the back wall behind the judge with no warning (and we heard old people whispering behind us that it was an 'omen' of some kind) and crashed to the gray stone floor and gave everybody a fright but the judge the most cuz she had to call a recess to compose herself and we joked that she wet herself maybe but we'd never be able to tell on account of the big black robe. Indeed, it all ended up being good news for the prosecution and bad news for the defendant and the media wrote it all down.

The real bang was the bang we all got out of seeing The Scarlet Pimp, Arnell, take the stand. When they called out his name, we froze. We hadn't heard that name since we'd played our Hooty Mack on the playground and frankly, it scared us. We started sweating, rubbing our hands on our shirts and slouched down in our bench cuz we didn't have the heart to look behind us and see where he was even though we heard big footsteps. Seriously, according to all the local lore we ever heard this guy was so evil he once killed a baby and ate it. We sat next to the sketch artist in the courtroom that day and we watched with dread as his head swiveled and his eyes got all big and his pencil started sketching hard lines into his pad while trying to take in Arnell's flowing velour cape that was all deep red and complemented the hat he had on his head that looked like a cross between a fur-lined crown and a wide-brimmed Three Musketeers-type chapeau. We heard the sounds his clothes made as they swished past us and it wasn't until then that we looked up from the drawing pad to see the worst villain we'd ever heard of. It wasn't just what he wore, or the long strides he took before two little short ones that mesmerized everybody, it was just him, his presence maybe and he kinda glowed and never more than when he talked. And somehow, it was like we stopped being frightened and crossed over into being mesmerized too, all by someone we thought was deader than canned tuna. Everyone had been sure that Hooty had killed him a long time ago in the uptown warehouse explosion.

Still very much alive despite what we had heard, Arnell worked his magic in the courtroom. You see, The Scarlet Pimp, Arnell, had a habit of adding an '-ah' to the end of everything he ever said and it sorta gave the impression that he was always rhyming, like when the Jos' lawyer asked if Arnell knew the defendant's son, he said, 'Yessir-ah, relatively well-ah,' and so on and so forth but it wasn't just the adding of the '-ah' that won over everyone in the gallery area of the courtroom, it was his ultra cool sense of humor. He knew the trial was a bit silly and he also knew that he was likely to incriminate himself on the topic of pimping if he left the subject of his relation to the deceased boy and what his knowledge of the boy's character was, so he always made these little innuendo jokes that just had people laughing, us included. It was kinda hard not to laugh when Arnell compared Monroe Mister to a certain part of the male anatomy in the most eloquent way and got away with it.

Nevertheless though, The Scarlet Pimp's testimony was quite damaging to Old Man Promised To (and his lawyer never objected once, which seemed kinda weird but maybe we watch too much TV and expect that sorta stuff) cuz Arnell made it real clear that Monroe Mister wasn't a perfect kid or anything even approaching that cuz he had actually consorted with the pimps in Upton and even conspired to 'turn Jo Mary out', and make her into a hooker and that was damn shocking to hear but it didn't surprise us cuz we always knew he was rotten on the inside.

Well, legends of so many rumors and urban folktales were coming alive for us that day that we could hardly contain our excitement when Leonard Prince 'Hooty' Mack, Jr. was called to take the stand. It was at that point when we forgot how to breathe and the room spun a little. Never in our wildest dreams did we expect to see Hooty Mack in person, in fact, some people like Beau were even saying he was 'dead by now' too, but hearing his name made our hearts beat all fast and we turned slowly to watch the doors to the back of the courtroom as we gripped the bench tightly in the worst kind of anticipation. Then the oddest thing happened, the first words from that play, HOOTY MACK, that we saw so long ago with Beau and Thorpe popped into our heads as fresh as the day we first saw it and promised to go to the next performance and write them down so we could memorize them:

Rage – Isaac Hayes, sing the rage of Dorothea Mack's son
   Leonard Prince Mack, Jr.,
'Hooty' to these be known, for his countenance resembled that
   of the ageless owl
murderous, doomed, that cost the virtueless countless losses,
Tossing the souls of so many sturdy bodies down to Hell
While their bodies lay as feasts for dogs and birds
And the will of Ms. Fortune was moving toward to its end.

Begin, soul brother #1, when the two first broke and clashed,
Arnellamemnon, lord of pimps, and brilliant Hooty Mack.

Sure, those weird old mixed-up words – like crap from our
high school English book with a bit of funk lyrics stirred in
– had come back to us clearly and still made us laugh cuz no
people we know ever talked like that (not even in movies unless
the movie is Shakespeare-ish or something), but never once did
we think they were true. Until that day in the courtroom when
we got a real big shock . . .

Barguss Has a Trial That Doesn't Kill Any Pimps or Mockingbirds (Somewhat Disappointingly)

After his name was called, the doors at the back of the
courtroom opened and we swear that smoke came in and
everything when Hooty Mack stepped through the door looking like Richard Roundtree on steroids. He was older than we
imagined him, and he had two silver patches of hair at his
temples but he wasn't any less imposing (and maybe even
more imposing) as he walked like a soldier to the stand,
with no hesitation. 'Arnell is only afraid of one man,' Candy
whispered too fast to us, so that some of her spit got in our ears
when she hissed the 'is' but she continued without noticing,
'and that man is . . . Hooty . . . Mack.'
  A showdown was unfolding right in front of us and we could
barely restrain our exhilaration cuz the day before we weren't
even sure that these two guys existed but there they were right
in front of us, headed on a collision course as Arnell stepped
down from the stand and took his two long strides and then
two short ones and he kept his big circus smile going like he
was still the ringmaster but he slowed a little when he saw
Hooty Mack coming up the aisle and not even bothering with

the gate as his knee banged into it and it flung open, smacking the back of Promised To's lawyer's chair and sending the front two legs clacking to the floor cuz the lawyer had been leaning back in it and looking pained but after that, he just looked surprised.

Hooty Mack didn't take any notice of that though cuz he was walking fast enough that he was through the opening before the gate slammed back again and then, right there, in the middle of the big courtroom, he and Arnell had a good old-fashioned standoff. We heard Donny Barn let out a yelp of approval just like he used to when we caught the special screenings of *The Searchers* or *For A Few Dollars More* at his theater with him on the last Sunday of each month. Was Hooty gonna snap his neck? Pull the pin on a grenade and stuff it under Arnell's hat? Punch him in the stomach and grab him by the shoulders and throw him out the window?

Time slowed down for everybody in that courtroom and the trial was completely irrelevant for what seemed like whole minutes but was probably only a few seconds, even the judge just watched to see if anything would happen and she kept glancing at the bailiff and maybe it was the kind of look where she knew that Hooty Mack had beaten up eighteen guys with nunchucks so maybe she shouldn't say anything to one bailiff cuz that might just make Hooty mad and he was definitely not the kind of person you ever wanted to make mad at you cuz deep down in your gut you knew just by looking at him that rules never really applied to a man that had stared death in the face at Hanoi and Nam Dinh.

There was an inherent righteousness in his movements, heck, even in his stillness, how he walked and hung his shoulders like a leopard as if he knew that the death of his prey was simply the natural order of things, just like we always saw on the nature channel and then we thought how great it would be if the guy that narrated those nature shows would narrate the standoff for us, but maybe we just got too carried away by seeing Hooty Mack and The Scarlet Pimp, Arnell, face to face . . . well . . . almost. Arnell had to look up into Hooty Mack's face and we could even tell from the second row that Arnell was sweating.

Then, real slow-like, Hooty moved his face to the side and whispered something into Arnell's left ear and we wished more than anything in the world that we coulda heard what Hooty said to him cuz all we could see was Arnell turning the shade of green that either means you're shit scared or you're gonna vomit everywhere with total disregard for what you vomit on, including yourself too, or maybe it was both and just like that, all of Arnell's coolness seemed to evaporate from him and his costume and he hunched his shoulders a little and moved to the side, out of Hooty Mack's way and then everyone in the courtroom (even the judge, we swear) went 'ohhhh' and with relief kinda too cuz it was immediately obvious to everyone who the bigger man was and we knew then that was true power and some bloodshed may have been avoided.

Nobody paid any attention as Arnell tried his swaggering best to regain some pride on the way out but his cape got stuck in the gate and he tripped forward and we heard fabric tear and everyone laughed out loud and some people were elbowing each other and pointing, even the court reporter giggled and the jury did too, even though they'd been pretty quiet up 'til then and so did the sketch artist (who had been feverishly sketching the standoff and trying to get the tilt of Hooty Mack's head just right so he kept erasing and swiping his eraser leftovers onto us without really realizing it) and the only one not reacting at all was Hooty Mack. He just dusted off the shoulder of his jacket. We looked at him and tried to burn his every feature into our memory so we could tell our kids and grandkids some day and we also secretly imagined that the shoulder he was dusting off had a huge scar on it underneath the leather where he had been surprised by a jungle Viet Cong pungi stick booby trap.

In a way, we were kinda disappointed that Hooty didn't take care of Arnell right there in front of everybody cuz there probably woulda been quite a few people that acted as if they hadn't seen it so Hooty wouldn't get in trouble cuz they didn't think that Arnell was 'worth his skin' at all. We knew Donny Barn was one cuz he actually stood up and said something pretty much to that effect just as Arnell was walking out the back doors and he froze and took Donny in with a true pimp's glare that sized Donny up, all the way to his bones and kidneys, and we realized that yeah, Arnell had lost out to Hooty, but he was still damn scary and not worth crossing, not even for a million dollars and a free trip to Mexico. At this, Hooty just laughed into his hand on the stand and put his ankle up on his knee and relaxed into the uncomfy wooden chair.

Arnell exited disgraced and the doors slowly closed and made a puffing sound and then everyone breathed and started whispering about what just happened and Her Honor had to bang the gavel for order but the state seal fell down again and we all laughed and figured this was the best thing we had ever seen, right up there with Thed and Thorpe's first concert, well okay, just behind it at number two, but it wasn't over yet. Her Honor didn't need another bathroom break though, so we went on.

When everything was in order, 'Mr. Mack's', as the lawyer kept referring to him, testimony was sorta anticlimactic cuz he just confirmed that Monroe Mister was a nasty kid and he detailed how he tried to set him straight but basically, he was disgusted cuz 'the boy was just too damn spoiled', and basically, we already knew that, so everybody just nodded and Old Man Promised To pretended like he didn't notice the public agreeing with such a dim view of his son. Then

Hooty Mack left the stand and people actually clapped, us included, and he just looked kinda embarrassed and dipped his head and went out the gate a bit slower than before and headed out the back double doors cuz Old Man Promised To's lawyer didn't have any questions for him at that point, and so we slipped out of our row and followed him. Lily asked where we were going and we mouthed 'bathroom break', and sped up behind Hooty Mack just as the doors were closing.

We stopped him in the big marble hallway and blabbered on and on about how he was our hero when we were kids and we really, really admired what he did in there with The Scarlet Pimp, Arnell, and he was so tough and we wanted to be just like him and could we please, please have his autograph on our t-shirts and he looked really embarrassed then but he signed our t-shirts anyway (with a ballpoint pen that kinda hurt our skin and he signed it 'L.P. Mack' and it was at that point that we learned that no one called him Hooty, maybe only his enemies) and we couldn't help it so we had to ask if he really did stuff like the grenade thing with Pimp Tall and all that and could we see his scar?

Well, Mr. L.P. Mack got down on one knee so he was closer to our heights (he must've been like six foot ten or something huge) and he just said, 'boys, that sure was a long time ago,' and he looked down before saying, 'some of that stuff happened and some of it didn't, it was just rumors . . . I don't have any scars from pungi stick traps like everybody says and I didn't beat up twelve guys with nunchucks [we didn't tell him we heard eighteen], and now, I'm just a grandpa that owns his own business and minds his own business [then we think he winked but he might've had something in his eye], I just sell insurance in Upton.'

Our mouths must have been open enough to show our broken hearts down in our chests if you looked hard enough down our throats into our lungs. We tried to squeeze out, 'but what about the play? What about all your heroism?' But it kinda came out as a series of separate chokes. Mr. Mack put his big hands on our shoulders and for a moment we thought of spitting on our hands and rubbing his autograph out of our shirts and we thought about how stupid we were to come out to the lobby and we just wished that we'd stayed inside the courtroom so we could have those amazing memories of Hooty Mack untarnished by the damn truth.

Maybe we even started to cry, imagine that, a coupla almost grown-ups crying, but we felt so much like kids at that point, maybe a few tears even squeaked out, much as we tried to hold 'em. We tried not to look at Mr. L.P. 'no longer Hooty' Mack and he got a look in his eye and a frown on his face and really all we wanted to do was go to the bathroom for that break, to wash our faces and walk back into the courtroom like nothing happened. All we heard was, 'I'm sorry, boys,' and just like that, Mr. Mack stood up and walked fast for the door to the outside and the insane hot street asphalt cuz they were finally repaving Gee Street, to the media people's extreme agony cuz they had to walk just about everywhere instead of driving.

We heard the door creak back and we heard it shut and we heard the glass shake and the latch go and we shuffled over to the bathroom and it was 'god's good luck', our mama always says that, that nobody else was in there to hear us cry or see our tears. Roo and everybody were gone and just when we'd felt a little bit of joy for the first time since they left, it got dashed on the rocks and it just didn't seem fair at all. As we tried to regain our breaths and wash the tears off our faces, we heard bootsteps outside the door and turned away and acted like we were peeing at the urinals, even though we really weren't. Our flies weren't even down.

The door opened and we could feel someone looking at us, then we heard the sound of crinkling leather and we turned to see Mr. Mack standing there, taking off his jacket and we felt really weird like we hoped he didn't want to do some weird sexual thing with us and our hearts beat faster and our fists clenched when he started unbuttoning his black dress shirt to the middle of his chest but our whole world changed back for the good when he pulled his shirt down to expose his right shoulder and the coolest-looking scar we have ever seen, apart from Roo's of course, and he just started talking all slow and said, 'I was in the jungle doing recon a few clicks west of Dong Tri near Châu Lang I guess, just scouting around, handling my business, when all of a sudden I heard a whooshing sound and some wet leaves scattered up into my face just as I felt the sharpest pain I ever felt in my life and I looked down and I had this huge fucking stick poking out of me . . .'

We never ever told anybody who we got the nunchucks from (we could bet a dime to a dollar that the Gee Street Girls guessed it in one anyway) but it probably would've taken a coupla really good hits with 'em to get the smiles off our faces as we re-entered the courtroom in the middle of Zeeda MarMartuchy's testimony and thankfully, no one really noticed that we had them stuffed down a pant leg and so they couldn't say anything about 'em. We're kinda ashamed to admit it, but after the talk we had with Mr. Hooty Mack in the bathroom (mostly we just listened), the trial wasn't nearly as cool since he'd gone back to Upton. And we really did try to pay attention to all the important bits but it was like the life and drama had gone out of the trial with him gone and The Scarlet Pimp, Arnell, gone too.

As it turned out, Zeeda ended up being the 'star witness' for the prosecution cuz he was there for the whole incident when it happened and even if he was drunk, he at least saw it with his own eyes. Well, as far as we could tell through our minimal attention paid to his testimony and cross-examination, Zeeda didn't waver under any of it. We didn't really listen to most of the testimony cuz we were still thinking about Hooty Mack and trying to remember every detail cuz that was definitely a story we'd tell our *great*-grandchildren if we ever lived that long.

As far as we were concerned the trial was pretty much over after that day and all Old Man Promised To's lawyer had to worry about was damage control as if that would win the trial for them. But to be honest, we were happy but didn't care a whole lot cuz more than anything we couldn't wait to get home and try out the nunchucks and hopefully not poke our eyes out or something.

One month later (and it was a really long month too, the media stayed the whole time and apparently nothing else was going on in the wide world cuz all we saw on the national news was rerun after rerun of the trial and expert people discussing it, dissecting it, talking way too much about it, and we can't really blame anyone else if they never wanted to hear about Barguss ever again after all that), we were proved right as the jury made the determination that Promised To had to pay the Jo family two million dollars for the loss of their only daughter. But in a silly twist, after the Jos got the money, all they did was move up onto rich people hill, which we would never have done if we had that kind of money but we don't, so that's life.

The next week was kinda slow and like most of 'em, there isn't much to say really. We went out with the Gee Street Girls a few times and caused trouble and we also went to our jobs and that's about it. But the good news for that week was that a date had been announced for the movie premiere of *Roo Kickkick & the Big Bad Blimp*! We all had the date on our calendars and marking off a day was like getting closer to

Christmas when we were seven and couldn't wait for presents, but that's really a good and sad story for the next chapter, so just turn the page.

20

As one last big thank you to the people of Barguss, Zeke and Norville Cline decided to hold the premiere of Roo Kickkick & the Big Bad Blimp right back in town at the Donny Barn Exclusive Theater. They made it a real big deal too: red carpets and everything, limousines cruising down Gee Street to get to the theater so people lined the streets and waved and took flash photography while people like Roman popped out of the limo sunroof and waved and threw flowers and beads to 'his adoring public', as he called them. It was actually kinda funny how it ended up being the place to be seen, well, even Steven Spielberg came to the premiere on account of how long he had been a friend of Zeke and Norville's. All the local TV stations and even a few national ones had people there on the red carpet to chat to the stars as they went by. And people came from all over the state to be there cuz we'd never had a film premiere here before.

We were real excited too, we got to ride in Roo and Florence's limo and the best part was we got to choose it cuz actually a coupla different people asked us if we wanted to ride with them and so we felt special. It sure was good to see everybody again. We all played pool at the Hitching Post earlier in the day and Roo won the $100 pot at the end of the round robin pool tournament, just edging out Madalick.

And it was cool just to catch up with everyone and see how they were doing and what they were up to. Sadly, Madalick and Roman had been fired from the Bruckheimer movie but they were auditioning for the new Schwarzenegger film so they weren't too upset.

Thorpe and Thed hadn't been up to much but sleeping and working on the score. They were able to make it to a coupla Fyodor's gigs with ReDeck, but mostly they just worked on the music at all times. We knew it was risky that Panazanc had decided to let them do the score and we couldn't wait to see the final cut of the movie so we could see how good it was. On the other hand, Florence was already getting super-popular, she landed two new roles and was good at being seen at all the hottest clubs and places to eat. Well, Roo seemed pretty proud.

And we all sorta stretched out in the limo and kept the tinted windows rolled up for a little bit before we decided to open them and let the wind pour into the car and we just had the feeling that we'd never see Gee Street from inside a limo ever again so we should enjoy it as much as we possibly could. Roo coerced us into sticking our heads out of the sunroof and we saw Lily and Luanne and we waved at them as they ran to Candy, Mandy, and Brandy and then all five of 'em chased our limo, screaming down the street like we were famous, like we were totally different people. They were just being silly but it felt kinda weird seeing people react like that to us. It was funny to see how the fancy car going to the fancy party touched off random pockets of screaming girls that seemed to roll toward us as the limo kept going, but then we got pulled down beneath so Florence could stick her head out and get all the attention but we didn't really care cuz we'd had enough of it already.

We were amazed to see how much work they'd put into the Donny Barn Exclusive though, it looked all nice and clean *with new paint and everything and they even had a prop blimp outside and the weirdest thing was that a stuntman jumped off of it every twenty minutes and we saw it and couldn't quite make sense of it but all the people in the little grandstands seemed to love it, with the way they kept 'oohing' and 'aahing' every time he jumped into a giant cushion. We guess he was supposed to be Raoul or something. Well, we can say that Donny Barn wasn't going to be one to let so many people show up in Barguss and not make any money off it. In fact, after the primo screening theater (the one with the actors and famous people) was full, he'd close off that section of the Exclusive and start charging the bystanders to come in and see the movie on the other screens. He sure was smart.*

The theater was totally full and we got to sit between Roo and Thorpe Thorpe, who just looked completely wiped out, even then. We think Thorpe was real, real nervous about the score and everything and we were gonna try and say something reassuring but Clue got up on stage and said a few remarks about how he hoped we enjoyed it and other stuff like that. Then it got real dark and it got real quiet so we could hear the projector click on behind us and the tension was kinda high and then it started with white words flashing up on a black screen.

Panazanc Film Partners, Inc. Present. A Zckwecy/Brush Film. Then the words faded into black and the huge title flashed up. Roo Kickkick & the Big Bad Blimp. *The music started right then and the title kinda looked like it had been written in blood. We recognized the music right away, it was from Autistik/Artistik's first album, track one to be precise: 'Angel of Death, Part 1: Stone Cold Chilling'. It's one of our favorite tracks of theirs cuz it starts out with this Run DMC-style backing beat and then Thorpe Thorpe's vocals come in over the top and it sounds like they've been strained through a sieve or even better, as if they'd been recorded* through a vent cuz that's what Thorpe Thorpe said he had to do to get his brother to turn the heat on in the cellar when he lived there: yell through the vent. Anyway, there is a really beautiful part to it when Thorpe Thorpe sings all forlornly that he is 'the last lost Christmas present / in the corner, forgotten and unopened'. The Gee Street Girls always swoon when he sings that line in falsetto at concerts and it's really kinda sad cuz the earlier part of the song tells us that the present was a pet hamster for his little sister (even though he doesn't have a little sister, it's fictional) and that line means that he/the hamster will die.

As soon as we recognized the song we started cheering and got goose bumps all over when a few other people started cheering too, right as the black behind the title faded away and it was a camera shot of the road speeding toward us and Barguss was in the distance and coming closer. We guess spellbound (like we didn't even remember large chunks of it) is the right word: a little confused but unable to turn away, that was how we felt through the whole movie, seeing our town and our stories and even us (we cringed and had to look away at those parts though) up there all big was something we never thought about. Never really made a connection to, believe it or not, we just didn't think when they were filming it, that okay, someday this will be done and blown up larger than anything we ever thought would be on a giant screen right in front of us. And we would be a part of that. We would be bigger than life, bigger than our lives in this small town that sometimes seemed too stupid for words or too boring to truly live through . . . it just wasn't anymore, not up there all big, even if it was only a small part of us. That night, some of us, a piece or two, was gigantic.

We try not to admit it to anyone but we cried when the closing credits came up and people started clapping sorta enthusiastically and the song in the background was 'Angel of Death, Part 2: The Heat Is On', and was the second track from Autistik/Artistik's first album, Talk Dirty to the Beep, and that made us feel good, like it was real authentic. Anyway, the song is especially genius cuz the boys grabbed the riff and the chorus from Glenn Frey's 'The Heat Is On' and then Thorpe Thorpe does a spoken word poem over it about waking up after he thought he was gonna die 'locked and alone in the basement' and how it is the most amazing feeling when the heat from the vent hits his cheek and wakes him and the poetic context makes the chorus of the original song actually sound kinda deep. When the house lights came on, we got more goose bumps and our ears were sorta ringing and we hugged some people and told them 'good job' and stuff like that and told them we'd meet them at the Prime Saddle Party in a little bit, we just had something else to do and it was like we sleptwalked right out of there and into another theater to see it again.

Well, we really wish we could say we had the same experience again but really, we didn't. Actually, we hated it. We hated seeing how real the curbing scene was and how it felt like we were having an out of body experience by watching it from another angle, in cushy chairs, like it was supposed to be entertainment cuz some people were actually laughing and that made us want to puke. Truth be told, as soon as that scene came on, we just started crying and couldn't stop even though our minds were wondering about how Clue and Thorpe and Thed had decided to score the curbing scene with the angry punk guitar riff from 'Fullyovergrown', one of their old songs, and we just aren't so sure it worked cuz we know the song's original meaning and didn't feel it fit exactly. See, the song was about a boyfriend and girlfriend who made a pact not to cut their body hair and after a few months, well, everything got 'fully overgrown' and actually it was a pretty comedic song, which is why we felt it didn't quite fit. But the song riff didn't go on for the whole curbing scene, it kinda faded in and out and actually long parts of it were completely silent (with tiny bits of sound fading in and out and Clue said he wanted the sound track to be 'almost like what Roo's ears were hearing at the time') and that was kinda hard to take cuz that's kinda how we remember it.

Mostly though, we hated seeing ourselves up there, so big. So big that we were like a giant target and we couldn't really think of a bull's-eye any bigger. That thought made us kinda nervous too, seeing as how the second time we watched it was with a normal audience and no one had anything invested in being polite. We heard some boos during a coupla poorly delivered lines and two people even walked out and we left our seats while J. Bart Roo and Florence were hugging in front of the mountain orange sunset which was a few seconds before the closing credits that had black and white photos with a few sentences typed below them saying what the characters ended up doing in the future, like most Hollywood-type high school/college movies do. But we didn't care so much about that, we were just relieved that no one threw anything at the screen.

We walked all the way to the Prime Saddle from the Exclusive and the streets were completely dirty from having so many people on them. Cigarette butts and gum and newspaper trash were everywhere and there was no one cleaning it up yet so we grabbed whatever we could on the way by, mostly just trying to clear our heads so we could be happy about seeing everyone for one last night before they went back to Hollywood but we still felt horrible when we got there. We shared a coupla empathetic glances with Roo but basically didn't talk to anyone about how we felt. Even though people were having a great time and dancing on tables and celebrating and stuff, we just had a bad feeling about everything, like we were all in real trouble but we couldn't totally explain it. At *least we were kinda prepared though. We think just about everyone else was surprised to learn . . .*

How To Bomb a Town To Bits Without Using Explosives

Later, we found out that the final box office gross take for one week (after that it was pulled from nearly every screen across the country, so if you blinked you pretty much missed it) was the eye-popping total of $38,762.50 and supposedly, nearly a third of that came from round-the-clock showings of it in Barguss. Considering the movie cost $45 million to make (turns out Ol' Krystof was pretty smart cuz he had a ten million dollar insurance policy written into his contract, payable to his relatives back in Eastern Europe, if he died while making the film so that counted against the budget kinda harshly), well, we're pretty sure it was the most horrendous loss ($44,961,237.50) in cinema history and it was expected to completely tank Panazanc Film Partners, Incorporated. That meant that it grossed way less than *Ishtar* and *Howard the Duck*. That was kinda hard for us not to take personally.

A buncha media people said it was 'the bad buzz' that killed it for everyone and really, we don't blame the public for not seeing it. If we lived anywhere else we wouldn't have gone to see it either cuz it was just about the most talked about movie in history before it got released, what with the directorial fiasco and Krystof's suicide that got caught on tape and Clue's high profile naming as director to take over and probably the worst of all was the Promised To lawsuit that got talked about twenty-four hours a day on some of the national news channels and had a lot of people saying bad things about Barguss before the movie even came out. Truth be told, we were pretty sick of the attention too.

So it really didn't surprise us that some critics went into their screenings with sharp eyes and pens and came out the next day in their newspapers saying it was 'pretty close to the worst movie ever made' (*The New York Times*) and 'the worst kind of fluff' (*Los Angeles Times*) and 'never in my career as a critic have I ever seen such boring, useless, over-the-top dreck that bears no resemblance to the America we all love to call home' (*Time Magazine*) and 'a wholly uninteresting movie about a wholly uninteresting place, Barguss is the undisputed asshole of America' (*Rolling Stone*). There were more though, exactly two hundred and twelve negative reviews in national publications, which we thought was pretty surprising cuz we didn't even know that there were that many critics. Well, we guess it goes without saying that the reviews kinda hurt the movie.

Then again, the protest probably didn't help either. The day after the premiere a number of militant-type Chicanos threw themselves into full protest mode (picketing Panazanc and pressuring national theater chains to pull the film) on account of Madalick appearing in 'white face' in the film. They referred to him as a '¡pinche vendido!' and a 'Tio Tomás' and even referenced his brown skin when they called him a 'self-hating Indian submitting to the conquistadores' for changing his appearance to act as Raoul de los Dios who was white when he was alive and we thought Madalick did a superb job in the role cuz he was real scary but we guess that fact didn't really matter. We knew they kinda had a point but it made us sad that they didn't see someone who was perfect for the role as Madalick actually was. Instead, they just saw an actor wearing make-up to make his skin lighter and they pointed the finger at Panazanc for 'making him deny his heritage when there are already so few positive portrayals of our people in the media'.

Maybe it's just us, but we thought it woulda been more

awful if the filmmakers had Madalick play the role in his natural skin tone and then sorta hurt his culture by doing so, cuz that way the bad guy would have been a person of color, instead of some crazy rich white kid that was actually a real person and not a character made up to 'demonize' (some placards said that word a lot) any race. Besides, we're pretty sure not many people got upset about Ben Kingsley darkening his skin a little to play Gandhi in *Gandhi* cuz he's a great actor and was right for the role and even won an Oscar® for it. But we could be wrong.

Well, none of that race argument stuff really mattered though cuz the film was pulled and the protestors considered it a victory, but that wasn't the end of it by a long shot. Politically, a national debate had been sparked off about portrayals of 'Hispanics, Chicanos, and Latinos' in cinema and television and Edward James Olmos ended up giving lots of interviews about the subject and we actually thought that that was something cool that came out of the whole fiasco.

What was truly bizarre was that even after the film had been pulled from theaters people didn't stop talking bad about it. Judging by the actual box office figures, it's most likely that a lot of the people who continued to talk bad about *Roo Kickkick & the Big Bad Blimp* didn't even see it, but that's just our guess. It was named the worst movie of the year in nearly every national publication that had a movie section but it wasn't until it became a sketch on *Saturday Night Live* (complete with small-town stereotypes about incest and everything) and the #1 place (ahead of Beirut at #6, and Chernobyl at #3) on David Letterman's Top Ten List of 'Worst Places to Vacation in the Entire World'. We didn't think it could get much worse than that, but a week later the Upton weather girl made a snide comment about Barguss in her forecast and we knew there was no turning back for awhile, not when weather girls got a backbone to kick us when we were down.

You know, it eventually got to the point where we didn't so much start believing everything that was said about us, even though we did laugh at the jokes cuz some of 'em were really funny, but more like we just stopped arguing. What we mean is, we figure most folks can't keep arguing if you agree with them, so we started agreeing with them just long enough for them to blow themselves out and give us time to pull ourselves back together.

Depression had gone through the roof in Barguss and the one psychiatrist that we did have was so overwhelmed that he actually had to recommend patients to Dr Nancy. One of those was Donny Barn. He'd been bad enough after Krystof's death but he was genuinely struggling after all the bad movie publicity and backlash. He honestly didn't care about living anymore and everybody could tell when he went out one day on his motorcycle and started zigging it up and down Gee Street. Well, some of us were happy to hear Donny back out there doing his thing, 'til we realized he was wearing his helmet on his right knee and leaning his head out over the handlebars as he gathered up speed and we figured he was fixing to put himself through a window or worse, the brick wall of the Taco Coleslaw Hamburger Hot Dog Apple.

The good news was the police got out there right quick and stopped Donny and forced him to put his helmet on his head due to there being new helmet laws and what not and by then, a crowd had kinda gathered around Donny to watch him put on his helmet and the whole time he was mouthing off to the officers calling 'em 'goddamn piggy pigs' and nothing much more original than that and we guess he couldn'tve known that they'd have the last laugh when Donny sped off around the corner and ran right into a parked car and ironically shattered his right knee all to pieces. It sure was hard to contain our laughter that day, but you can bet we did. That incident with

Donny and the helmet and the knee was pretty much the only thing worth laughing about though.

For a long time after the movie, it was like the whole town fell asleep and didn't wake up for awhile, kinda like hibernation except some parts of Barguss fell asleep permanently if you know what we mean. The suicide rate went up like fourteen hundred per cent after that. We usually had about ten or so per year, with most of them being depressed kids we went to high and junior high school with or old people with cancer or something horrible who didn't want to live anymore, but it skyrocketed the year the movie bombed and more than a hundred and forty people killed themselves that year by jumping off the water tower or drowning in the memorial park lake, but by far the most common ones were pills, bathtub electrocution and gunshot wounds to the head or heart. The most baffling one was Hasselzwell Smol's disemboweling, like hara-kiri style in his living room and the oddest thing was, he didn't even die, it was just an attempt cuz his neighbor heard him groaning something awful and usually that's pretty normal Hasselzwell after he's had a fifth of the 'Gourmet Russian Vodka' that they got down at the Coopermarket for $3 a plastic bottle.

Anyway, the neighbor comes over to the house and bangs on the door and Hasselzwell is screaming for a damn ambulance like you'd never wanna hear someone scream for an ambulance in your life and next thing he knew, he was getting rushed to Barguss General Hospital for emergency surgery. They were able to put all his guts back in and somehow he lived. Well, to hear Hasselzwell tell it, all hunched over a beer at Paulson's, he didn't even intend to do it, straight off anyway. Turns out he actually fell out of his recliner onto the steak knife he had been using to cut up his TV dinner when he dropped a frozen-and-reheated pea onto the carpet.

Now, anyone knew from looking at Hasselzwell that he

didn't waste food as his belly indicated to anyone not blind, so as he was bending over to snag the pea with his fork, the knife slipped off his plastic tray and as he readjusted himself to catch the knife with his foot, he missed and fell out of the chair just as the knife rebounded off the floor and the blade sunk right into his stomach as he was falling down on it and the hard floor plunged it all the way in to his spine (Hasselzwell hated tiny steak knives).

Having gotten that far, he had a quick think about his life through the burning pain and decided it just wasn't worth it to keep living: he had no wife, no family, not much money, he was fat, out of shape, and had no real friends. In fact, the one person that used to talk to Ol' Smol all the time was Roo and he had up and moved to Hollywood, so they no longer talked about the 1976 Volvo 244DL (navy blue with sunroof) that Roo had purchased from Hasselzwell who had finally decided that he was the town's 'designated drunk' and didn't need a car on account of how he should never really be driving anyway. So Hasselzwell somehow found the courage inside him to turn the knife sideways and cut across his belly 'til part of his guts fell out. 'Cept now he guesses that only people really committed to dying that way should ever try cuz it's a real long and painful way to go, at least, with a serrated blade

So, with people jumping out of windows, drinking themselves to death and deciding to go for a swim and not breathe any more air while they were at it, we really didn't think it could get any worse in Barguss. Heck, we even considered moving or ending it all ourselves, but just then, 'they' started coming to town and everything changed.

21

Pretty much a year slipped by in this kinda fashion: sleep, eat, work, eat, sleep, watch Roo Kickkick & the Big Bad Blimp on the weekends, then do it all over again. But that wasn't just us, that was most of the town. It actually got to the point where everyone had a regular seat at the movie theater on Saturday afternoons. We actually had taken over a whole row, us and Beau Thorpe (sometimes) and the Gee Street Girls. The best Saturdays were the ones where we managed to sit next to Luanne and Lily without looking like we were trying to and then getting all excited when we made 'accidental' contact with them while reaching for popcorn or trying to tie a shoelace.

To be honest, we didn't really enjoy the movie all that much but we kept going, out of habit. We had to. After pretty much internalizing everything negative the critics had said about the 'fictional' Barguss depicted in the movie (even though it was based on a true story), a lot of us had trouble separating it from the real one that still existed and still had to keep going despite the setback, or the 'speedbump' as Mrs. Kickkick always called it. In some ways though, we think we kinda took a sick satisfaction from going to the theater every weekend and revisiting our greatest disappointment/horror, we guess pretty much everybody did (Dr. Nancy said so anyway when we got sent to her on account of our depression, and she said it 'isn't *so uncommon' to do stuff like that). There was an attraction to it, like magnets, that drew us there that we really can't explain. So we'd just sit down and shut up every Saturday and cringe nearly throughout the whole thing then look in everybody else's eyes when it was over like we'd been through a bloody war and only they could truly understand what we had just gone through cuz they'd been through it with us. Welcome to Barguss, population dwindling, saddest place on earth. At least, we thought so.*

Anyway, the next year was kinda the same though the suicide rate dropped from the previous year and that in and of itself was cause for celebration although no one really seemed to notice. There was more sun that year due to the greenhouse effect or some such thing and we never really thought that sun could affect people positively mental health-wise, maybe that's cuz as a personal preference we always loved clouds more, but we're pretty sure now that more sun helped some people pull out of their depressions and those that kept going found it a little bit easier. The Saturday Night Live *Barguss jokes got stale and were dropped. Letterman never mentioned us again. In an odd and reassuring way, we laughed harder when those guys and girls found new things to ridicule and left us out of it. Sure, people in Upton were still uppity but they always were anyway so that was no real change. The good news was we were being forgotten on a massive scale, time went on and we never thought that would feel so good. Funny, how things worked out that way. We can only just admit it now, but when we first found out that a movie was gonna be made here, we thought, 'wow! Everyone will know where Barguss is and they won't ever forget us.' Thank heavens that that's no longer the case.*

In late 1998, *when there was snow on the ground and the plows were out making the streets a little bit safer, we finally decided to celebrate the making of* Roo Kickkick & the Big Bad

Blimp *on the three-year anniversary of the film's release. Well,
it wasn't exactly the three-year anniversary of the film's release
but it was pretty close and trust us, it didn't really matter that
we hadn't celebrated the first two anniversaries. It was mostly
Donny Barn's doing really; always the financial genius, he
decided the First Annual Florence Mink Film Festival went so
well that it had actually given us hope, so why not throw one
just for 'the movie that started it all'? We weren't exactly sure
what 'it' he meant, maybe 'it' was Florence's career or 'it' was
our suffering, but come to think of it, it didn't really matter
which 'it' it was.*

*That decision did make some of us uneasy, though, and we
aren't quite sure why, maybe everyone watching* Roo Kickkick
& the Big Bad Blimp *at the First Annual Florence Mink Film
Festival made it okay. Sorry we had to lie about everybody
having a good time during the first showings, see everyone
watched it all those times but nobody laughed or smiled like
we said they did earlier. The whole reason Donny threw the
Florence festival in the first place was cuz everyone was so sad.
Indeed, Florence had been successful and, for a time anyway,
was the only real person to drag herself out of that career
wrecker and so it was kinda like we were celebrating Florence
and putting all our faith in her, instead of in an entire movie
cuz the movie had let us down but she sure hadn't. Pretty
amazing how she had gotten out of it all without a scratch.
Florence was always lucky but maybe people just treated her
a bit different and a bit better just on account of how she was
so much more beautiful than anyone else. Sure, Roo had been
the main target of the jokes, of the sketches, some really mean
stuff too, mostly about his curbing. We talked to him on the
phone a few times and we can tell you, he took it all in stride
somehow. We always did admire that.*

Ever eager, Donny took out a huge ad in the Upton
Chronicle *and some little ads in a few magazines and we*

all laughed . . . we were absolutely sure nothing would come of it. We knew that the population of Barguss was the only one that could be counted on to attend but we let Donny make a big fuss out of it anyway. It was the first real big fuss he'd made since Krystof died and he finally looked happy again now that he had a purpose, a big 'to do' to put on. We had no idea how wrong we were about to be.

Two days before the Big Bad Blimp Festival, gangs of young kids and even older adults showed up from out of town and started roaming the streets dressed as Roo, Florence, Thorpe and Thed, Raoul, Monroe Mister, Doctor Dinner and Mrs. Kickkick. At first, we just called them the doppelgängers and there were only a few of them, okay, so we'd seen a few in town for the First Annual Florence Mink Film Festival, but they were less conspicuous then and we really didn't think much of it cuz even people from Barguss did that, so we didn't make too big a deal out of it. Heck, every so often Candy and Mandy dressed up as Florence and we never said anything about it. If we did, we'd have gotten a punch. Anyway, just as we thought we had a handle on things, they got even weirder.

We were shocked to find that some of the more hardcore ones had dressed up as us (!) and even the Gee Street Girls thought that was really, really scary but not quite as scary as the doppelgängers taking lots and lots of pictures of everything, including the fire hydrants and garbage cans. But it wasn't until we found out that a group of fifteen people had flown over from Germany to attend, and there were at least twice that many from Japan and they all had pompadours like Roman as Monroe Mister had in the movie, even the girls. Then the news came that the Prime Saddle Hotel was full, completely. They had even run out of cots. People were going to be sleeping on the floors. Some had paid fifty bucks a head per night to sleep on the couches in the lobby.

There was no way we coulda predicted it, nothing like this,

not quite on this scale and we're pretty sure Donny didn't know how big it would be either but we did know one thing for dead certain after everybody showed up: there was about to be a whole lot of trouble . . .

The Mystery of the Donny Barn Night Fire Party

On the first day of the Big Bad Blimp Festival, the largest screening room in the Donny Barn Exclusive Theater was crammed almost to the rafters with clones. There was a pack of Raouls in the back corner cavorting with the Monroe Misters in the back middle. There were some Roos up in front and a whole buncha Florences right next to 'em. And that really was the most interesting thing, how people seemed to leave their social groups (except for the Japanese who were all dressed up like Monroe Mister Promised To anyway) and gather with the others that dressed the same as they did.

We listened as many people told each other where they were from and we were real surprised to hear so many different names: Alaska, Pennsylvania, Ohio, Hawai'i (that was how they pronounced it), New Brunswick, Singapore and Northern Ireland were just a few that we heard. 'Course we were all real confused about why all these people would travel so far to be here. It was so unexpected and so weird to have so many fans of the film show up out of nowhere. Well, not exactly nowhere cuz they all came from somewhere but we were speaking more metaphorically really. Maybe one of the problems was we weren't even sure we were still fans of the film anymore, after all that we'd been through here anyway.

But then all these people showed up and we'd even gotten asked to autograph someone's arm with a big thick permanent pen which was real creepy for us cuz the only things we've ever been asked to sign are speeding tickets, paychecks, and tax

214

forms and really, we didn't even want to do it but the group of people got these super pouty looks on their faces like we were hurting them by not submitting to their request on the corner of Hotblack and Gee when what we wanted was just to get something to eat and not be bothered. We did it anyway and they thanked us but it still didn't feel right. People like us should never be anything approaching famous. That's for the Florences and the Theds and Thorpes and people that can handle that kinda thing.

Although the fact that Donny convinced almost the entire cast to come out for it was a reason so many people showed up. We say 'almost' cuz that's what the advertisement said but it really wasn't true. Florence couldn't make it on account of being up for a Best Supporting Actress Oscar© that night and that actually accounted for the odd scheduling: we were to watch *Roo Kickkick & the Big Bad Blimp* at four in the afternoon so everyone could scramble back to their homes or hotel rooms to see if Florence won for her role in *The Burning Bend*. Donny had managed to convince Roo to come though and we were so excited to see him that we picked him up at the airport earlier in the day along with Thorpe and Thed, who were supposed to play a mini-concert before the movie started. Apparently that was one of the big reasons why so many people showed up.

By the time some tech guys were setting up a small stage for Autistik/Artistik in front of the movie screen, us and Roo took our seats in a little box in the middle that Donny had specially constructed so it looked like we were special and we aren't sure we could tell you just why, but we kinda had a problem with it. It didn't feel quite right was all. In retrospect, we feel silly for not having noticed earlier that Roo shoulda been in L.A. that night with Florence celebrating her achievement. It didn't even cross our minds then. He confessed to us later that he and her were having 'some problems' and that was kinda strange cuz he never talked about stuff like that to us so we just listened and then gave him a half-hug but the news made us real sad. We were sure it was her mistreating him almost certainly. Nothing more was said about it though.

We asked Roo if he planned on being around for the big city ceremony the next day and he said yeah so we were happy about that. There was a little something planned for putting up a totem pole in the memorial park that happened to coincide with honoring our town founder Zebulon P. Barguss, which was kinda funny cuz the present of a totem pole was from a famous modern artist that happened to be a Native North American-type Indian and lived in our Canadian sister city and Z.P. Barguss is known to have killed a few Indians back in his day. Actually, we used to be really bitter cuz everybody else in our state has exotic sister cities in China or India or somewhere cool in Europe – like Upton, the capital, has a sister city in Brest, France, and we always laugh about the name but we're really just jealous inside – and we only had one in silly old British Columbia.

Anyway, Donny Barn came crashing through the little gate into our box and he had the strangest grin on his face that we ever did see and then he looked to the right with just his eyes a coupla times and we thought maybe something was wrong with him, that is, 'til we noticed that The Scarlet Pimp, Arnell, was lingering in the aisle just as a buncha kids were fighting with each other to sit on the stairs in front of him. 'Man, that guy couldn't hide in the jungle if you gave him camouflage and buried him under a tree,' Donny said, and it was true too. Arnell wore a bright blue fur coat and the same crazy king of the musketeers pimp hat and he looked real nervous cuz he was rubbing his hands a lot.

Donny was starting to act nervous too cuz he sat up all straight in his chair and we just figured that he was scared of Arnell and we didn't blame him none either. We knew that, on the sliding scale, Arnell was a badder dude than Donny, just not quite as bad as Hooty Mack. We scanned the audience to see if Hooty Mack was around and maybe that's why Arnell was acting so nervous. We're pretty sure Roo didn't notice any of this cuz he got up to go to the bathroom and that wasn't such a good idea on account of how he got mobbed right away and didn't come back for about twenty minutes which left us time to watch The Scarlet Pimp out of the corner of our eyes but he didn't move from the stairs.

When Roo got back, he told us he had made an extraordinary acquaintance, a young girl of about sixteen who had been curbed too, by her brother actually, and she had come all the way from Boston to see the movie cuz she 'felt a deep connection with his story' and that was obvious . . . it was wrote big on her face (we thought, but didn't say). Honestly, hearing Roo tell it made us cringe real hard just to hear about how this girl from Boston got curbed, cuz even though Roo's scars made him look dignified in a way we never thought would happen when he was younger, he'd actually grown into them if such a thing is possible and they certainly made him look really tough too but we were so sad that what he went through could ever happen to a girl and mess up her face for life like that. We must've said something out loud or mumbled it anyway cuz Roo responded, 'I think she looks beautiful just how she is,' and the simple, direct way he said it almost made us cry, you could tell he wasn't lying and really did believe that she was beautiful still.

To tell you the real truth we were caught up in our conversation about the girl when Thorpe and Thed walked on stage and we saw them in our peripheral vision and we thought it weird. They *always* had huge dramatic entrances and wonderful costumes and something going on at every moment, but this time they didn't and that confused us. By that point, we weren't looking at Roo anymore but we were listening real hard to how when this girl (and her name was Millicent) had gotten her drug addict brother mad somehow, he dragged her outside but we were looking on stage as Thorpe and Thed fidgeted. That was when we felt something in the pit of our stomachs . . . they never fidgeted on stage and it was then we knew that something was real wrong.

Just as we were about to interrupt Roo, Thorpe brought his left hand down hard on his brand new Neolix® Super Jam 650 portable guitar/keyboard and everyone in the audience who had been cheering pretty loud cheered even louder but then it just turned to screams as something among the amplifiers popped like someone lighting off big firecrackers at ground level cuz sparks went everywhere and people started screaming but they thought it was a part of the show, 'til they could see flames anyway. Then it was chaos. Everyone running for the exits, even Thed and Thorpe and people getting stomped on and we turned to our right expecting to see Donny but he was gone, long gone. We didn't even see him in the crowd, or Arnell either, but it didn't really bother us cuz we knew we had to get out too. You know, put on your own oxygen mask before assisting children with their oxygen masks, exactly like that.

So us and Roo jumped the box and got down low. The flames had already spread to the screen and up the curtains on the sides and even to the soundproof carpeting on the walls and as they spread they blew sparks when they reached each speaker of the sound system and it was just like in the movies. We picked up a few of the smaller people that had been pushed aside by overzealous fans steaming for the exits and it didn't matter how much we yelled 'stay calm!' real loud it didn't work so we gathered up a small group and pushed for the door to the outside, which, at that moment, had a fist fight in front of it between two Raouls over who would go first.

Smoke was starting to fill up the room and even if it wasn't at eye level yet we could taste it and it got in our eyes and the loudness of the flames grew as they did. It was an ocean-type roar and it reminded us of Krystof torching himself and we didn't like that sound, that sound is nails on a chalkboard for us, we don't ever use the fireplace anymore cuz we can't even stand the little sounds, they are just the opposite of comforting.

By the time we got to the exits, the Raouls had been shoved through by a Roo and we thought that was great and just as we were exiting into the night to realize that it was snowing, the real Roo must've turned around to go back without any warning. All of a sudden, he just wasn't there anymore and we panicked after getting the last of our group through the exit cuz for whatever reason and we don't know why exactly, we just had the feeling that he was dead and how awful that would be when we scanned the smoke that was taking over the theater and by now had probably spread to the other ones through the vents or something.

We got down on our hands and knees to avoid the smoke and started crawling back to the front row of seats to look for Roo and it was a damn good thing too cuz there was a scared little boy hiding under there and then we figured that was what Roo was doing, looking for people who might've been trapped, trampled or stuck. We had to drag the little boy out by his leg and rushed him outside and slipped on the snow and fell hard on our asses and believe it or not, some people actually laughed, a life or death situation and we just saved some kid and they laughed and that just really made us mad. That was something Monroe Mister would do, when he was alive he never understood how important anything was.

We dashed back in just as the Barguss fire department rolled up and yeah, we were scared more than we've ever been but it was like being on autopilot in our own bodies. By then we couldn't hear anything but the shaking loud roar of the fire and we crawled and crawled in two different directions and still couldn't find Roo and just as we were trying to head back toward the light of the open door and the brightness of the snow, we felt someone's hand on our shoulders and it was Roo's and he was inching forward in a soldier's crawl with a girl in his arms and her leg looked all twisted up and nasty.

As we got within five feet of the doors, the other one got kicked open and we saw some of the smoke above our heads vacate into the air and two firefighters grabbed our arms and rug-burned us out into the snow so that the white stuff felt soft and cold and good on our hot skin. When we could at least sit up, us, Roo, and the girl got taken to Barguss General. Turned out the girl had a broken leg from being pushed down the stairs by the stampeding crowd and it also turned out that this girl was the same one Roo had been telling us about, the Millicent girl who had been curbed just like him.

We looked at her face as she coughed and it was obvious that she hadn't gotten it anywhere near as bad as Roo had, her thin scars barely got up to her cheeks but Roo's dominated his whole face and anybody could tell from fifty yards away what had happened to him but Roo was right, she was beautiful. And not like Florence was beautiful in that almost scary way that kinda gave her the power over people and made them do stupid things sometimes (us included) but a soft kinda beauty, even all smoke-stained and hair everywhere and shot up full of valium when she smiled and showed her fake front teeth that were whiter than the rest and we knew that her and Roo had a special bond that only a few humans on this earth had any idea about, and even though we knew that was for the good for that moment, it made us a little bit jealous not to have a bond like that with anybody.

An interesting thing about that Millicent girl's smile though was that her eyes smiled too and it was just like Luanne and Lily smile with their pupils getting hugged by their irises and sending out good feelings to anyone lucky enough to be caught in that beam. It was then, riding super-fast in an ambulance that didn't pay attention to bumps or traffic lights while it slid over the snowy roads, wearing masks over our mouths and noses and coughing the occasional bit of gray stuff into them by accident, that we knew that Florence could never be as pretty a girl as Millicent cuz we had never noticed, and it made us feel sorta stupid cuz we must've been so mesmerized by her perfect nose and all the rest to actually see that Florence had never really smiled with her eyes before, and probably never would, ever. It occurred to us just then, that it wasn't something she was capable of.

At the hospital, us and Roo got treated for smoke inhalation and released but we waited in the waiting room for the nurses to get done setting Millicent's cast so we could go in and see her and the nurses almost didn't let us but Roo explained that she was far away from home and probably scared so it would be good if we could just see her for a little bit and they let up cuz Roo is as persuasive as anybody we know.

We didn't talk much in the waiting room, just sat there thinking, hoping everybody was all okay, especially Donny and Thed and Thorpe but the fans too, of course. We just sat around the bay window that looked into the parking lot as the snow fell down all slow and it was almost funny to think we'd been in a fire not too long ago and how different the snow was from the fire, so slow and comforting. The Academy Awards were gonna be on in a little bit but we turned the television off. Can't say why exactly, just felt right. A few more ambulance loads showed up and got shepherded right into the emergency room but mostly, it was quiet.

Before we got to go back and see Millicent, the lights went out for five minutes and then the hospital's emergency generator kicked on, but in those brief minutes of being in a room only lit up by the fading light from outside reflecting off the snow, sitting next to Roo, we've never felt so peaceful in

221

our whole lives. Just after the emergency lights buzzed on, a nurse took us back to see Millicent. We went through the door first and then stood off to the side on the wall as Roo came in and walked straight to her bed and sat down beside it like it was his place and he was meant to be there. She was smiling with her eyes without even smiling and if we didn't know any better, we'd have thought she was in love with him.

The nurses shooed us out after a little bit and an off-duty ambulance driver that was two years ahead of us in high school drove us and Roo home cuz Roo had to stay at our house on account of his mom was remodeling the apartment. We promised Roo we'd go back to the hospital in the morning and pick up Millicent before the totem pole ceremony and it wasn't 'til after we said that that he looked more comfortable. Our mama was forced to cook steak and eggs for us over the fire that night (but we had to be in the back room when she did) cuz she was so happy we made it back safe on the night that the Exclusive burned pretty much to the ground.

We never did see Donny Barn again and to add insult to injury for a lot of the fans that attended the screening, the fire at the theater had popped a few power lines and that caused an entire blackout of Barguss and not a single person was able to see if Florence won the Oscar® or not that night.

22

We were up kinda early the next morning and we didn't wanna wait for Roo to wake up, so we snuck into the living room with our breakfast and popped on the TV. As luck would have it, public access channel 8 was showing the Gee Street Girls' documentary about Barguss. The panning image of the plains got cast brightly on the far white wall in the living room cuz we hadn't turned any lights on. Lily was narrating and saying how the land Barguss was built upon used to be 'Indian land' just like everywhere else in America, we guess.

It's actually kinda funny that it wasn't 'til we were in high school when we found out the real history of Barguss and America too, how it used to be 'Indian territory' and all that stuff. The funny part was that we didn't learn any of this information in history class where we shoulda learned it, about how basically all white people did back then is make treaties and then break them. We actually learned that information in art class of all places. That was cuz we had a hippy art teacher named Miss W, that was it, just W, cuz she said she refused her white name (we weren't sure but we guessed the white letter was okay). She used 'Miss' too cuz she never married but she'd been living for twenty years with some guy named Howard who was a masseuse and part-time science class substitute teacher at our high school and he taught our biology class once and blew up a Bunsen burner by accident, which was classic. Miss W also said she had an Indian grandparent on her mother's side but we really never believed her even though she had a ponytail down to her butt with beads in it and everything and it swayed when she walked, so you could never really walk next to her but instead, you'd have to walk in front of it, or behind, cuz otherwise it would hit you.

Well, she had us make pots as our year-end projects and the whole time spouted off on how this land came to be 'ours, quote, unquote' going through everything from Columbus and his genocide to the 'Trail of Tears' and Andrew Jackson to the 'Battle, quote, unquote' of Wounded Knee. It was real eye opening especially when you're hearing all this awful stuff while trying to throw an 'authentic Indian pot' (which we knew it never really could be, but Miss W insisted) and her words kept messing us up on the wheel cuz you can't quite keep your hands steady when hearing about how U.S. soldiers killed women and children asleep in their tents but honestly, you can only listen to somebody ranting all righteously for so long before your ears kinda shut off after a while.

By the time we finished our cereal, Lily's silky voice was going on about our town founder, Zebulon P. Barguss, and it was about then we figured the girls were right, the documentary they did was surprisingly good and we decided to tell 'em so, but without the 'surprisingly' attached to it. Anyway, Zeb Barguss was a kooky explorer/spy/military man who ventured westward mostly for glory just like Lily says as the camera slowly pans over the frayed old black and white picture of Zeb and his huge army coat double collar and slightly matted hair. It's actually pretty funny how Barguss got to be called Barguss cuz Zebulon never actually set foot on this land. As he was out exploring with his men one day, Barguss got transfixed by some mountains in the distance and decided to go up and have a look. After two days' hard climb through the snow they

224

reached the top of a peak but then Zeb saw an even bigger peak adjacent to it and he tried to reach it but gave up on it cuz all he had was summer clothes and was getting real cold in the snow.

Modern day Barguss now sits at the foot of the real big mountain that Barguss wanted to climb but couldn't. As it turns out, he didn't name it Barguss either. A couple of later explorers who came through referred to it as 'Barguss' on account of his journal entries or something, but the name wasn't popularized until around 1840 when another explorer came through and named it such. The Barguss story is something we're all taught in elementary school, we were even forced to put on Discovery of the Frontier, a play in which we depict Z.P. Barguss as a steady hero who actually did climb the peak he wanted to, instead of settling for the smaller one. Thorpe played Barguss back then and to this day, when given the opportunity, he'll make a joke about how everyone from Barguss is doomed to climb the wrong mountain and never meet their expectations or goals. We always laugh at the jokes, cuz they are funny, but still, we hope it isn't true.

We were caught up in Lily's voice so much that we didn't hear Roo enter the room and didn't know he was there 'til he put his hands on our shoulders and that gave us a shock. He said he wasn't hungry after we offered to cook him something for breakfast cuz the power was back on but it was obvious he just wanted to go pick up Millicent from the hospital, so we shut off the TV, much as we still liked Lily's voice in our ears, and borrowed the keys to our mama's car.

At the time that we filed out of the house and locked the door behind us and opened up the car and started it up and headed down Gee, we really couldn't have known it was a 'day for revelations', as our mama would repeat later, all solemnly when we returned the car keys and told her the shocking news. She also said another thing after we got the whole story out and

*it was kinda cryptic and we guess a little symbolic or something
even though we didn't get it at the time. She just said,*

**'Yes Indeed,' and then Mama started rocking in her
rocking chair before completing it, 'Every Totem Pole
Does Tell a Story.'**

When we got to the hospital and parked, Roo was already
out of the car and making a beeline for the entrance with us
trailing behind. Some of the snow had melted overnight, so we
just followed his slushy clear footprints to the double doors
of the entrance without really looking up. We kinda knew he
wanted a little time alone with her and it was cool to see a
side of Roo we'd only seen a coupla times before with how
he treated Laura and Florence the night she went sorta crazy.
He was acting like a big brother, like a parent kinda. He was
very protective yet real quiet about it, not like Beau at all, who
always let everyone know that he was 'busting his goddamn
ass off' raising Thorpe Thorpe and how much trouble it all
was. Nope, Roo was certainly the opposite of that. We know
Beau loved Thorpe a lot, just the tough kinda love though.

   We stood outside of Millicent's assigned room before the
nurse told us not to loiter, we either had to go in or back
to the waiting room. So we knocked and got no answer. So
we knocked again and got a faint 'come in,' then entered.
Millicent looked totally different than she did the day before
in the ambulance. She had cleaned up and taken a shower
and pulled her hair back tight in a ponytail kinda bun but
not really. We aren't sure what it was called but it looked
pretty and she didn't have any soot on her face either. Roo
was helping her into his jacket and she was shrugging it on.

   Underneath it, she was wearing a long dress that she said one
of the nurses had brought for her cuz it used to be the nurse's

daughter's and 'she didn't need it anymore', and Millicent had needed clothes due to the fact that the doctors had had to cut her jeans off in the operating room to fix her leg. So then, Roo put his name on the paperwork to sign her out and the four of us made our way to the car and we let them walk ahead. With her on crutches, Millicent left these cool little circle prints with one shoe-toe print patterned in the slush. We can say she wasn't really like most sixteen-year-olds though, cuz she knew when to just be quiet instead of talking all the time and we could kinda see why Roo was attached to her apart from their bond. They sat in the back together as we drove to the memorial park without even listening to the radio.

We figured lots of the out of town movie fans didn't want to go to the totem pole dedication and ceremony on account of the fire at the Exclusive the night before, but we went anyway cuz our honored guests from our sister city would be leaving that afternoon just after the dedication. As we found a place to park, we noticed a huge semi-truck with Canadian plates that said 'British Columbia' and they looked kinda like ours but had blue in them and just said 'Beautiful' at the top and it was even spelled right. A big long trailer extended behind the semi and a cylinder that must've been at least sixty or seventy feet long and five or six feet in diameter was wrapped in white cloth and secured in a series of brackets that had to've held it steady during the journey.

Indeed, that was the totem pole that was to be put up on the foundation that used to support the old statue of Monroe Mister Promised To, god rest its soul. Getting out of the car, we had to wait cuz Millicent had a little trouble pushing herself up and out with her crutches and all but Roo was helping her, so that gave us time to realize how much we loved the idea of putting up something decent in the stone of Monroe Mister's vacated foundation.

We joined the group of people surrounding the reconnoitered logging truck as it backed up onto the slushy snow grass of the memorial park, so as to be closer to the foundation for us to put it up. There was a small old man with dark hair darting around the pole while the truck was moving and we just figured he was the famous artist cuz he was securing ropes for us to raise it. That was when we heard through the mutters in the crowd that Florence had lost the Academy Award the night before and we aren't exactly sure why, but it really didn't bother us that much. We made a mental note to tell Roo but then decided against it when he looked so happy next to Millicent.

It was a really beautiful thing how pretty much everyone in town helped put the totem pole up. Everyone pulled and pulled 'til it was fit into place in the specially drilled hole made in the former statue foundation so it would fit the full diameter snugly. Millicent couldn't help but she shouted encouragement and that was kinda nice cuz it brought a smile to Roo's face and we always did love to see that smile. A few people fell over in the mush and laughed cuz they couldn't quite get a grip or didn't wear the proper work boots or clothes like we did.

When the pole was up and still clad in white, a big shout went up from everybody and we were all so glad to have done it. That was when we noticed the large group of movie fans gathered off to the side who were watching the whole thing with interest and we realized we were wrong and they had come to see it after all. But we didn't have much time to pay attention to them cuz Mayor Yermo was giving a speech on a makeshift stage to the left of the totem pole. All in all, it was a pretty good speech cuz he said all the right things about 'brotherhood and sisterhood' with our other city and how honored we were to receive a gift this priceless and so on and so forth.

At the end of his speech he said that the city council had

voted to rename Gee Street 'Union Boulevard' in honor of the union between the two cities that existed now. It was a really nice gesture even if we figured it was mostly cuz of the gift that they had decided to do that when we had nothing to give in return.

So then Mayor Yermo gave another little speech about how Zebulon P. Barguss would have approved of this unity and it didn't make much sense to us anyway so we just stared at the big painted face of Zeb Barguss on thirteen feet of canvas set up behind Mayor Yermo and it looked eerily like the one in *Citizen Kane* when Charles Foster is running for election and we might have said something to Roo about it but then the mayor gave a signal to a worker sitting up on the white-covered Gee Street sign (just like the totem pole, really) and pulled it down to show a brand new green street sign that said 'UNION' all big in capital letters.

Nice as it was though, it just didn't look right to us, not at all. Maybe cuz to us, it would always be Gee Street. The street we grew up on (close enough), the street we walked on everyday, the street Maria died on, the street Donny broke his collarbone on twice, the street that the Taco Coleslaw Hamburger Hot Dog Apple was on, the street that had pretty much been the same as long as we could remember, and at that moment, we realized that some things in life were just gonna change anyway, whether we liked it or not, and somehow, that made us feel like adults, but sorta bitterly. Everybody clapped anyway and we did also, even though we didn't really want to.

After the clapping, the little old man took the stage and started singing a low chant into the microphone in a language we couldn't understand and we figured it was a blessing so we bowed our heads 'til he was done and then, without saying anything else, he pulled a big rope in his hand that extended all the way to the top of the totem pole, and as he did, the white sheets fell away with a flapping sound and crumpled to the ground, so much whiter than the slushy brown snow around it and as we caught sight of the naked totem pole we lost our collective breath for a moment of awe and regained it as a sound of disbelief rose out of the onlookers, including us, cuz it just didn't look like any totem pole we'd ever seen.

We looked to the old man artist, who had a great big smile on his face and then back to the pole and we couldn't really believe it. At the very top was a bulbous representation of the blimp with a figure riding it, and we knew it was Roo, we didn't need to study the face to know that, but below the blimp and Roo was Florence with shining knot-holed cheeks carved and rounded all perfect and below that was a real tender 3D portrait of Krystof staring off into the distance and below that was an upside-down Raoul de los Dios and we figured that that simulated the fall cuz below him was Monroe Mister Promised To and the tops of their heads touched at the hair point and just below that was a little doorway carved into the wood that you could actually walk through, to the other side.

By the time we had taken it all in, people were already pushing forward as a mass to touch it and put their hands and faces on it and pass through the doorway and for whatever reason we heard Donny's voice in our heads and he said, 'sublime'. It reminded us of the time that he tried to teach us what it meant in relation to *The Magnificent Seven*, like how something could be so beautiful it was terrible and vice versa, so heart-strikingly terrifying that it was gorgeous to look at. *That* was what this totem pole was, the most perfect expression of everything that happened that day all those years ago and what it had led to, carved right into wood that had once lived as a tree: it was a memorial fit for the memorial park and it was a memorial for everything Barguss used to be, cuz that was the day everything changed for us here but then our heads started spinning and we had to sit down. Fast.

Plopping down in the slush, we didn't give any mind to our jeans getting dirty, we just had to not be on our feet for a moment. Roo plopped right down next to us as Millicent hopped up and down on her crutches above us, trying to see over people's heads. For about five minutes, we couldn't even look at Roo but we knew he was feeling something similar. When we did look over to him, we hoped to hear something good, something reassuring, something to tell us, or show us, that everything was gonna be okay, but the opposite happened, and our world got turned upside down just like Raoul's head on the totem pole when Roo spoke, still looking at the ground, his tears falling to the slush and melting it a little on contact, 'Raoul was my brother and I couldn't save him.'

Hearing those words was like getting punched in the stomach without having to double over, no, it was more like getting punched real good behind the ear cuz our ears started ringing and we felt a little sick to our stomachs and it was like Roo and us were the only people in the world for that moment cuz our vision was kinda getting fuzzy and narrow and we could only see Roo as he shot a quick look to us out of the corner of his eye and we had no choice but to believe him cuz we felt deep down that it was true.

Then Roo started talking again and we just listened through the ringing, 'we're all just raising everyone else's children now,' and we didn't quite understand what he was trying to say but he continued and we were relieved we didn't have to ask him to clarify, 'with divorces and parents running off, people turn into parents that weren't supposed to be [like Beau, we thought], then we're more related to people through halves and steps than we ever thought possible [like Shoe and Laura, we thought, though it was difficult for us to put awful Raoul in that category too], you know, when I was up there, he actually asked me, "why should I hang on?" and I just said cuz we're brothers and then he just smiled and let go.' Looking at the side of Roo's downcast head, for the briefest of moments, it was like we could see Raoul falling from Roo's perspective and it made the back of our necks cold through our jackets and we had to look away.

We found the details out later. How Roo's dad had grown up in the same town as Miss Fern before she tacked a Micklewhite on the end of her name, who just happened to be Raoul's mom and somehow one thing had led to another at some point and even with the pieces in place, it was still the hugest shock of our lives to hear that Roo's dad was Raoul's dad too cuz we'd never seen two more different people in the whole wide world (at least you could see similarities between Roo and Shoe and Laura), and that Roo and Raoul were half-brothers and Roo was just trying to save his brother and not trying to get Florence Mink to like him at all, which was what we had thought all along, screwed us up a bit and made us think about things for a real long time afterward and we were real distant for the rest of the ceremony where we got to eat what was called an 'authentic venison stew' but we barely tasted it.

Roo took Millicent home the next day on a flight to Boston. Turned out her mother had asked that he do so and she even paid for the ticket cuz he had taken 'such good care of her' and she wanted to thank him in person. We didn't see Roo for a long time after the day that he laid it all on the line and even still we wonder why he told us that news right then, and we keep coming back to the totem pole and how it moved us inside and we're sure it did the same for him and he just had to stop keeping his secret.

As it turned out, the totem pole became highly controversial and deemed a 'sacrilege' by many of the Indian nations on account of it not telling a traditional Indian legend and instead, told an unbelievable but true story of a buncha nobodies in a tiny western town in what passed for the United States of

232

America nowadays. Many people came to take pictures of it and write articles about it and the artist got even more famous for it, even though many people questioned his motives and what exactly he was trying to say for years and years after that. There was even a peaceful protest by the Cheyenne and Ute nations right there in the memorial park not two weeks after the pole was raised.

But we're pretty sure most people missed the plaque that the artist had installed in a secret compartment in the base of the totem pole at the foot of the doorway. You had to know how to wedge it up just so you could read the plaque hidden underneath a little plank of wood that looked just like everything else. Us and Candy, Mandy, Brandy, Luanne and Lily uncovered it one night when we were all wrestling in there for some dumb reason. Now we're pretty sure Mayor Yermo never read it cuz he certainly wouldn'tve let them put it in if he had seen the plaque beforehand, but he didn't and it was only for people who could find it, as we came to believe anyway. As for us, we didn't really understand it at first but somehow, we knew it was wise and we came to see it not really as moralizing or anything but more like a kinda gentle reminder to be as good as you could, and we told Roo so, much later, and read the exact words to him over the phone after we'd written them down and wedged the piece of wood back in place for the last time.

After All That

We never did figure out who burned down the Donny Barn Exclusive Theater, even though the cops investigated for like five months but still couldn't determine if arson was involved even though the wires to the instruments 'seemed to be frayed in such a deliberate way so as to facilitate flammability', the police report said. For our money, it coulda been any one of three, make that four, suspects. Since Thed's and Thorpe's instruments started the fire, we wouldn't put it past those two for a second to make one last big bang just like they did with the blimp, although it wouldn't be like them to endanger so many people. But then there was also the really suspicious-looking pimp lurking about. Maybe The Scarlet Pimp, Arnell, had decided to take revenge for Donny's hugely disrespectful outburst in the courtroom. Or Donny Barn coulda done it, whether he died in it or not. Some folks think he lit out for Canada on his motorbike or something and had his brother collect the insurance money, or maybe he really did go out in a 'blaze of glory' (for some reason, every time he said it, it reminded us of that Bon Jovi song) like he always drunkenly said he would, or maybe he was just finally fulfilling his promise to Krystof. We're pretty sure that Donny was the most likely perpetrator, though we'll never really know for sure. To this day, the accepted and official cause of the fire was that 'the movie print in the projector became unstable and caught fire', that's what the police report says, but we don't buy it even if everybody else does.

Believe it or not, *Roo Kickkick & the Big Bad Blimp* actually made money, eventually anyway. Somehow it ended up being a modest box office hit in the United Kingdom despite limited release and it was even a huge box office hit in Germany (where it was acclaimed as 'Neu Posten-Realist Amerikanisch Zeitgeist Cinema' or something), and a big hit in Japan as well, where it grossed more all time than *Godzilla, King of the Monsters*! One Japanese journalist actually wrote in his review that the movie was 'a gentle true parable of modern life and our misadventures as human beings played out against the surrealist landscape of hidden America' (translated by Shoe, of course) and eventually became quite the cult hit in the United States and Canada after being released on video. Four years after its release, it even turned a profit for Panazanc Film Partners, Inc., which meant that Zeke and Norville didn't have to shut down the bizness after all.

As for everybody else, well . . .

Roo Kickkick and Millicent eventually got married and had one son, Joey. You'd think he was cute despite his name and scarless too, as Roo was always real quick to point out. They live in a suburb of Boston now but still come back for Christmas and New Year's.

Florence still lives in Hollywood and is still making movies. She even got some critical recognition recently but it's mostly come from Europe. We saw her most recent one, a quirky art movie called *How To Be A Litmus Dancer*, and we didn't really understand the title even after seeing it and we aren't exactly sure why, but we felt that she seemed real sad underneath her acting and we figure maybe it was cuz Roo isn't in her life anymore but we could be wrong.

Raoul de los Dios is still dead, thankfully. Though sometimes we do wonder if the information that Roo told us would've changed Raoul's life, but then again, he did decide to let go after hearing it, so maybe that's the answer right there.

Thorpe Thorpe eventually left the band after a disastrous world tour in which he was nearly electrocuted in Belgium and had to re-evaluate his life. After which, he married Staceyleene and moved to a commune in Hawai'i, though he never forgot his roots and comes back to Barguss sometimes to play charity concerts for autism, cuz, he says, 'it's the least' he can do. Due to his accident, he's scared to use the telephone, so he never speaks to . . .

Thed Teldut anymore. Thed moved to Westminster, we think that's in England, with a girl he met in Hollywood and continued to pursue musical interests there before going back to school to become a scholar of the ancient and dead Sanskrit language.

The statue of Monroe Mister Promised To was never found and plans to construct a larger statue were never put underway. Old Man Promised To died in his sleep at the ripe old age of eighty-one and was not found for three weeks due to the size of his house and the lack of visitors. Word was, he worked himself to death, nearly exhausting his fortune by trying to find the missing statue (odd little flowers grow there now) even though it was at the bottom of the hill that he drove past nearly every day. Sorta sad really.

Sassa Medusa Belle surprised everyone when she shacked up with Beau Thorpe. They now have one boy, Chad, and two little girls, Mali and Mozambique (Moz for short). They've left Barguss and the drug trade behind them and coincidentally they now do relief work in Africa. Last we heard, they were in Lusaka but we still aren't exactly sure where that is.

Mrs. Kickkick continues to live in Barguss and is content with a monthly stipend from Roo, which means she doesn't have to work two jobs anymore. She took on a supervisory role at the apple factory and finally remarried, this time to a perfectly normal elementary school teacher named Ken A. Hall who treats her great and that makes us real happy.

Major Lem Kickkick received a dishonorable discharge from the armed forces after going AWOL from his post in Germany in a frantic attempt to convince Juanita Po-Hutchins-Kickkick to come back to him. Unfortunately, a street sweeping machine struck him when he fell into its path after a botched attempt to climb her window trellis. We hear he ended up in a mental ward after he failed to recover from the head injury he suffered and never spoke another word.

Juanita Po-Hutchins-Kickkick got bored of Wolfgang the music producer in the early 1990s cuz he wouldn't stop smoking Turko-Portuguese hashish or shut up his big mouth about 'post-Jimi Hendrix guitar expressionism' and 'the treacherous path of melding classical and avant-garde musical backgrounds with psychedelic rock'. Just after that, Juanita left Germany for a vacation in Nepal where she met a mute herbal healer. She lived with him for four years, maybe cuz she was sure he had the secrets of the universe, but if he did he never shared them with her. We guess that disappointed her somewhat, as she moved back to Germany alone and now hosts a late-night talk show in Munich where the people sometimes wear clothes and sometimes don't when they talk about right-wing politics.

The whereabouts of Donny Barn are still unknown and though most folks presume he's dead, some believe that the infamous 'rogue bandit' currently terrorizing Eastern Europe with motorbike speeds exceeding two hundred kilometers per hour is actually Donny fulfilling the last element of some bizarre promise to Krystof. Wherever he is, alive or dead, we'll never forget him.

'Smarty' Marty Mindy sold The Golden Ring in late 1999 and moved to Las Vegas where he collapsed while screaming, 'ooooh yeah! It's time for peanut butter, motherfuckers!' for the eighth consecutive time at puzzled bystanders when he struck the jackpot at Caesar's Palace's giant slot machine. Turned out he had a massive heart attack and died with his face in the lap of his girlfriend of two years. She threw him a lovely funeral.

Hasselzwell Smol has recovered fully from his self-inflicted wounds and continues to live on the same diet of cheap beer and TV dinners that he always did. Our mama says he'll probably outlive us all.

The Gee Street Girls had to change their name after Gee Street got renamed, and they tried the Union Boulevard Girls for a while but it just didn't work cuz the word 'Boulevard' was too long to fit on the backs of their jackets, so they ended up dropping it. They kinda broke into two groups though when Mandy Mulryne won the Barguss Blue Kitty Cat Queenship just after she graduated from high school and promptly moved to Upton to go to college. Candy and Brandy eventually followed and that was the end of the quintet, although their documentary still runs on public access local channel 8 late at night, mostly on Sundays.

Mayor Yermo Nastich retired from politics and left Barguss for his hunting lodge in the mountains. Sadly, he broke his back in an unfortunate weightlifting accident while training for the senior division in the state weightlifting championships. While laid up with the injury, he had quite a lot of time to read *The Tao of Jeet Kun Do* and he must've really connected with it cuz now he owns the only Jeet Kun Do dojo around. It's built into the side of a mountain and looks really cool at night when the lights are on.

Krystof Zckwecy is still resting as peacefully as possible in his coffin underneath the cabin museum dedicated to him. We put flowers there every so often, but we're always surprised by the amount of tourists that come to pay their respects.

Some girls even left their panties there once. We never really got that.

Despite never landing the role in the coveted blockbuster, Natalie Darling kept acting in a buncha B-type horror pictures and quasi-independent movies where she had to take off her shirt a lot. But we guess she got tired of acting after awhile cuz she eventually married a big-time entertainment lawyer and became a party hostess pretty much full-time. Sometimes, we catch ourselves wondering if she still has that ivory cigarette holder that seemed so much like an extension of her hand in the breeze that glided around the curves of Roman's 1937 Super-charged Cord the day they first showed up.

Roman 'Herc' Stevens quit acting to become a stuntman, which he then quit in order to turn his father's converted ranch back into a working ranch for disadvantaged children. This news surprised us the most on account of we never thought he was capable of such a good thing, but the truth is the truth. He is now the president of 'Horses for Hearts', a nonprofit organization founded in his father's memory that teaches children who have been victims of abuse, rape, drug addiction and violence how to ride and take care of horses and also of themselves too. 'Horses for Hearts' also has a scholarship fund, and to date has sent three hundred and twelve former participants to colleges and trade schools throughout the country. Roman still keeps in touch with . . .

Madalick 'El Peleador' Pinchone. Madalick continued acting for five more years and starred in such films as *My Daughter, My Daughter*, which was Clue's next independent project, as well as *Bulletriders 9* where he co-starred with that guy from *Beastmaster*, we forget his name. Madalick walked away from acting though and has since concentrated on his artwork, which, not surprisingly we guess, has gained a more political tone. His recent exhibit, 'Crossing Over, Living Under', was featured at the Los Angeles County Museum of

Art and also traveled to the Whitney Museum of American Art in New York City as well as taking a six-country traveling tour of South America. He is a loving single parent with one daughter, Zurina Sophia, and is at work on an autobiography tentatively entitled 'Congratulatinos!' He still remembers giving a switchblade to . . .

J. Bartholomew 'J. Bart' How, who was unlucky to have his movie career fizzle as it did, due to his premature male-pattern baldness at the age of twenty-four. From what we hear though he still works in television and has recently completed a pilot for a new television situation comedy in which the line between reality and fiction is quite fuzzy. Supposedly the show deals with four formerly famous child TV stars who happen to be all grown-up and living together in a loft in L.A. as they try to resurrect their careers separately and grow together through their hardships. Personally, we can't wait to see it.

Fyodor Dearnt Rheeves never acted again after many of his fans tagged him a 'sell-out'. He returned to ReDeck and they recorded thirteen albums without a break and without ever actually signing a major label deal. He now makes tribal acoustic dance music singles (but he calls it 'organic bump') for European radio stations in his downstairs studio in his hermitage in Clear Lake, Oregon.

Mr. Link 'Doober' Stubbs continued producing hot new acts in the music industry 'til he had a mid-life crisis and decided to move to Guam and learn how to surf, sail, and ocean fish. Nobody has heard from him since.

Morloine Harrison Westleycake died shortly after the filming of *Roo Kickkick & the Big Bad Blimp* due to a severe brain hemorrhage. If you look real hard at the tiny white print at the end of the film, it says it's dedicated to 'Speedy', that was Morloine's nickname. Indeed, his last and best movie role was playing . . .

Doctor Dinner. The Doc still lives in Barguss and is still

the town freak, though he has added a new concubine in Dr. Nancy, who, despite all her initial protestations, must've really gotten off on the Doc's foot worship thing. Dr. Nancy still operates her beauty salon and Doc Dinner continues to practice, though the townsfolk still gossip when a young waitress/dancer from Dixie's Gypsy Den is invited up to the house on the hill for an evening meal with the doctors.

Raw Mike Tall still lives in Upton and recently won a large settlement from the Upton Police Department from when they forcibly detained him and demanded he 'talk' about the missing statue. This event took place before the trial forced Old Man Promised To to forget about the statue hunt for a while. Raw Mike bought a dance club downtown with the settlement and named it 'Brutality' just so he'd never forget. Though they hardly see each other, he still keeps in contact with . . .

Dance LeRoy, who is now an author of highbrow literary fiction since writing *Bells In The Distance*, some book about mythology or something stupid like that. He can frequently be found acting all pretentious while in franchise coffee bars all over the country, using his meager fame to pick up weak-willed, slightly batty women who read way too much. So if you ever see him, beware, cuz we told you so.

Shusaku 'Shoe' Kikukiku is now a record producer and owns his own label, 'Barguss Records', and we were really flattered by the name when he told us. Shoe was greatly honored recently when he fulfilled his lifelong dream by performing live with Ryuichi Sakamoto. Mr. Sakamoto had personally extended the invitation for Shoe to join him on stage at an all-star Tokyo benefit concert for world peace. The good news is that Shoe is still married to Moira and Ru is doing great in school and wants to be either a sumo wrestler, a samurai, or an astronaut when he grows up. Word is, Moira is pregnant with their second, a girl, and they were considering naming her Laura after . . .

Laura Mon Alzar, who eventually became Laura Mon Brush after she married Clue (they had kept in constant contact ever since she left) in a private Hollywood Hills ceremony at his home on her eighteenth birthday. She attended Clue's alma mater, the University of California Los Angeles, on a soccer scholarship and led her team to a national championship in her junior year there. She is now a real estate analyst/appraiser and she draws in her spare time. We think about her a lot and hope she's happy.

Wayne Newton is 'still a damn legend and always will be', so said Thorpe Thorpe last time he was in town with Staceyleene for the autism concert, and we were all out at Paulson's for a drink. At the time, he was trying to get Wayne to come to the next benefit concert and do another duet with him of 'Daddy Don't You Walk So Fast'. We told him we'd pay twice to see that and he smiled big while Staceyleene rubbed his arm and said she loved him.

As for The Scarlet Pimp, Arnell, well, he was never heard from again after his shadowy appearance at the Donny Barn Night Fire Party. We'd really like to think he made it out of there alive only to receive his final comeuppance from . . .

Leonard Prince 'Hooty' Mack, Jr. As far as we know, he still leads a fairly boring existence, now retired from his insurance business since handing it over to his eldest son, Leon. L.P. runs his neighborhood watch and regularly wears a 'Badass Chef' apron while orchestrating holiday cookouts from the super-size grill on his back porch. To this day, none of his neighbors even suspects that a hero lives just next door.

As for us, well, we told you as much of the truth as we know. So there's really not much more to tell, 'cept not too long ago, we finally got lucky after getting up some nerve to ask Luanne and Lily Lukash out on a double date to the Taco

Coleslaw Hamburger Hot Dog Apple where we all ordered the #16 with carrots and laughed about the weird coincidence. We've been together ever since and still all live in Barguss. Perhaps most importantly though, we've had a few 'just bang' moments ourselves since Roo first told us about his, and we'd love to tell you all about them but Luanne and Lily would really pound on us if we did, so we guess that's . . .

PRETTY MUCH THE END